PLEIADIAN RESCUER

BOOK 1

IN THE

NEW PARADIGM SERIES

BY

BENEDICT STONE

Disclaimer

This book is written for an adult audience as it contains strong language and graphic violence

All characters, conspiracies, organisations, and events are written in a fictional context, and any similarity to real-world situations is purely coincidental

Reader Discretion Is Advised

Book Cover Design By BespokeBookCovers.com

Prologue

Ingolstadt, Bavaria

Germany

Earth Year 1784

"We must yield to their commands," said Brother Spartacus, "they have both the ability and the armies to do as they say. We have no choice." He was shaken by what he had seen, they all were. Never had any of them witnessed such acts of barbarity.

"Are you suggesting that we just hand over control of everything we have built?" replied Brother Ajax. "You cannot be serious, Brother."

"I see this as no matter for debate. To do anything other than their will, would be to sign death warrants for all of our young and you all stood witness to how they intend to carry out such a warrant. No, brothers, there is no alternative. We must yield." Spartacus knew there was nothing they could do but to give in to the awful demands of their new overlords.

"I cannot stand by and idly watch our creation turned against not just *our* goals, but that of our entire species." Ajax was furious that the founding members of the Order of the Illuminati could cave in so easily. "We began the Order to bring not only humanity but the *entire world* into the light. To bring about equality to all. To free the masses from their miserable lives of hidden slavery, and you give up at the first true hurdle? No sir, I will not yield."

"Then you and your bloodline will perish, Sir," replied Brother Philo.

From the corner of the dimly lit room, a man spoke quietly for the first time since the start of the secret meeting. "If you'll permit me to speak?" he asked. Receiving a nod, he continued. "Brother Spartacus is right; there is no recourse to this demand that has been placed upon your organisation. You *must* yield, or you and your families will suffer a death most horrible. However, there are alternatives to trying to fight against it. With the amalgamation of both your organisation and my own, we may be able to do things in such a manner that we can do some good. All is not lost quite yet, brothers."

"Of course. The *Mason* has all the answers," Ajax said with as much sarcasm as he could muster. "Your dying lodges *would* know what to do, wouldn't you? Or maybe you are in league with the devils and wish to aid the monsters in destroying us."

"Come now, Brother. The Masons have undergone the same demand as us. Why do you think they brought about the Independence of America?"

"Personal gain of wealth and power. To control their own country thereby creating their own laws that would, in time, see them as the most powerful nation on the globe, and with us no longer in a position to stand in their way, as we have been, they could dominate the entire planet. I see no other meaning behind any of this." Ajax hated the Masonic Knights Of Dark Light with a passion that stemmed from his very soul. For centuries they had kept the path to illumination secret from the world and used esoteric mysticism to further their own power and wealth beyond imagination. Ajax had aided in the foundation of the Illuminati to use those very tools to free the planet of the Masonic death grip, because, in his eyes, that's exactly what it was, a death grip. It might take a thousand years, but ultimately, they would destroy civilisation. Of that, he had no doubt. Now that there was real speculation that his order joining with one of outright evil, he felt nothing but pure, unadulterated rage.

"No, Brother, that is not the truth," the Mason said firmly. "Where it may be true that we *may* have amassed wealth and power for our own deeds, we have *not* entered into this accord for any other reason than we have been forced to. As have you. Your Order has gained influence in areas of society that we have not, and if I were to be honest, I would have preferred to have removed that influence properly and taken control for ourselves. Alas, that is not to be. Circumstances have forced all of our hands into an alliance, and our hands *must* grab that alliance with all of our might if we are to survive. Those monsters are truly evil. Satan's very own. You saw it *eat* that poor child with your own eyes, sir. You must realise that you nor we could be in league with such actions. No, sir. We must ally and do what we must, do what we are forced, and where possible, do what we *can* so that we might be able to put some semblance of safety to the world. If we try to stand against them, they *will* land their armies, and they *will* rain destruction upon us until we are, as a species, extinct."

The conversation continued long into the night, and by the time it was drawing to a close, the candle-light by which they were talking started to flicker as the flames came to the ends of the wicks. It was agreed. They would join their respective organisations to try to guide a safer coexistence with the monsters. There was nothing else to be done. They couldn't stand against the evil before them; all they could do was survive.

Only the very top one per cent of either group would ever know what was going on and why. Anyone who gained such a position would have to be eliminated should they refuse to abide by the Orders decree. This was to be the way for the foreseeable future.

Pleiadian Scout Ship

Low Earth Orbit

Earth Year 1784

"Traton Saf, I am detecting energy signatures that are not consistent with the current technical abilities of the planet's inhabitants," reported the systems analyst.

"Elaborate," replied Saf.

As the Commander of the ship, it was his job to ensure that the mission was successful. They had been tasked on a scouting mission to ascertain the status of the planet that the inhabitants called Earth. The world below was still using fire to light their homes, which meant that any real power sources that were detected were due to either human advancement or more probable, as in this case, off-world intervention. That would be a massive breach of Galactic Law because Earth was currently classed as undeveloped. That didn't mean that the planet didn't have any development in terms of buildings or houses, or even people, but what it did say was that the Beings that resided there were not developed sufficiently enough for contact with an *alien* species. The repercussions for such a breaking of the non-interference law could be extreme and range from economic sanctions to military action, depending on the severity of the crime that was committed.

"Well?" Saf demanded impatiently. He wasn't accustomed to waiting for answers.

"Traton, apologies, I am finding the readings… confusing. They appear to be Draconian, but that cannot be. We are too far from Draco spa…" Elda trailed off. "Confirmed. Draconian shuttle leaving the surface."

"Thank you, Elda," Saf replied. Turning to the PRD controller, he added, "Keep the Phased Reality Drive at 100 per cent, and track that shuttle; there are no shuttles without mother ships – find it."

"There are no other ships in orbit, Traton," said Orlon. "They could be using another planet to shield themselves."

"Acknowledged, keep scanning," Saf ordered. "Bring the ship to battle stations. I want to be prepared, in case we find ourselves in conflict."

The command crew burst into life as the ship came to battle stations. Each crewmember knew their jobs and was instinctively getting on with their tasks. Throughout the vessel, it was the same, each person moving to their assigned positions and preparing for war.

"Traton, I think I have found them... energy readings are being immitted from the far side of the moon," said Elda several minutes later. "Yes, there is definitely a Draconian ship on the far side of... oh my, Traton, it's a battleship. Cruiser class."

"Prepare a communication drone. Include everything we have on the humans and more importantly, what we've got on the Draco in the system. Do not release until I order it and keep updating the information load until the last second." Saf needed to prepare for the eventuality that his ship could find itself fighting for survival, but he also needed to ensure that the Pleiadian Council of Light were aware of the situation in Sol System. It might not change anything on a Galactic level, but at least his own people would know.

Saf was convinced that the Draconians were here to exert their influence on the planet below. It wouldn't be the first time. The trouble was that with the limited information they had, the Galactic Council wouldn't act. It always seemed to be the way. Although they *knew* that there was an illegal act being committed, being able to *prove* it was something else entirely. All proof would need to be absolute, completely undeniable. All they had right now was proof that the Draconians were in this particular solar system and had visited Earth, but nothing to prove that they were doing anything wrong. After all, the Pleiadians were here on a scouting mission, so couldn't that be why the reptilians were here? No, Saf knew they weren't here to scout, but that didn't mean the Council would believe him. He needed proof.

"I have a suggestion, Traton," said Orlon. "If we send a ground team to the area where the shuttle landed, we might be able to ascertain the reason for the reptilian's appearance here."

"Well done, Orlon. I was thinking the same thing. See to it." Saf gave the order as he walked to the bridge door. "I will be in my compartment preparing a report regarding the situation."

Saf knew that once he had determined the Draconians reasons for being on the planet, he should take his ship to the nearest point in space to allow for real-time communications. That was the rule. But he couldn't shake the feeling that wouldn't be possible. He felt his intuition telling him to get as much information uploaded to the drone as possible. He had completed his report, ending it with, "We must consider instigating the Earth Born Project as soon as possible."

The comm beeped on Saf's desktop, indicating a message from Elda. "Traton, the ground team is on the surface and will be on the scene of the landing area momentarily."

"Acknowledged," he said. "I am on my way."

Making his way to the command couch, Traton Saf demanded a report. In front of him was the holographic display showing that the ship was in a geosynchronous orbit above the team on the ground. He watched as they made their way towards a building that was situated on the edge of a forest. As they moved, the team were taking scans of the area, and that data was scrolling down the right-hand side of the holo-screen. Everything seemed reasonable; the only exception being the radiation levels were not in line with regular background readings. They were not dangerous; however, they were not rooted in planetary norms. The patterns matched those that would emanate from the reactors of a spacecraft, specifically, a Draconian combat shuttle.

The video feed from the Bretar, the leader of the ground team showed their movement as cautious and deliberate as they got close to the building. There appeared to be a large dark patch in the dirt to the front of the property.

"Bretar, get a better view of that." Saf gave the order already knowing what it was.

"Traton, it seems to be blood." Having given the initial report, Bretar got closer and held the scanner over it. "Confirmed, it is blood. It appears to be fairly fresh. I'd say within the last ten, maybe twelve hours."

"Acknowledged, Bretar. The cellular diagnostics make it clear that the blood's owner would have been a human infant," Saf replied as he read the information coming from the ships analytical systems. "Proceed with extreme caution and do not hesitate to use deadly force if the Draco attack."

Saf had seen this before. The Draconians had used this tactic on other worlds. Sacrifice the young to force a response from the old. Be it conflict or submission; any reaction would allow them to formulate a way to proceed with their plans. Whether that be a clandestine insurgency or an all-out invasion, the reptile's would know one way or the other. But even with all the knowledge and experience from past Draconian indiscretions, the Galactic Council still needed undeniable proof. Currently, everything they had found so far was, at best, circumstantial.

Under cover of what little remained of the darkness, the ground team slowly made their way to the house and attached small listening devices to the windows. The small machines not only recorded what was said but relayed it in real time to the ship, allowing the command crew to hear what was going on. After a few minutes, the conversation inside one of the rooms made it clear that the Draconians had slaughtered an infant to force the humans into submission.

The people in the house were apparently of some importance and from what Traton Saf could make out, they were the head of some sort of secret society whose influence spanned the globe and appeared to be free from the elected government's laws and opposition. The Draco was here to engage in an insurgency using the underground cabal to further their own agender. Allowing this to happen would have devastating consequences for the planet.

Saf wouldn't stand by and watch this, he would intervene.

"Traton, I think there may be Draconian's in the forest..." Elda reported knowing full well that the ground team would be in imminent danger. "Shadows are appearing in the treeline. I think they have matched their body temperatures to that of the environment; it's difficult to see, but I recommend we withdraw the landing team."

Watching the display, Saf saw what Elda had been talking about, and switched through the various visual settings on the spectral analyser but could not say with any degree of certainty whether or not the shadows were anything other than that, shadows. Still, it was better to be safe than sorry.

"I agree with that assessment Elda. Pull them back to the stable but have them leave the listeners in place." Saf wanted as much intelligence as he could get before releasing the comm drone. "Does anyone know if there is any native wildlife that could mask its body temperature in a way such as we see here?" he asked, opening the question to the entire bridge crew.

"Some animals can change their temperatures, but not in the way we are witnessing, and not on this continent."

"We will assume the worst then and prepare for emergency extraction of the ground team." Saf couldn't take any chances. He wanted to be ready to pull his unit off the surface at a moment's notice.

"So, we are agreed," said Brother Spartacus with some degree of relief. "I will prepare a dispatch immediately," he added as he made his way to the desk.

Brother Ajax had reluctantly come to terms with the situation. There was nothing else to be done. They had to agree to the demands, and in doing so, they may be able to do some good. He had hated every second of his deliberating on the matter, but what else could he do? If he had gone against the Order, he would have been dead before sunrise. Not just him either, his entire family would be killed, and probably in a manner most horrible.

Their plan was simple and elegant. Infiltrate every facet of human society, particularly government and pave the way for peaceful coexistence with the reptilian species from another world. None of those present believed the monster at his word that they only wanted to take a few of the planet's resources and then move on. The alien had told the men gathered that they were a peaceful race that desperately needed certain minerals to ensure the survival of their dying world. He had also said that they were aware that the inhabitants of Earth were not ready to accept the knowledge of Beings from other planets; therefore, their presence should remain secret. The men knew that the show of force was made to prove to the humans that, if necessary, the Draconian's would invade and take what they needed by force, leaving the humanity no choice but to capitulate.

By having Illuminati Masonic members in top leadership positions, they could dictate the New World Order that was needed to ensure the survival of the human race with as few casualties as possible. They knew there was always the risk that the Overlords could change the terms of their agreement, but in the meantime, they would gain technological advances that would otherwise take centuries to create. That was reason enough to go along with the demands. By getting advanced technologies, they thought they might eventually be able to use it in such a way as to combat the monsters and drive them from the Earth. But they also knew that would be something for future generations to deal with - if humanity survived that long.

With the dispatches complete, both Spartacus and the Masonic Grand Master added their respective wax seals before they were handed over to the rider. Both of the wax prints carried the emblems of the secret societies from which they derived; the Cap Stone of a pyramid with the All-Seeing Eye for the Illuminati, and the Circle and Compass for the Masons. Both men had also signed their names in ink to alleviate any doubt as to the authenticity of the new orders. The manuscript was to be shared between only the top echelon of both societies and no one else. Any who saw the contents, who were not positioned to do so would be eliminated immediately along with anyone they had told. Secrecy was the key to success. Forget the accord with the aliens; if *humanity* found out, they would all hang just for the conspiracy of being a part of a secret organisation that was influencing the world stage.

"Do not stop until you reach the French capital." The tone that Spartacus used was one of utmost severity. The consequences of failure clear in implication. "Reveal to no one what you have on your person and guard it with your life."

"I will, Brother. My life is forfeit before the cause, Sir." The rider set off at best speed. His journey would be long and arduous, but Spartacus knew he would succeed. He wouldn't have chosen the man if he had any doubt. Although the document he carried highlighted the new amalgamation of the two most powerful secret societies, it also laid out a plan to start a revolution in France, which in doing so meant they could begin the process of replacing that government's leadership.

The sound of the horse hooves faded as the men made their way back into the house. A shot of whiskey was in order. They had set into motion the greatest conspiracy in human history. Only time would tell if they were successful.

"May God have mercy on our souls." It was the only toast the men could think to say.

* * * * *

"Two more enemy combat shuttles on approach," Elda shouted over the rumbling of explosions.

The Draconians had somehow made a stealth approach and targeted the Pleiadian scout vessel in a devastating move. The ship had lost its Phased Reality Drive and was visible for the world to see. How had the Draco been able to detect them while they were phased? It shouldn't have been possible, but that didn't alter the fact that they were currently being hit with a barrage laser fire.

"Return fire and continue evasive manoeuvres." Traton Saf was still composed enough to sound confident. However, he knew that they would not be going home. The ship had sustained catastrophic damage that could only be repaired if they made it to a space dock and they couldn't do *that* if they couldn't get back to the Pleiades star cluster. They were venting atmosphere and fluids, which made the job of the enemy tracking systems that much easier.

The landing team had been engaged at the same time as the ship, and they had already lost two of the five men. The firefight was still raging, but Saf could see from the displays that the unit on the ground had moments to live before the sneaky Draconian warriors finished them off. He had assigned one of the ships turrets to provide cover fire for the landing party but had to countermand the order to fight off the number of enemy combat shuttles.

"Traton, the Draco battleship has broken its moorings and is on an intercept course. Estimated time to weapons range is three minutes." The fear on the bridge was palpable.

"Acknowledged, Elda," Saf said. "Release the drone, the battle is lost. We must get the reports back to command."

"Drone away, Traton."

Smoke and sparks had started to fill the command deck, obscuring the view of the holo-screen, but Traton Saf would never leave his people behind. "Target any shuttles between us and the surface and fire at maximum. We are going in to pick up the landing team. Have them ready to evacuate as soon as we're down," he said.

Having received the notification of extraction, the commander of the landing team gave his reply. "Acknowledged. We are ready to go as soon as you touch down," Bretar shouted over the sound of weapons fire. The ground team was surrounded by enemy warriors, and the battle was more intense than anything they had trained for. Almost relentless incoming fire had annihilated his men. Only two were left fighting, including him. The covering fire from the ship had ceased about ten minutes ago, and the enemy had exacted a devastating toll. His team had performed admirably, killing at least twenty of the reptilians, but it wasn't enough. They were still coming, still fighting, still trying to destroy the Pleiadians by any means necessary.

The pain was instant, and as Bretar looked down to his right, he saw the claw had come through his back and exited the front of his chest. Blood poured away from him as his vision began to close in and darken. He knew he was dead; his body just hadn't realised it yet. His last companion had taken a plasma round to the face a moment ago. It was over, and he knew it. His life signs would still be visible on the ship, and that meant that Traton Saf would continue his decent to extract him, and that would expose the craft to more enemy fire. He couldn't allow that.

"Traton, abort evac. We're finished." His voice was barely a whisper.

"Acknowledged, Bretar. Thank you for your service. May your soul join the galactic light, my friend." The recognition that Saf couldn't save his men was devastating. This brought with it another realisation, get the ship away. "Rodan, get us out of here."

The ship lurched as the pilot engaged the engines to full and aimed for the stars. In routine flight the Antigravity Drive provided a field that engulfed the vessel, which meant that the G-forces exerted were negated because it was the drive that created a portal in front of the ship, effectively pulling it along in whichever direction they wanted to travel. However, the system had sustained damage during the battle, and now the ship was running on its back up, ION drive. The craft was moving at 12G and the force it exerted felt as though the weight of several swamp dogs were crushing Saf's chest. He had to tense every muscle in his body to keep some semblance of consciousness.

No sooner had they broken through the atmosphere than a massive explosion hit the trailing edge of the little scout ship, causing it to lurch.

"We've lost the engines, Traton. We're dead in space," Elda said with an edge of finality.

The holo-screen was still just about working, and Saf saw the human dispatch rider making his way across the countryside. He knew what the courier had in his possession and that it could change the face of the planet below.

"Weapons, target that human on horseback; we can't let him reach his destination." Before he'd even finished the order, he felt the vibrations as the weapons fired towards the surface and he saw what appeared to be lightning strikes hit the besieged man and his horse.

Traton Saf watched as the enemy battlecruiser opened fire on the drone that was trying to escape to free space. "NO!" he said quietly as he saw a bolt of plasma score a hit. The feed died shortly after. If that drone had been destroyed, all hope was lost.

He wouldn't get to find out, as a moment later everything turned black as his ship disintegrated into the void.

1

London

England

Present Day

Today's the day I take my life back, Archie Hammond thought as he finished emptying out his locker before making his way over to his mail draw and clearing that out too. His time serving the public was over. As much as he loved the job, he just couldn't take another day of managerial shit. It was time to move on to pastures new before he punched his boss' lights out. After one final check that he had everything that belonged to him and stuck anything that belonged to the service outside the door of the station office, he moved into the section of the building that housed the Human Resource office.

"What's this?" asked the HR Manager as Archie handed over the envelope and the cylindrical package.

With a big smile, Archie replied coarsely, "Read it, and you'll find out." He'd had enough of the Ambulance Services bullshit, and he hated the woman that was stood in front of him. Dressed up like a superstar wife, in high heels, very short miniskirt topped off with a revealing blouse that pretty much put her tits on show. She had gotten to where she was by sleeping with anyone with enough importance to achieve her goals and anyone else for that matter. Not only was she one of the biggest hypocrites in the service, but she was nasty and vindictive, as well as a terrible liar.

A look of shock and surprise came across her face as she read the resignation letter. In it, Archie had been blunt and to the point. He had pointed out the failings of the Service for all the stress they had caused him over the past seven years. The job itself was easy, and he could do it standing on his head with his hands tied behind his back, but for more than half a decade, the management had stitched him up at every turn. From being told that he had leave granted, only to be disciplined upon his return, because they had lied. To having his shifts changed continuously at short notice and being sent from pillar to post and forced to work all over the service rather than where he was actually based. He was continually being called into the boss to answer questions about bullshit allegations from other managers and the control centre - none of which was true.

Generally, Archie's life had been made so difficult that he could no longer put up with it. The pressure had been total and constant. And on top of that, there was the general stress of being run into the ground just with the standard workload of life on the world's most prominent Ambulance Service. Every time he spoke to the stations Ambulance Operations Manager, he was lied to, and that in itself was cause for stress. But for all of that, the worst thing for him was that constant policy changes. None of which were of any benefit to the staff nor the people they served... the public. The incompetence of the management for not being able to see that these changes were costing lives was unbearable, and he could no longer be a part of it.

It had taken Archie some time to come to the decision to leave the job, but it was inevitable – the victimisation, bullying, and harassment had become overwhelming. He had been living on roughly three, maybe four hours of broken sleep per night for years. The constant worry of how they would get him next was causing him to wake up multiple times through the night, and it was making him ill. He started to feel like he was permanently angry, and if he wasn't angry, he was anxious – it had all taken its toll.

He had worked as a Paramedic for just under twenty years, and it was a job that he absolutely loved, not only that, but he was bloody good at it. But things change when the management has a person on their radar, that's it, game over. In that situation, there is only ever going to be one outcome – resign or get sacked, the result was the same...you were gone. You might win a battle, but you'll never win the war, and it's only ever the war that matters.

For the first time in years, Archie was in control of his own fate – he would be the one to determine his future.

"Well, at least you'll get a reference from us," was all she could say.

With a laugh, Archie replied, "Do you really think I would put any future job in your hands after everything you lot have done to me? Don't be fucking stupid. I'd never ask you people for anything. Now, I've cleared my locker and my mail draw, so there's nothing else to say, so if you don't mind, I will be on my way."

"What's this parcel?" she asked as Archie turned to leave.

"Oh Yeah, I nearly forgot," he replied with a wry smile. "You can share that with the rest of the management team."

"What is it?" she asked again as she opened the packaging that contained the giant Dildo.

"Now that I don't work for you people anymore, you can all go fuck yourselves!" It was a childish thing to do, but it made him feel good, and that made it worthwhile.

And with that, Archie had ended his twenty-year love-hate relationship as a Paramedic. Now he was free to do whatever he wanted, the only problem he had, was he didn't know *what* he wanted to do… absolutely no idea!

Having spent several weeks doing odd jobs for various people, he was offered a week of training work, explicitly teaching First Aid. It wasn't a job that he was particularly interested in, but it was something that a lot of former ambulance personnel found themselves doing. It contained public speaking, and Archie hated that with a passion, but with nothing to lose, he gave it a go anyway. After all, he had a unique background in the subject, his knowledge and experience were of the highest order. And he couldn't keep hoping for labouring work for the rest of his life.

Archie was as nervous as he'd ever been as he opened up the 3 Day First Aid at Work training course, he felt as though he was entirely out of his comfort zone. He found that strange considering the amount of life and death emergency situations he'd previously found himself in. Standing at the front of the class, he felt self-conscious, and he was sweating as his nerves threatened to overwhelm him. Before him, were 12 people, men, and women of various ages. They had all been put on the course by their company to be in line with the governing body for the industry.

After giving the group an introduction to the course and a brief history of himself, he found that the students seemed to be hanging on his every word as he went through the input. Speaking to several of the group during the morning break, he found out that their interest had been piqued because he was a trainer that had actually been there and done it, whereas previous instructors had learned their trade from a manual. The realisation that he was able to hold their attention so effectively gave him the confidence to relax and pass on the knowledge and skills needed for the people in front of him to achieve the standards required to pass the course.

Three days later and with the course drawing to a close, Archie realised that he'd not only enjoyed teaching the subject, but he also felt some measure of satisfaction in helping others improve their abilities in life-saving skills. The achievement was in no way comparable to that of actually being on the front line and doing the job for real, but it was there, nonetheless. Closing the course down, he was pleased that all of his students had not only met the required standard but well and truly exceeded it.

Over the next couple of days, Archie thought about going on and teaching First Aid for a living, and the more he considered it, the more it made sense. He seemed to have a natural ability in teaching. The only problem that concerned him was the regularity and the amount of work he would get from week to week. First Aid at Work courses are typically three days long, most of which were run during the working week, Monday to Friday. That meant that he would only be able to do one full course per week. Though, he might be able to make up the other two days by teaching First Aid Refresher courses as they consisted of one day's input. He might need to do a bit of juggling of days here and there, but he certainly felt that it was possible. Providing he could get at least one full three-day course a week, financially, he should be able to pull it off.

His decision was made a few days later after he received a phone call from the owner of the company that had contracted him in to teach. The man had received feedback from the students that attended Archie's course... it was good. No, it was excellent. The best feedback any of the company's trainers had ever gotten. The praise was followed by the offer of more work. Although the company was not doing as well as they could, it meant that for a time, the number of jobs would be limited. To Archie, it didn't matter; it was a foot in the door and a step in the right direction. He took it.

After a few weeks, the lack of work coming in made it evident that the company was on its last legs, probably in its death throws. Archie made the decision to go freelance and put his name on the books of several other firms. He couldn't believe his luck, as the reception he got from most was that they were trying to rip his arm off. They all wanted someone of his experience on their books. In some cases, he even wrote his own pay grade. Which was good... really good. So good in fact that after several months he decided that he could only work three days a week and still have extra money at the end of the month. It was an option that he just couldn't refuse. He'd worked hard his entire life and sacrificed his work-life balance for only work. The realisation hit him one night when he was having a family night, with old pictures and videos of the kids playing on the Television. Watching the family birthdays and Christmas footage, he noticed that he was either not in them, or if he was, he was wearing his uniform, and that meant he had either been to work, or he was going to work. It dawned on him that life on the Ambulance Service had robbed him of the intimacy of his family. He'd missed out on so much, that he couldn't even begin to recall what. With the amount of money he was now making, he decided that enough was enough; he'd work only when he had to and no more.

This new freedom of working meant that Archie found himself with plenty of time on his hands and he soon rediscovered a past passion for fishing. Spending as much time on the bank of a river or a lake as he could, usually freezing his nuts off and catching nothing but a cold. Days, nights, weekends and even weeks at a time were lost fishing. He loved everything about the sport, and also the fish. Where possible, he tried to return any fish to the water in a better condition than when they came out. To this end, he carried a full fish care kit and treated every fish as though it was a pet from a home aquarium. As much as he loved being at the water, the sport could get extremely expensive. He could make the money, but that defeated the object of working a three day week. No, he'd prefer to have the time at home.

It was during one of these periods away from angling that Archie discovered the UFO phenomenon. It happened entirely by accident. Out of sheer boredom and with nothing to do, he had been flicking through the television channels and found a documentary on Unidentified Flying Objects. After watching the show, he found himself intrigued and began thinking more and more about it. He couldn't figure out if the people featured on the programme had actually had some kind of unexplainable experience or if they were just nutters. Eventually, it turned in to an extensive research campaign that seemed to go on and on. He found that the more he looked into it, the more he felt there was something to it. He thoroughly researched the more significant stories such as the *Roswell Incident, Rendlesham Forest, and the Phoenix Lights,* to name but a few. He was well and truly hooked, and it got to the point that when he wasn't fishing, he was researching UFOs. And if he wasn't doing either of those things, he was looking into the sky for strange lights or flying saucers. His interest verged on obsession.

It didn't take long after beginning the Ufology research for Archie to notice that there seemed to be some sort of strange connection between UFO sightings and spirituality. So much so, that he felt it warranted further investigation. This project was ongoing, however, after about six weeks of research, Archie had become convinced that there was indeed some sort of link to a lot of sightings and decided that he would begin his own spiritual journey. He began meditating regularly and started to follow certain Buddhist philosophies – not the religion, he was in no way religious – but he did implement some elements of the ideals. He combined these with the Ju-Jitsu he had done since childhood. Soon after he began his walk down the spiritual path, he realised that they all seemed to pay into each other and he'd started seeing results, particularly during his martial arts training. He appeared to be able to see things before they happened; like he could anticipate what was coming. It seemed to be the same with life in general, and it was as though the new practices had sparked something within his own intuition.

Within three weeks of combined work in both Ufology and spiritualism, something strange happened, not to Archie personally, but rather to his wife and his brother. Lucy was still working for the Ambulance Service, and Jeff was a hospital porter. They were both working night shifts on the same night, but at different hospitals, the locations of which were approximately five miles apart. Archie had spent the evening meditating for quite some time, and he had been focusing on the UFO subject. During this session, he kept seeing something that he couldn't explain. It was like there was a light that would get brighter and more prominent at specific points of the meditation. Eventually, he came to think that the light was trying to tell him something. He noticed the intensity change when he concentrated on specific things, such as questions he might ask during the sitting. Questions like *"Are UFO'S real?"* or *"Are UFO's alien in origin?"* His intuition was telling him to pay attention to it, but even though he felt there could be something to it, he tried to push it from of his mind because he thought it was more likely to be the onset of a migraine. He'd had experienced visual disturbances similar to this before, usually as a precursor to a blinding headache. Usually, the disturbances took the form of a streak of light through his vision from left to right, a bit like horizontal lightning that only he could see.

Eventually, after several hours of meditation, with the light glaring and not feeling the excruciating pain that he usually felt, he came to realise that there was more to this light than just a headache. The lightning Archie had experienced in the past was trying to tell him something, and the pain was the result of his not understanding it. During meditation, if he asked a question and received the light in response, then the answer would be *YES,* and if the light didn't show, the answer was *NO.* He had to prove this to himself time and again before he put any true faith into it, but once he was convinced of what was happening, he never suffered a migraine, ever.

It was at approximately 1 am on the night they both saw, what could only be described as a UFO. Jeff managed to snap a couple of photos of it on his mobile phone. They were blurry, and the object was obviously at high altitude. They were the typical *can't quite make it out* UFO picture's, but at least it was something to go on. However, Archie wouldn't find out about this incident until three days later when Jeff phoned for a chat, during which he hesitantly said he had seen something weird in the sky while he was at work. But fearing that his brother would think he was a mental case, he wouldn't elaborate any further, even when Archie pushed the subject.

After the call, Archie was talking to Lucy about family matters, and he happened to mention what Jeff had told him, immediately she apologised, saying that she had meant to tell him that she had seen something similar but forgotten all about it. She said it was a light that didn't act like a normal plane or helicopter, explaining that it behaved like a fly – zipping one way then the other but at incredible speeds. Her telling of the incident was free, she knew about her husband's research into the UFO phenomenon and was more than happy with relaying her tale. As he questioned her, he realised that this could well be the same object that Jeff had seen. It was also the same night that he had been meditating and first experienced the light. Was this coincidence? At this point in time, he hadn't told either of them about his spiritual journey. In fact, he hadn't revealed it to anyone, instead opting to keep it secret.

Archie felt like he needed to speak to Jeff more about what he'd seen, but for some reason, he didn't feel safe talking on the phone. He didn't know why and couldn't explain it, but he just felt that someone could be listening in. Instead, he made his way to Jeff's house, where they discussed the incident at length.

When the conversation started to die down, Archie told Jeff about Lucy's sighting and a look of relief swept across Jeff's face as he revealed that he had begun to think he was losing the plot. Once he realised that he wasn't going to end up in some sort of institution, he went into the timings of the event, where he was at the time and the direction he was looking in when he saw the object.

After leaving for home about 2 hours later, Archie kept going over what he had been told. There was nothing else for it, he would give it a day or so and speak to Jeff again to further confirm what he'd been told. Meanwhile, he would talk to Lucy and get some more details of timings, where she was exactly, and what direction she was looking in when the event took place.

After an in-depth conversation, it appeared as though they had indeed seen the same thing in the night sky.

A few days later, Archie spoke to his brother again, although this time, Jeff seemed more composed, and he was able to express a lot more detail about the event. The result of the conversation seemed to make it definitive – they had seen the same thing. Archie had already worked out the distances and angles from both of their respective positions that they were viewing it from, and he had even visited both sites and verified the angles with a map and compass. He was sure they had seen the same thing at the same time, on the same night – it all matched. The event itself lasted for three minutes before the object *blinked out* – which is exactly how they both described the end of the sighting.

Was it a mere coincidence that the same night that he focused a meditation session on the subject of UFO's, the two people closest to him both happen to see one? Could it just be circumstantial that their sightings had occurred on the same night he starts to see a light that seems to answer questions during meditation sessions? No, Archie didn't believe that for a second. There seemed to be some sort of divinity involved – some kind of guidance to it all. He concluded that he was being pulled in a particular direction for some reason, but what or why he didn't know. He only knew that he had a guiding light and that it was sending him somewhere – he just had to figure out why.

There was one thing that he was sure of; fate was now the driving force in his life. He stopped believing in coincidence from then on, and this caused him to completely re-evaluate his life and the experiences he'd had through it. Did everything that had happened to him all happen by chance, or was there a reason for it all that went beyond his understanding?

Through meditating on specific questions, Archie got some answers, but he couldn't seem to find the right yes or no question to ask that would reveal the answer as to how it all linked together. The time he had spent working for the Ambulance Service had turned so bad, was to teach him patience and more importantly, to force him away from any Governmental influence, causing him to question and research everything the Government said and did. It also showed him how to keep his head in times of extreme stress and emergencies. The compulsion to follow the Buddhist philosophies was to open his mind to the fact that there was more to reality than he'd previously perceived. And the UFO research had spawned an entirely new era in his life that had absolutely opened him up to the probability of there being other intelligent life in the galaxy. He didn't know how, but he *knew* that alien life existed, and he realised that if *he* knew about it, then the Governments of the world would know, which in turn meant that they had been lying to the world for a very long time.

The conspiracy - there was no other word for it, but conspiracy - that had been perpetrated to hide the existence of alien life opened the door to different types of conspiracies and hidden agenda's, such as the Illuminati and their New World Order. Chemtrails sprayed in the sky by planes as a means of geoengineering the planet. The Banking System, and a whole host of other theories. Hell, he even looked into religion, and he came to the same conclusion regarding them all; they were all mechanisms to control the world's population. Although he knew there had to be one, he just couldn't find a reason as to how it all fitted together. He decided to continue to do what he was doing, but with one exception – he would tell those close to him about the spiritual journey he was on.

Six months later, during the height of summer, Archie and his family were having a meal at a local restaurant. The place was hot – sweltering, and the open kitchen was bellowing heat as if he was standing before the gates of hell. It got to the point where he just couldn't take it anymore, and with sweat pouring from his face, he decided to go outside for some relief and fresh air. His son insisted on tagging along, probably because he was bored more than anything else. The time was getting close to 9.45pm, the temperature outside was beginning to drop, and the light was starting to fade to full darkness.

The fresh air was a welcome relief as Archie made his way into the beer garden. The night was clear with not a single cloud in the sky. The moon was full, and the stars were shining brightly. Behind him was a group of about twelve people enjoying a quiet drink after their meal. After a few minutes, Archie felt compelled to look into the sky, his son following suit as he did so. They both saw it at the same time; a bright light dancing around the blacker Eastern sky. It was like nothing he'd ever seen before. It manoeuvred in the same manner that Jeff and Lucy described during their sighting...moving from point to point in the blink of an eye as if it was a flying bug. There was a gasp from the table behind them as the group saw the same thing, and several people were saying "UFO – it's a UFO!"

Archie knew that they were right – it *was* a UFO. As quickly as it came, the light blinked out and was gone.

From that point on, he made an even more significant effort to step up the spiritualism and as a result had more UFO experiences. It got to the extent that at one point, he felt as though he couldn't go outside the front door *without* having a sighting.

2

2 Years Later

London

England

It seemed to take hours to get all the kit ready to go, but then it didn't help matters that when Archie moved on to a fishing lake, he liked to set up the proverbial home from home. It was the middle of winter, which meant that he would be taking more equipment than usual because he liked to be prepared for any eventuality – better to have something and not need it than to need it and not have it. The lake, situated in the West Midlands, England and was literally in the middle of nowhere. There was nothing around for miles - no towns, cities or any other form of civilisation, which was precisely why he'd chosen this place. Peace, quiet, and tranquillity... bliss.

As well as all the usual fishing gear, Archie had decided to take an extensive medical kit which contained the usual stuff like bandages and space blankets, but it also had advanced equipment like Intravenous Fluids, heart stimulating drugs such as Epinephrine and Atropine. The pack also contained an Automated External Defibrillator. The AED was the machine that sent an electrical charge through a patient's body to stop the heart from quivering at times of cardiac arrest. Usually, Archie wouldn't take this kind of gear with him to go fishing, but while he was making an equipment list for the trip, he felt compelled to take it for some reason. Since discovering the guiding light, it hadn't steered him wrong yet. So, trusting his intuition, he packed all the gear up for transport.

Along with the first aid stuff, Archie had decided to take the survival pack from his hiking and mountaineering days as well. Quite why he would need this equipment, he didn't know, but he took it all anyway.

He also packed two tripods for his video and digital camera so that he could film or at least get some photos of his catches. He had been planning this trip for a while and wanted some photographic memories of it. Both of the cameras had interchangeable lenses for close and long-range shots. He also took a thermal imaging camera, or TIC, that he had borrowed from a friend that worked for a Search and Rescue team. He didn't know why he'd need such a device, but that compulsion had got him again, and he knew better than to ignore it.

He had more bait and lures than you could throw a stick at, and with all the kit crammed into the van, Archie set off for the venue. He would be driving through the night and should hopefully arrive at the lake just before dawn. He couldn't wait to get there and set up.

The journey itself was fairly mundane and uneventful, with one exception; Archie felt like he was being watched but couldn't seem to find a source as to why. Pulling up next to the massive expanse of water, he decided to break the usual routine that he would employ when he arrived at a new fishing venue. For him, the norm would be to walk around the entire lake while looking to see if he could find any fish shoaling up and target those before setting up camp. But this water was immense, walking it would take ages, and he was dead tired from the long journey.

He noticed that he could drive the van about halfway around the lake, which he did slowly, taking his time to find the right spot. The lake itself was lined with various trees and bushes, while the margins of the water contained plenty of reed beds. Every so often, there would be areas where the property owners had cut away the foliage to create swims that allowed anglers access to the water.

He eventually stopped at a lovely looking horseshoe bay that had a small beach of compacted sand and mud. The area was situated down from the embankment, about 12 feet from the dirt road. The cove itself was lined with bushes, shrubs and evergreen trees, like conifers or ferns. Most of the other trees on the lake were barren, with no leaves or foliage, nothing but just bare branches. With the combination of the shape of the bay and the evergreens, it meant that the water here was shielded from the wind – it was flat calm and looked like a mirror. *Perfect*, he thought as he turned the engine off.

Getting out of the van, he found a small path through the bushes that led down to the potential campsite. He couldn't help but marvel at the frosty spider webs that were attached to the various shrubs and blades of grass. He imagined that the area was like a little city for the spiders, yet a death trap for any other insects. When he reached the water's edge, he realised just how fortunate he had been in finding this place. It was shielded from the elements more than he could have hoped.

After having a good look around and finding his preferred spot, Archie made his way back up to the road to get his gear together. After he pulled what he needed from the back of the van, he turned away from the lake and noticed another large body of water approximately half a mile away. In fact, the entire area was littered with lakes and ponds of various sizes. It appeared that the place was faithful to the advert – the anglers heaven.

He couldn't see another single person, either fishing or in the surrounding area. Maybe he was the only one brave enough, or more likely, stupid enough to fish in this ridiculously cold weather, or perhaps everyone else knew something he didn't. Either way, he was here now, and he wasn't about to go home because of a little cold. Nope, there were fish to catch, and Archie was in for the long haul.

Time was getting on, and at about 10 am, he knew it was time to crack on with putting the camp together. Having found a piece of flat ground about twenty yards back from the water's edge and under the lip of the embankment, he set up the bivvy. That wasn't too much of an issue, he'd used the thing so many times that he had become quite adept at erecting the tent in short order. As soon as he finished the last touches, he got the gas heater going inside, it was absolutely freezing. After he had set up his little home and got the heating on, he set up a second, smaller tent that would house the bait. He didn't fancy having dead fish and maggots in his house for the week, that would really mess up his Feng Shua, and there was no way he could have that!

With the two shelters and the bait squared away, he got all the gear he would need and put it outside the main bivvy while he set up his bed and sleeping bag so that it was ready for the night ahead. It didn't take long, but with the homestead sorted, it was time to get on with why he was there... fishing.

He managed to get his rods together reasonably quick and started working the water, trying to find the best place to put his baited hooks. Although he was there to fish for pike, he used a carp fishing tactic as he worked the water. He plumbed the depth of the water with a marker float at about a hundred yards range, directly in front of the swim. The idea is that the angler attached a free-running lead to the line before tying the marker float to the end. When it had been cast out, into the water, the weight would drag the float to the bottom. Once there, the angler would strip off, or payout, 12 inches of line at a time from the reel, and the buoyancy of the float would then pull the line through the eye of the free-running lead on the bottom of the lake, allowing the float to rise towards the surface one foot at a time. Meaning that if the angler stripped off line 10 times before he saw the float on the top of the water, that the depth of the water was 10 feet.

After a few minutes of paying out line, the float bobbed to the surface. Archie was surprised at how deep it was. At nearly 35 feet, it was just too deep for what he had in mind. He wound the line in and recast to about fifty yards and *feeling* the lead to the bottom, he knew it had landed on gravel - perfect for bait presentation. After repeating the process of paying out the line, he found this area was around twenty-five feet deep – "That'll do" he muttered to himself.

Leaving the marker float in position, he made a note of a large tree on the opposite bank that lined up with the float, then he cast the other rod around it and found that the area was reasonably free of weed and other obstacles. Decision made; he would fish here.

Now that he had the range, he put the line into the clip on the reel spool and wound it in. Laying the rod on the ground, he staked out two posts at a distance of the length of the rod. That way if he broke the line in the middle of the night, he knew that he could fix a rig to the end and use the posts to get the required distance by wrapping the line around the posts four and a half times and slotting the line into the reel clip. With that done, he measured out the second rod in the same manner before he cast the baited hooks either side of the marker float and felt them down to hit bottom and confirm they landed on the gravel. With each cast, he noted a landmark on the far bank to help with casting in the dark, something to line up with. By lining up with and aiming at the landmark and casting hard enough for the line to hit the clip on the spool, he should find the same spot every time. When he'd finished, he wound in the marker float and put it away, he didn't need that anymore.

By the time Archie had set the lines in his preferred spot, it was mid-afternoon, and the weather was getting colder; it was time for a brew. The warm cup of coffee was a welcome relief to his cold hands, and for a time, he just sat there holding it as he sipped at the hot liquid. Once he'd warmed up somewhat, he set up the tripods and cameras and set them to the side of the porch to the bivvy. The main reason for the photography equipment was to capture a few self-portraits of himself with any fish he might catch, and if he was lucky, he might be able to hit the record button on the video camera to get some footage of the fight as he reeled in the fish.

Happy with the camp set up, Archie sat down on the bedchair and almost immediately felt the effects of the lack of sleep as exhaustion started to take hold. It had taken him most of the day to set up, and darkness was already beginning to reach across the sky as night set upon the landscape. Looking above, he noticed that there wasn't a single cloud to obscure his view of the stars, which were as bright as he had ever seen them. The lack of light pollution was doing its bit to allow more stars to be visible. That was one of the things he loved about being in the middle of nowhere. Both the view and the quiet was genuinely breathtaking. It was a memory worth keeping, that was enough to get him to set about taking some photos. By the time he had finished, the hands of the clock must have plodded on because he felt ravenously hungry and absolutely freezing cold. It was time to eat - on the menu tonight was chilli and rice, which he started cooking up in the porch of the bivvy.

During the cook, he felt compelled to look into the night sky, causing him to divert his eyes upward as he stirred the spicy mince. There, he saw what he thought were three *new* stars that he hadn't noticed earlier. They seemed to be brighter than any of the other lights in the sky and Archie couldn't seem to look away, he was transfixed. As he watched, he thought one of them moved, but he couldn't be sure. The sound of the chilli bubbling in the pan pulled his attention back to the stove, looking away from the sky, he resumed stirring. Happy that his meal wasn't burning, he looked back and was startled to realise the three brighter stars had moved position significantly. Initially, he thought they might have been balloons that were tethered together, but after a moment, he felt his heart rate quicken as he watched them move around each other in a circular motion before zipping around in the darkness of the night sky.

With this display, and the kind of movement he was seeing, it became apparent that the objects weren't simply balloons. He realised he was watching a UFO event and he scrambled to get the photography equipment pointed upward in the hope of catching some footage for later review. The first thing he did was to set the video camera to the sky and start recording before grabbing the stills camera and snapping as many pictures as he could. The event continued for around five minutes before the lights all blinked out simultaneously.

For a moment or two, Archie could only sit there in stunned silence as he recalled the display of aerial acrobatics he'd just witnessed before he remembered the chilli and rice were still cooking. This pulled him out of the immediate bewilderment, and he set about serving up his dinner, his mind continuing to race. After pouring the chilli over the rice, he sprinkled a bit of grated cheese over the top and started scoffing down the grub. He was hungrier than he initially thought.

As he leaned forward to put the bowl down, he heard the unmistakable whomping of helicopter rota blades. At first, he didn't think much of it until he realised they were getting closer. Getting out of the bivvy and turning towards the approaching noise, he saw that there were at least three of the flying machines heading directly toward him, or towards the lake, at least. Archie instantly felt panic creep through his body as he realised they were all blacked out; the only reason he could actually see them at all was that the moonlight was glinting off of the windows. Black helicopters were commonly associated with nefarious activities around UFO encounters. His intuition was screaming at him to hide, to not let them find him. There was confusion in his mind as he thought back to the UFO sighting; craft that he felt, no, *knew* were alien in origin, from another world. During which he felt elation and wellbeing, but now with his own kind in helicopters, he felt fear and dread. *Shouldn't that be the other way around?* He thought to himself. *NO, trust your feelings – HIDE!* He immediately realised he had to sort out some way to hide himself, but what could he do? He had about two minutes before they would be overhead.

The first thing he did was to turn off the heater and tried to get as much heat outside as possible by fully opening the bivvy door flaps. That wouldn't be enough to hide the heat signature alone. What else could he do? His mind was racing as he tried to think of something and in a moment of inspiration or maybe madness, it came to him… *SPACE BLANKETS!* The survival pack contained several space blankets – the type that marathon runners used after the race. They had no thermal properties other than to reflect heat, meaning that they didn't generate heat, they merely rebounded the users heat back at them. Hopefully, they would reflect the heat back into the tent while reflecting the cold outwards. He didn't know if it would work, but he had no other cards to play.

Frantically, he ran around one side of the bivvy and unhooked the rain cover that sat over the top of the main tent and pulled it over to the other side. Ripping open the three space blankets, he laid them over the roof and replaced the rain cover over the lot. Jumping inside and shutting the door flaps, he hoped that his hiding spot looked like a bush from the air. Fortunately, the tent was sat at the bottom of a twelve-foot bank that led up to the road, and he'd had to park the van in the designated parking area, which as luck would have it, was under a large clump of trees. He hoped that those factors combined would provide a bit more cover.

Looking through a small spy hole in the flaps that formed the bivvy doors, Archie watched as the helicopters circled around the lake and local area for the next half an hour or so before they finally left in the same direction from which they had come. Breathing a big sigh of relief, he turned the heater back on. A few minutes later he got out of the tent with the Thermal Imaging Camera and moved towards the water's edge, turning back, he checked to see how effective his little heat hiding house was. To his total surprise, it was hidden quite well – even with the heater on...not perfect of course, but it was definitely better than a kick in the nuts. As he thought about it, he decided that if the choppers came back, he would repeat what he did the first time and turn everything off and stay out of sight. He couldn't explain it, but he felt like the occupants of those helicopters would do him harm if they got hold of him. Maybe he was just paranoid, maybe he'd seen too many science fiction movies or perhaps he was right to be concerned.

Archie spent the rest of the waking night in and out of the bivvy, checking out the sky or reviewing the photos and video footage. He couldn't believe what had happened and still felt agitated about the helicopters. He decided to have a meditation session to try and find his centre and settle himself down. Hopefully, his guiding light might have something to say on the matter. Whenever he posed the question of the helicopters being dangerous, the light shone so brightly, it was as though there was a torch pointed at his face - they were dangerous alright. By the time he'd finished, Archie realised that the session had lasted a lot longer than intended. Archie thought he had been meditating for about an hour but was shocked to find he'd been at it for two. He had lost all concept of time during the sitting, but the upside at least was that he found himself more relaxed. Eventually, he fell asleep around 01.30 am, a lot later than he would have liked, he was knackered.

3

Fishing Lake

West Midlands

England

Archie was woken at around 9 am by the buzzing of a bite alarm and a screaming reel… fish on! Jumping off the bed chair, he fell flat on his face – he was still wrapped up in the sleeping bag. After scrambling out of the binds and getting to the rod, he engaged the drag, and lifted into the fish, laughing at his misfortune of smacking his face in the dirt as he did so.

The fish tore line from the reel like nothing he had ever experienced, he just couldn't seem to get a handle of it. The drag was set to full, but the line was peeling away as if it was in free spool. Within seconds it was down to the backing line. BANG! The rod was ripped from his hands and started skipping across the water. He stood there, frozen in disbelief as he watched it go.

"What the fuck was that?" he asked himself, helplessly watching his £400 rod disappear. He was absolutely dumbfounded. He was there to fish for predators, but that meant the Northern Pike, not a Great White fucking shark! Archie didn't know what it was, but what he did know was that the violence involved in taking the rod out of his hands in that manner just couldn't be done by a pike.

After a few minutes of feeling sorry for himself, Archie remembered that he had stuffed the rod butts with buoyancy foam, causing them to float if he ever dropped them into the water. That meant he might actually find it. Looking around the bay, he saw a tree with very few leaves and plenty of low hanging branches, it appeared to be reasonably climbable. Making his way up, he stopped after reaching a height of about twenty-five feet and got himself stable enough to start scanning the lake through binoculars. Initially, he couldn't see anything but open water, although he did find an old rowboat in the next swim. *That might come in handy – if I ever find my bloody rod*, he thought to himself.

He spent the next ten minutes looking around the lake before finally spotting something poking out of the water. It was the butt of the rod, approximately 200 yards out, and to the right of the bay. As it bobbed up and down, Archie lined the rod up with a focal point on the far bank, so that he'd have a fair idea of what direction to go once he started making his way out to it. Now that he knew roughly where he was heading, he started making his way down from the tree, which to his surprise, was a lot harder than going up. Eventually, after falling the last ten feet, he was on the ground with a bruise on his arse to match the one on his face. Cursing as he got to his feet, he just hoped the boat was usable. A lot of lakes in the U.K have small rowboats on the water so that an angler could use it to aid them in landing a particularly big or snagged fish. It just happened to be a stroke of luck that this fishery had one. But with the way his morning had started, Archie wouldn't be surprised if he sank halfway across the lake.

Limping, he made his way to the next swim to check out the wooden vessel. He was thankful that the thing was in pretty good order. At about eight foot long, it had oars and even a little makeshift anchor in the form of a large brick attached to a fair amount of rope. And as an added bonus, there was very little water in the bottom. *Thank heavens for small mercies*, he thought as he started getting ready for the row out to his rod. Just as he was about to get in, he had the sudden realisation that if for some reason, he ended up in the water, the thick winter clothing he was wearing would be a severe hindrance. With that in mind, he opted to strip down to his underpants. He didn't want to fall at all, but if he did, being fully clothed would probably mean he wouldn't come out again. As soon as he was ready, Archie sat in the boats only seat, taking his fish knife with him. He started rowing in the general direction of the landmark he had spotted while he was in the tree.

As he made his way across the lake, Archie was going over what had happened in his mind. What could have pulled the rod from his hands like that? After all, he was on a lake in Britain, not fishing on the Zambezi river. He was trying to think what kind of fish could have done that and as far as he was aware, the biggest freshwater predators in the U.K were the Northern Pike and the Wells Catfish. Neither of those grew to the size that could strip line from a fully engage drag and pull the rod from the anglers hands that violently. Although the European Wells Catfish did grow to enormous proportions, the British species didn't come to anywhere near the size of their European brethren. All of a sudden, another, more horrible thought popped into his head – he was predator fishing, which meant that whatever it was, it took a sizeable dead bait. Therefore, it *must* have been a predator, and it was big enough to literally tear the rod from his hands. That made him wonder if the fish could eat him if he fell in. *Fuck it – I should have kept my clothes on so that I could drown before being eaten!* As the thought come to him, he started laughing – that scenario would be just his luck today.

The journey took about eight minutes, save for a few minutes it took to find the exact spot. The physical exertion had actually kept him warm, but as he got to the rod butt and stopped, the cold hit him immediately, and it hit hard. It was absolutely freezing. Hesitantly, Archie reached over the side and gently gripped the rod, he didn't want to rush in case the fish was still attached to the hook and bolted away, pulling him into the lake, and eating him before he had time to drown. With one hand gripping the butt, he reached beneath the surface with his other hand and gently pulled on the line to see if there was any tension, which would indicate that the fish was still on. The line was still attached to the reel, but there didn't seem to be any weight there. *Good*, he thought as he got both hands on to the butt and gently started to lift it out of the water, all the time feeling for any tightening of the line. *So far so good*, he thought as he got his fish knife and forced the blade into the side of the boat – he wanted it to hand and ready to cut the line if anything untoward happened.

Once he was ready, with the rod in his right hand, he took the reel handle in his left and slowly started to rewind the line on to the spool. After winding a significant amount of line back onto the reel and checking that it was still slack, Archie decided that the fish must have spat the hook and was gone. He started winding harder. That was a mistake. The rod bent double, and a heavy weight began to pull the line off of the reel again, causing the boat to shift as it was dragged across the water.

"FUCK THIS!" Archie shouted as the bow of the boat started dipping under the surface. Struggling, he reached out for the knife and cut the line, the sudden release of tension, causing him to fall backward, into the bottom of the boat.

"Time to go," he said to himself as he picked up the oars and frantically started rowing toward the bay. He wasn't about to mess around. The amount of force he had exerted to just try to hold the rod for those few seconds had been immense, and he was already out of breath. Whatever that thing was, Archie didn't want to play its game. Nothing in British freshwater angling should be able to do what this thing had, and if he was honest, it scared the life out of him. He wanted to get off the water – sharpish. He didn't think he had it in him, but he was like an Olympic rower as he got back to the bay in quick time.

No sooner had he grounded the rowboat, he got dressed and laid down on the beach to catch his breath. As he lay there, he decided that he would change his target fish. There was something in this water that he didn't want to fuck with. Nope, he was definitely going to switch to a gentler bit of course fishing. *Yeah, a few Roach, Rudd and maybe a Carp or two will be lovely*, he thought as he lay there looking up at the sky. With that in mind, he jumped up and wound in the other pike rod and packed it away before whatever it was out there took that line as well. He wouldn't need his predator gear anymore on this trip.

After he set up a course fishing rod, and with the adrenalin leaving his system, he realised how cold it was. He was freezing and felt like he had been chilled to the bone. Looking at the time, he had no idea how late it was, 2 pm already. He got a brew on, and as he sat there waiting for the water to boil, he realised that for the first time in his life, he was actually pissed off with fishing. So much so, that although he had just set up his rod, he didn't bother to cast it out, he'd had enough for one day.

Every muscle in his body ached as he lay out on the bed chair. He picked up the cup of coffee and took a swig as he thought about what had happened over the past twenty-four hours and remembered the UFO sighting. *Did I dream that, or did it actually happen?* He wondered as he reached out for the video camera. He was so tired that he couldn't quite remember. Upon reviewing the footage, it all came back to him – it was no dream, it definitely happened! There was some great video footage of UFOs zipping around the night sky. Better still, there were some fantastic high-quality photos on the other camera. What a trip – an epic UFO event, falling out the bivvy, falling out of the tree, and nearly getting eaten by a monster fish! No-one was going to believe this – people would think this was just another one of those *Fisherman's tales,* like; "The One That Got Away". What was his life coming to?

Night had set upon the landscape by the time Archie had cleared away after eating. He decided he would just lay out on the bed and relax to some tunes. With the heater going full blast it wasn't long before fatigue had him. He was woken by the sound of static that had somehow pushed its way over the music, pissing him off because he realised that the song that was playing was; "It came out of the sky", and he loved that tune. After another minute or so the player cut out altogether and at the same time the bivvy lit up as though the sun had just risen right above him.

What now? He thought as he got up and stuck his head out of the door flap. Looking up, the light was absolutely blinding, he couldn't make anything out through the brightness. He noticed that there was no noise, just what seemed to be an electrical charge in the air, causing the feeling that every hair on his body was standing up. After a few moments, the light shot up into the sky, and the camp was again in darkness. In the same instant, the music restarted before Archie quickly turned it off. As he put his head out of the bivvy again, he heard the sound of splashing coming from the lake. It sounded as though heavy rain was falling into the water. Using the video cameras crappy excuse for night vision setting, Archie looked towards the waterline and was startled to see hundreds of fish jumping out of the lake. Assuming that the bastard predator had come back and was chasing the prey fish around, he returned his attention to the sky.

Three, what he could only describe as Lightships were dancing around the sky again. Having the video camera in his hands already, Archie just pointed the lens up but didn't really pay much mind to filming. Instead, he just watched and enjoyed the show. He felt happy, content, but most of all privileged to be witnessing such a spectacle. The craft spent the next fifteen minutes zipping across the sky from point to point before they just blinked out and were gone.

The splashing continued for another five minutes and then started to move farther out from the beach and eventually faded completely. It was as though the predator was swimming through the shoaling prey fish and they were trying to jump out of its path. The weird thing was that a lot of these fish were not prey at all. One landed on the beach, and it was a big Carp; more specifically, it was a Common Carp. Archie couldn't believe what he was seeing. Never in all his years of fishing had he seen or heard of such a big Carp beaching itself to get away from a predator. Being that he was so surprised at the size of the beached fish, he decided to get his scales out and weigh it. 22 Pounds of Common Carp had beached itself to escape a predatory fish - unbelievable! His amazement turned to curiosity as the fish's size confirmed that it was no prey fish. What was in this lake that could force a fish like this to be scared enough to make it act in this manner?

While he had it on the bank, Archie decided to give the Carp a quick once over with some anti-septic cream specifically designed for fish. After cleaning up and treating a few ulcers on the Carps underside, he released it back to the water. But his astonishment went further as he watched the thing repeatedly trying to beach itself. It was only when he took it along the bank to the next swim and try to release it, that it actually returned to the depths. It was weird, he'd never seen nor heard of fish acting in this way. Archie couldn't help but think that the fish didn't want to go back and would prefer to take its chances on land. But that was stupid, it would mean certain death.

As he walked back to the bivvy, he heard the distant sound of rota blades, the helicopters were coming back. He ran back to the tent, turned the heater off and used the doors as a fan to get as much heat out as he could before they arrived. As soon as he felt he'd done enough, he went inside and zipped the door flaps, leaving a small opening to see out of. The noise became deafening as the choppers flew over the top. At one stage, he thought they might actually land on his camp.

Looking through the hole, he watched as the bait tent went flying into the bushes as the downdraft hit the bay. The rush of air was so intense that the roof of the bivvy was bending inward. *They're going to find me*; the fear was building in him as he watched the choppers circle the lake in the same way they did the night before. Just like they did previously, they disappeared the way they had come from after about half an hour.

Looking at the clock, sometime after pulling the bait tent out of the bushes, he realised how late it was, and decided to meditate over the situation. During which he asked the light if he should leave, the answer he got was not the answer he really wanted... *No*. He also asked if there was a reason to stay to which he received a light shine so bright that the response was unmistakable – *YES*. Once he had finished the session, he made the decision to keep the heater off and just get into the sleeping bag and try to get some sleep. But it didn't come easy, his mind was racing with questions like *Why was he here?* And *What am I supposed to do?* He eventually dozed off about 2 am.

The following morning, Archie awoke to feel remarkably refreshed, more than that he felt terrific, which was surprising considering what he had been through over the past couple of days. Getting out of bed, the pain from the bruise on his arse flared up, and the memories of the previous day flooded back into his mind; falling out of the bivvy, then the tree, and rowing across the freezing water in his pants the morning before. The memory made him laugh aloud as he thought about it. Surely today couldn't be any worse than yesterday. He undid the door zips, opened up, and nearly fell over, this time for an entirely different reason. The beach was littered with dead fish - lots of them, of all sizes and species. Something strange was going on, but he just didn't know what. He didn't like it one bit. Why would so many fish beach themselves like this?

Moving the fish into the next swim, he thought of the old saying *If you can't take a joke, don't go fishing*, to take his mind off of the situation. It was short lived though, as he realised that a lot of these dead fish seemed to have some sort of... burn marks. Pulling out his knife, he cut one open and gasped at what he found; it was cooked. Unable to believe what he had seen, he cut a second one open, and this time it was actually burnt on the inside. How had this happened? What could do this? Was this why they were trying to get out of the water last night? Was there something in there that was burning them? The questions filled his mind thick and fast, but he just didn't have any answers. *Fuck it, I'm having a brew*, he thought as he threw the last carcass into the bushes next to the bay.

While he waited for the kettle to boil, he decided to test the temperature of the lake with his hand. Dipping his finger, he was shocked to find it was reasonably warm. It wasn't hot enough to burn him or the fish, but it was definitely warmer than it should have been. Something was wrong on this lake. With the kettle whistling, he put the strangeness out of his mind and made a cup of coffee, using the rest of the water to make up a bowl of noodles. He was starving.

The weather had turned in to a bright, albeit cold, sunny day and as Archie stood on the bank eating his food, he contemplated whether or not to stay and fish or cut his losses and go home. Looking around at all of the fish scales on the beach, he couldn't help but think that this place had something seriously wrong with it, like there was some kind of bad mojo going on. In the same moment, the fish started jumping again, and as he watched, he thought he saw some kind of bow wave push through the surface of the water – some sort of strange ripple. Maybe he was seeing things, he wasn't sure, but he made the decision to pack the gear up and leave for home tomorrow morning – he wouldn't be fishing here anymore.

With his mind made up, he set about stowing everything he wouldn't need back in the van. The only things he kept out were what he would need to have a relatively comfortable night; bed, sleeping bag, cooking gear, and the medical pack along with the survival pack, would be all that remained of the camp. Everything else was packed into the van, ready for a quick departure first thing in the morning.

Little did he know that *everything* would change that night!

4

Fishing Lake

West Midlands

England

Archie had a sense of foreboding as he sat watching the sky outside the bivvy. He couldn't shake the feeling that something dodgy was about to occur. He didn't know what, he just knew things didn't feel right. The night was cold, the air was still, and the natural sounds of the wildlife and the rustling of the leaves on the trees had stopped. Even the sound of the water lapping against the beach had ceased. The only noise was the gas cooker burning away next to him.

A few minutes later, he heard the sound of bubbling and assumed the kettle was boiling. He noticed a low humming sound coming from somewhere across the lake. Thinking it was a plane off in the distance, Archie picked up his cup and made himself another coffee. Once he replaced the kettle, he turned off the stove, but the bubbling sound continued. It seemed to be coming from the lake. Taking a swig of his drink, he immediately noticed that the kettle hadn't actually boiled, and the water was only just warm. Concentrating on the noise, he realised that the lake was definitely the source of the sound, and after a moment or two, the bubbling turned to splashes. Archie knew precisely what that meant - the fish were jumping again.

As this realisation set in, three lights appeared in the sky directly above the lake. This time they were close – really close. They made the same pattern as they had on the previous nights – circling each other and zipping about the sky. After a few minutes, one of them came in really close and held a position about fifty feet above the water, at a distance of around forty, maybe fifty yards. Archie was awestruck as he sat there in amazement. For a second, he thought that the lights in the water were a reflection of the craft hovering above.

WHOOSH

WHOOSH

From beneath the surface of the water, two intense beams of light erupted out toward the hovering ship directly above. As the rays struck the craft, its lights flickered, revealing it to be a typical saucer type spaceship, the sort you would see in a movie. Almost instantly the stricken ship listed towards him before crashing into the lake no more than twenty yards from Archie's beach.

To the right of the downed Lightship, a Dart or Arrowhead shaped craft exploded from the lake, firing multiple bursts of the same intense beams at the other two Lightships still in the sky. At the same time, from across the water, another Dart burst through the surface. A moment later, Archie heard another crash from the other lake behind. He assumed that the noise was another one of the hostile ships.

The instant the first Lightship was struck, the cogs as to what had happened the day before all fell in to place in

Archie's mind. These Arrowheads must give off some sort of radiation, which had been the cause of the dead fish. And it must have been one of them that had snagged the hook and carried off his rod.

Watching what could only be described as a battle, Archie found himself shocked to the core. Was he dreaming? The two remaining Lightships seemed as though they were ready as soon as their enemy had fired at their first ship. They manoeuvred quickly out the way of the incoming fire as the Arrowheads reached out with their weapons.

Getting quickly to his feet, Archie started calculating his next move. What should he do? Should he hide? Should he jump in the van and drive away? What *could* he do? There was nothing in the fisherman's handbook to prepare a person for this shit!

The two remaining Lightships pulled back, seemingly to lure the Arrowheads away from the immediate area, before they started fighting back. Beams of light, obviously weapons, flew across the sky seeking their targets. Archie looked at the downed ship and thought about the people inside. *No, not people*, he reminded himself - *Beings*. Were they alive, or were they dead? *Fuck it, I'm going to row out and see if I can help*. He didn't know what he could do, but he had that compulsion again.

Archie saw two of the Arrowheads destroyed as he rowed like a mad man towards the flickering ship. As he got closer, he noticed that there was an open hatch on the left-hand side of the craft. Making his way to the opening, he saw that the battle in the sky had intensified significantly as more and more Arrowheads seemed to appear from nowhere. As the Lightships destroyed one, it was replaced by another two. He couldn't believe that he was witnessing two alien nations fighting in Earth's sky. *And I'm in a poxy rowboat about to jump on to an alien spaceship – what is the world coming to?* He couldn't help but snort a laugh at the surreal situation he had found himself in.

He was about five feet from the floating saucer when another Lightship simply appeared out of thin air. Archie jumped so hard that he nearly fell out of the boat. The new craft was extremely low, almost touching the roof of their downed brethren. It held that position for some time. With everything that was going on, the only audible sound was from the whooshing of the weapons fire from battle overhead. There was no real engine noise from either of the alien ships other than a slight whine from the Arrowheads.

As he reached the rim of the saucer, the now familiar sound of rota blades filled the air. The helicopters were on their way. With the rope and brick anchor in hand, Archie slid on to the edge of the craft and almost slid straight into the water, but somehow managed to get a grip of the hatch just in time to stop himself from going over the side. He threw the brick into the opening, hoping that it would keep the boat in position for when he got back. As he was about to drop into the ship, there was a mass of heavy machine gun fire from behind. Instinctively, he dived to the rim of the ship to limit the potential for being hit. The cracking from above told him that the helicopters weren't shooting at him but at the Lightship overhead. The noise was horrendous. He couldn't help thinking that at any second he would kop an unfortunate one as the high calibre rounds ricocheted off the intended target above him. The knowledge that staying where he was would mean that he would probably get shot prompted him to hop into the hatch. At that very instant, his feet touched the deck inside, the Lightship above moved away from the location, drawing the helicopter with it. Archie realised that the vessel had been shielding him so that he could make it into the cover of the alien craft.

That thought led to another – he was standing inside an alien spaceship. He couldn't just go inside and start searching. He had to be sure the enemy of this ship wasn't going to just blow it out of the water with him on board. No, he should stay topside for a while, and if it looked like they were going to destroy this thing, he'd jump into the water and swim like a crazy man to get away.

He watched the interstellar dog fight going on above in utter bewilderment. He was amazed at the capabilities from both of the alien ships as they fought. He'd never seen anything like it - even in films. It seemed as though the Lightships had the upper hand, but the problem was that the more of the Darts they destroyed, the more that appeared. Over the noise of the rota blades, Archie heard the distant rumble of fighter jets. He guessed it was only a matter of time until the Air Force got involved. They streamed in and immediately set about trying to attack the Lightships with missiles and strafing runs... unsuccessfully. Their targets just seemed to hop out of the way of the plane's weapons.

Laser and tracer fire were streaming all over the night sky as each side tried to get the drop on the other. The Arrowheads and the humans were apparently working together as they tried to coordinate their attacks. That made Archie wonder if he was doing the right thing in trying to help the aliens inside the crashed vessel. *Should I rethink this? NO, I'M DOING THIS.*

He was just about to enter the ship when the dreaded WHOOMP of the rota blades returned, stopping Archie in his tracks. The downdraft felt like some unseen force was trying to crush him. Looking up, he saw someone fast roping down from the helicopter to the rim of the saucer. As the soldier touched down, he immediately brought his rifle to bear and started screaming for him to get out of the ship.

Archie knew full well that this soldier wasn't concerned about his welfare…he was there to kill him, but he wanted him outside to do it cleanly. Slowly, he started to raise himself out of the hatch as the military maniac moved quickly towards him. Archie knew precisely what he was going to do, and as he got to the lip of the opening, the soldier was about five feet away. Without hesitating, Archie performed a forward rolling break-fall towards his enemy, as he came out of the roll, the rifle started firing on full-automatic, but the soldier wasn't fast enough - Archie was on him. The roll brought him to the left of the shooter. Reaching out with his left hand, he grabbed the barrel of the man's weapon, forcing it away from him so that he couldn't be shot as it kept firing. With his right hand, Archie immediately started repeatedly punching the left side of the shocked soldiers head. From there he moved the punches to the left side of the enemy's chest and instantly felt the ribs cave and crack under the weight of the blows. His victim yelped in pain as he fell to his knees. Archie's actions were so fast that the gunman couldn't react in time.

The wounded man tried to use his elbow to smash Archie's face in, but his attacker was just too fast. He caught the elbow and manipulated it until he had the wrist and pulled the arm out straight, at this point Archie put the palm of his right hand through the back of the soldiers' elbow with a satisfying crack. The soldier screamed and howled in pain, but Archie didn't care as he continued to punch the guys face to a bloody pulp. From nowhere, he saw that the beaten soldier had a pistol in his right hand and was desperately trying to get a bead on him. He had to get away before the bastard shot him. Diving to the side, Archie performed another break-fall but in the process, pulled his fish knife from its sheath on his belt and as he came out of the roll he spun back toward this murderous piece of shit and threw the blade. From this distance, there would be only one outcome as the knife buried itself into the man's eye. The soldier fell backwards and started twitching on the deck, Archie realised he had just killed him.

It all happened so fast that he couldn't quite make sense of it. His martial arts training was so intense that it seemed like he'd been on autopilot during the fight. His senses were always heightened when it came to clobbering time, but tonight was a shade beyond anything he had ever experienced.

Suddenly he heard shouts over the noise of the rota blades above. Looking up, he saw two more soldiers preparing to come down the ropes. He ran over to the dead man, pulled the knife from his eye and cut the sling that attached the rifle to his body. Touching the weapon brought with it some kind of flash - knowledge of how to use the thing. Bringing the stock into his shoulder, he took aim on the first man roping down. Flicking the switch from auto to single shot felt as if it was completely natural. A single pop sounded out as the round left the chamber, the target fell from the rope and landed with a sickening thud, head first onto the rim of the saucer before sliding into the water.

He was about to line up another shot at the second figure when a blinding flash hit the helicopter. There was no big explosion. The aircraft just tilted over and fell into the lake as though it had been frozen in mid-air. Even the rota blades were stationary before the thing hit the water, where it sank almost immediately. Archie looked over his shoulder to see where the blast had come from and saw a Lightship about a hundred yards away. A second helicopter started moving in from the left and opened up on the alien vessel with its minigun. The chopper had absolutely no chance as the Lightship blinked out and reappeared about fifty feet to the right, then blasted it with the same weapon it had used on the first helicopter.

The remaining heli's started bugging out – they'd had enough of this game. The pilots were way out of their depth, and they knew it.

As soon as he thought it was safe, Archie lay against the dome of the saucer and gathered his thoughts. *Fuck, I've killed two people!* He felt kind of guilty but as the thoughts swam through his mind, he couldn't help but realise that he'd had no choice. They would have killed him if they'd had the chance. *It was them or me – screw those guys*, he thought. He turned his mind to shooting the second guy with the rifle; how the fuck did he hit him? He'd never fired a weapon in his life. Looking at the gun, he seemed to know everything about it – even down to its maintenance. Hey, maybe he was a natural or more likely, he'd seen too many war films.

Climbing to his feet, he pushed all those thoughts aside as he made his way over to the dead soldier. He searched the now still man and took anything that could have been of use. Without even thinking about it, he ejected the magazine from the rifle and replaced it with a fresh one. Grabbing the pistol, he did the same thing. He then stuffed as much spare ammo as he could fit into the pockets on the side of his trousers and started making his way back to the hatch. While he was walking, he realised that he knew exactly what he was doing when it came to the firearms, but he didn't have a clue as to how or why.

Looking up it was clear that things weren't over as the Arrowheads and the Lightship were still duking it out. As he got to the hatch, Archie decided to leave the now strapless rifle in the boat. He felt like it would be more of a hindrance rather than an asset. After all, he had only fired the thing once, and as far as he was concerned, he'd got lucky hitting the target. He tucked the pistol into the front of his trousers and decided that he would probably always opt to use the knife as his first choice of weapon. With that, he had experience and was more than competent with it.

5

Inside The Crashed Alien Ship

Fishing Lake

West Midlands, England

The inside was absolutely massive, far larger than it looked from the outside. Peering down the corridor, Archie noticed the way was extremely dark. In fact, the only area that was actually illuminated was the immediate vicinity in which he was standing. Turning on his head torch, he nervously stepped forward, and as his foot touched the floor, the lighting followed his movement through the walls. Slowly, he took another step, this time there were sparks as the light tried to follow. Jumping back to his original position, he realised that the ship's power was shorting out and there was an acrid smell of burning electrics as smoke began filling the air.

It was evident that there wasn't much time before either the ship caught fire, or it sank beneath the water. The thought made Archie nervous, but it also made him realise that he had to get a move on. If there were anyone on board, they would surely die if he did nothing. He took another step forward, this time there was only light, no sparks. He took another, and another with the same result... light. Slowly, he made his way forward through the corridor and after about ten paces, the thought reoccurred to him that he could be saving hostile Beings. It ran through his mind that the helicopters and fighter jets did attack the other ships of the same design as this one, but then again, the human forces had attempted to kill him as well.

Pulling his fish knife from its sheath, he thought *Fuck it – I'll deal with any hostile intent if and when it appeared – but I've gotta check this out, they might be friendly*. After all, they had plenty of opportunities to attack him over the past two nights, but all they did was dance their ships around the sky, which he was sure they had done for his benefit. He was the only person on the fishing lake, which was in the middle of nowhere, not a town or village for around twenty miles in any direction. So, the appearance of the Lightships could only have been for him to see. It was as though they were saying "We're Here". But even with that thought process, Archie would be taking no chances. If he had to start wind-milling, he'd be doing it with a blade in his hand, intent on doing as much damage as possible before getting the hell out of there.

Moving on, the noise of the ships electrics shorting out was still going on somewhere, but at least the lights were still working. After what felt like fifty feet into the craft, Archie came to a door on the right. This seemed to be where the crackle and pops of the electrical system were coming from, and there was an intermittent flashing of blue light. Psyching himself up to enter the room, he wondered what he would find inside. With his mind racing, visions of the typical pop culture "Grey" alien were prominent, although he did have a flash of Klingon go through his head. How would they react to him? Would they attack him? Would his martial arts be any match for them? Hell, were they even alive?

Upon entering the room, he found nothing, it was empty. There were no aliens, no bodies, nothing. The noises were definitely originating from this room, and the flashing light was actually coming from the walls, but there were no light fittings as such. In fact, at that moment he realised that he hadn't actually seen a proper light source since entering the ship. Clearly, there was light, but it seemed to emanate directly from the walls and the ceiling, though he couldn't see any bulbs or anything that could remotely be described as conventional light sources.

Leaving the room, Archie resumed his search back down the corridor. This place was massive, there seemed to be no end to this hallway. Eventually, he came to another doorway, this time on the left. Confused, he couldn't figure out how there could even be a door or room on that side of the hall. Going by human understanding of spatial awareness, there shouldn't be a room on that side at all. The ship was saucer-shaped, and he had entered the craft through a hatch on the left side of the vessel and turned immediately left into the corridor, which he assumed would run around the circumference of the entire craft and that meant that through our understanding, the only place for compartments *should* be on the right-hand side of the hall. It just didn't make any sense. Archie had to put it out of his mind and get a move on as he felt the craft lurch.

Psyching himself up again, he moved into the room, which was extremely dark. The only light came from his head torch. Scanning around, he saw a bank of crystals and loose wires all over the place. The compartment was hot – really hot. It felt like his head was burning, but he couldn't figure out why. After about ten seconds he realised his hat was alight. Tearing it from his head, he threw it to the floor and stamped out the flames. Looking up, he noticed a bunch of wires hanging down from a hole in the ceiling and like a fool, he must have snagged the hat on one and set himself alight. Cursing, he left the room and carried on down the hallway, very quickly approaching another door on the right. He hoped that this room was the one he was looking for. He was getting seriously concerned about safety; the vibrations and rumbles made it painfully clear that the ship was becoming more unstable by the minute.

Moving inside, he had to shield his eyes. This was by far the brightest room he had been in. The light was so bright it hurt. So much so, that he had to wait for his eyes to adjust before he could do anything. It was like walking out of a pitch-black room into bright sunlight. Moving around the outside of the room, he realised how big this place was. He found what appeared to be four double beds. He was feeling more than seeing, the room was *that* bright. By the time he had found the fourth bed, Archie's vision had adjusted enough for relatively normal vision. From the edge of the room, he looked inward, there was a table, several large chairs, and what looked like cups or drinking containers, but that was it - no aliens and no bodies. He was beginning to think he might be wasting his time as he moved back into the dullness of the hallway, where again, he had to wait for his eyes to readjust.

The electrical issues worsened as he made his way down the corridor, and the farther he went, the more the light seemed to dim. After a short time, he apparently found the end of the hall as he approached the last door.

How was this possible? The ship didn't seem big enough for this kind of layout. He looked back up the corridor to confirm his suspicions – the hall was straight. What was going on here?

The smoke was getting worse, time was a critical factor, he had to crack on with the job. As he was about to enter the last room, there was a loud rumble, and the vessel seemed to vibrate and shift worse than it had previously. *Fuck, is it sinking into the lake?* He had to pick up the pace, or he was going to find himself neck deep in shit. Quickly, he moved into the last room… *Gotcha!* There were four wrap-around chairs or couches with what looked like *normal human beings* sat in them. He was shocked, he didn't see that coming. He'd expected to find some type of alien.

Switch on you dickhead! He needed to get a grip of himself as he made his way to the chairs. There he found what appeared to be a normal, blonde haired human man. Going through the primary survey, it was apparent that this one was dead, so he moved on to the next chair… again, dead.

BOOM! There was a massive explosion, and a significant shift rocked through the ship.

Looking around, Archie noticed approximately eight, maybe ten view screens moulded into the wall. He didn't know what the explosion or what the shift was, but he could see through the displays that the ship was still on the surface of the lake. However, it was listing badly. It was time to *really* get a move on.

The third person was actually alive, albeit unconscious. After making sure the casualty had a secure airway, Archie moved straight on to the fourth man. The brain matter hanging out of the massive hole in the right side of his head meant that this casualty was number three on the dead scale; One - DEAD, Two - PROPER DEAD, and Three - FUCKING DEAD!

Two loud explosions ripped through the vessel, announcing that it was time to get out of there.

Moving back to the only one of the four... *men,* that was still alive, it dawned on him how big the survivor was. He was like the proverbial man mountain. At least six-foot-tall, and well built, which meant he had to weigh about 17, maybe 18 stone. Archie was only five foot eight and a fit 13 stone. He knew this was going to be a monumental lift, but fuck it, he had to try. He couldn't in good conscience leave him to die. Looking at the casualty, memories of life on the ambulance service came flooding back as he muttered to himself "Why do I always end up with the big fucker?"

Pulling the big man forward to get into a position to lift him, he started to groan, prompting Archie to lay him back into the chair, where he began trying to wake him using both verbal and pain stimuli. Well, trying was the right word to use, would standard pain stimuli actually hurt a giant like the one he had in front of him? After several seconds the man seemed to start coming round. *Great, hopefully, he can walk out of here.*

"Wake up!" Archie said, nearly shouting as he slapped the casualty's face, "Wake up. Open your eyes, mate, come on wakey fucking wakey."

Getting no further response other than the same groaning, Archie thought that he was probably wasting his time trying to talk to him. After all, would he even understand English? Was he even human? Just because he appeared to be a man, didn't make it so. Putting that out of his mind, he knew he had to get moving as the angle of the deck started to change. He pulled the casualty forward again and got him into a position on his shoulders and braced his self for the inevitable weight that he was about to lift. Taking a deep breath, he pushed up hard with his legs, but as he did so, he nearly threw the injured man against the ceiling. He weighed next to nothing. Archie had held fish that weighed more. Feeling like the world's strongest man, he assumed it must be the adrenalin running through his system that was making him stronger. He'd read and heard many stories of people achieving superhuman feats in times of emergency.

Moving back into the hallway, Archie immediately saw the smoke had gotten considerably worse, and his eyes started to sting straight away. His throat had become thick as he began to choke on the particulates in the air. He had to get out of this shit before they both died of smoke inhalation. Hunching over, he managed to get as close to the floor as possible and started a crouched run back up the corridor as fast as he could. The big blonde backpack started choking and vomiting almost straight away, and Archie knew that he had to get lower or the man would be dead before they got to the hatch. Lowering himself further, he found himself on his hands and knees as he half carried, half dragged the unconscious casualty toward the exit by crawling as fast as he could.

He had been moving for a minute or so when three massive explosions erupted from somewhere behind him. *Fuck this – if I stay on my knees we're dead*, he thought as he stood back up and started running. Every few steps, he dropped his head below the smoke layer to gulp some air. On the way into the ship, Archie had been confused about the layout of the craft, with the corridor being so straight and long for what, on the outside, was such a small ship. But right now, he couldn't have been more grateful because it meant he had only one direction in which he had to run.

As he moved forward, he noticed a terrible sound; a cracking noise. The lighting was gone entirely, and the smoke was awful. He found himself feeling more than seeing his way, but when his head torch did occasionally penetrate the gloom, what he saw horrified him. The walls were seemingly being stretched to the extent that gaping holes were being ripped through them. At the same time, he realised that the load on his back was getting heavier and heavier the closer he got to the hatch and freedom beyond.

After what felt like an age, Archie felt a doorway to his right, which meant he was making progress. The ship was now listing severely, so much so that he had to run uphill. His lungs were burning, and every muscle in his body was on fire as the demand for oxygen increased continuously.

Boom!

This explosion felt different, and it was followed almost instantly by another noise. It took a few seconds for

Archie to realise what it was, and another few seconds to come to terms with just how much shit he was in as the sound of rushing water got worse. The angle at which he was running seemed to get more dramatic, and the man on his back got significantly heavier. Something had changed. He realised that it couldn't have been adrenalin that made it so easy to pick up his casualty because the surge of adrenalin he now had was by far stronger because he knew the ship was sinking, yet the weight on his back was getting worse.

With panic well and truly setting in, Archie reached his right arm over his shoulder to hold on to the unconscious man, leaned forward and started running with his left hand feeling the left wall as he ran. He was desperately trying to find the door that he knew would be coming up on the left. From there, he knew he only had about fifty feet to go. Archie kept his hand on the wall as he moved, he was feeling his way until his hand disappeared through an opening. He instantly had a surge of hope run through him until he realised that the sides of the doorway were serrated. This wasn't the door he was looking for. This was one of the holes he'd seen being ripped through the ship's structure back down the corridor.

The sound of water was getting louder and louder, exacerbating the panic Archie was feeling. He could hear someone shouting, "KEEP GOING, KEEP GOING, DON'T STOP!" For a second, he thought that Blondie was awake and could get off of his back and get out of the ship under his own steam, it took a moment before he realised that the shouting was actually in his head. He pushed forward using every ounce of strength and determination he had.

Finally, the smoke seemed to clear enough for him to see the hatch about ten feet in front of him. He must have missed the doorway to the left of the corridor entirely during his rush for freedom. Reaching the opening, he bundled the unconscious form of the blond giant through and climbed out after him.

As soon as he was outside, he started searching for the boat, quickly realising that the lip of the ship had risen about ten feet from the surface of the water as the other side sank. The small craft had started to drift away; it was now roughly ten, maybe fifteen feet away. *So much for the shitty anchor*. He knew what he *had* to do, although it didn't make the decision any more natural. He really didn't want to do it but jumping into the lake was the only option. The temperature of the water was the main concern for himself, but his real worry was that if he dropped the unconscious casualty in from this height, there was every chance that he'd go under and never come up again. As the thoughts raced through his mind, Archie knew it was all irrelevant, there *was* no other way to get off the sinking ship.

"Fuck it, here goes nothing," he grunted to himself as he heaved the dead weight of the unconscious survivor over the side. He waited a few seconds to see where the unconscious form would resurface and mentally noting the position before taking the plunge into the icy soup himself. As Archie broke the surface, he immediately started swimming to the face-down Blondie.

There was a terrible sound and light show as the ship finally lost the battle to stay afloat and started going beneath the surface. As it went down, it seemed as though it was imploding, folding in on itself. It looked like it was inside an invisible car crusher. Eventually, it went down in an area that Archie knew was roughly fifty feet deep – not deep enough to exert the kind of pressure to crush a vehicle. He had no time to dwell on it, he had to get to Blondie and get out of the water before they both succumbed to hypothermia.

After turning the hulking form on to his back, Archie got behind him, put his left arm over the casualty's left shoulder and grabbed him under the right armpit, as though he was a lifeguard. He swam backwards in the direction of the boat. He was absolutely shattered and started to really struggle with the exertion of it all. Both of them kept going under the water as he tried hard to stay afloat. Getting to the boat, he realised that there was no way he could get himself inside, let alone lift the dead weight of the giant. The only way forward was to stay in the water and use the boat as a float, that way he'd have the leverage to keep both of their heads above the waterline. As he started to swim while trying to push the boat, he realised that the brick anchor was preventing the small vessel from moving. It must have dislodged from the hatch as that side of the ship started to rise out of the water, now it was stuck fast on the bottom of the lake. Temporarily, Archie let go of the big man and pulled his knife from its holster to cut the rope attached to the brick. When he'd finished, he thought about just dropping the blade in the water but decided against it. So far that knife had been a godsend, an invaluable bit of kit. No, he wasn't going to just bin it now. Surprisingly, he managed to re-holster it on the first attempt. Grabbing hold of Blondie and the now free boat, he started kicking hard for the bay.

It felt like it took an age to get there, but finally, he reached the safety of the shore. For a moment or two, he just lay on his back, gulping hungrily for air as the water gently lapped against him. A few seconds passed before Archie struggled to his feet and pulled Blondie from the waterline and up the beach. The man was still unconscious and deathly quiet – too quiet. Archie knelt at his head, opened his airway and checked for breathing and a pulse – he had neither – he was clinically dead!

6

The Beach

Fishing lake

West Midlands, England

Archie had come too far and done way too much to just let the supposed alien die now. He went through the primary survey again. If the Beings anatomy and physiology were human, then the man was in cardiac arrest. He surmised that because the casualty was alive before being dropped into the water that he must have drowned, so ensuring the airway was clear, Archie gave five initial rescue breaths before starting chest compressions, doing thirty before stopping and giving two more breaths. Then repeating the process for a minute. After there was no change, Archie stumbled to the van and grabbed the medical kit; what he was currently doing wasn't going to be enough. He needed to perform the more extensive treatment as soon as possible.

Once he got the kit and arrived back at Blondie's side, Archie gave him another minute's worth of CPR before starting the more advanced stuff. He quickly laid out the airway management gear, opened out the laryngoscope and slid the blade into the mouth so that he could lift the tongue. This allowed him to have a good look into the patient's throat. In doing so, he realised that he would need the largest endotracheal tube he had to fit this monster throat. With the right tube in hand, Archie re-inserted the laryngoscope, then slipped the ET tube along the groove of the scopes blade, and through the larynx. As soon as it was in place, he withdrew the scope. Using a 10ml syringe, he inflated the cuff that sat on the outside and near the bottom of the tube. Once the cuff was inflated, it would mould to the throat, and close off any space so that the only way for anything to pass into the lungs was through the inside of the tube. It also meant that if the patient vomited, it couldn't get past the cuff – stomach acid in the lungs was never a good day out! ET tubes were not always 100% effective, but they were definitely better than a punch in the tits.

With the airway as secure as it was ever going to get, he attached the Bag Valve Mask to the top of the tube and started inflating the lungs with air. The Bag Valve Mask is basically a rubber or plastic, oval shaped bag with a valve fitted to the top. The valve fitting would be attached to either a mask that was placed over the mouth and nose, or it could be mounted directly to the top of an ET tube. When the bag was squeezed, it would force air through the valve and into the airway, oxygenating the lungs.

Archie gave five long inflations before beginning chest compressions again. For an ordinary *human*, the compression rate should be between 100-120 per minute at a ratio of 30-2. That meant that the rescuer would do thirty compressions, two lung inflations, thirty compressions, two inflations – and you aim for a compression rate of 100-120, thereby simulating a heartbeat of that number per minute. It worked out to be roughly just under two compressions per second. But this man wasn't an *ordinary human*, so Archie decided to change the ratios to 40-4 at a speed of 160 beats per minute. The truth was, he didn't know whether the patient's heart rate should be higher or lower, and he was just too cold and tired to think clearly enough to figure it out. He didn't even try. He made his decision and just got on with the task at hand.

After a couple of minutes, fatigue started to set in as Archie became more and more tired. What he was doing wasn't having any effect; it was time to change it up. It's hard enough to do a resus at the best of times, but with everything he'd been through to get to this point meant that he was absolutely knackered, and his CPR was becoming less effective as time went on. He decided to cut away the clothing to expose the chest so that he could attach the defibrillator. While it was analysing the heart rhythm, Archie put an intravenous cannula into a vein in the right arm.

The defib gave a No Shock Advised signal, so Archie pushed a double dose of adrenalin through the cannula and re-started chest compressions. It was a much larger dose than he should have given for a *normal human*, but Archie didn't know if this man *was* human. Furthermore, he was really feeling the effects of the night's events, so if he could simulate a shockable heart rhythm quicker by giving more adrenalin than he should have, so much the better. His shoulders were cramping, and his triceps felt like he was receiving electric shocks to the back of his arms. Two minutes doesn't sound like a long time, but when you're doing a resus on your own, it feels like an eternity. Thankfully, just before he felt he couldn't carry on, the defib announced that it was going to analyse again, which meant that Archie had to stop CPR - he was grateful for the momentary respite.

About twelve seconds later, the analysis again revealed that nothing had changed. *FUCK!* Archie pushed through another dose of adrenalin and got back on the chest. He was feeling disheartened with the fact that there was still no change, but he had to carry on. *He's a big man – fuck it, I'm gonna give him another dose*, Archie thought to himself as he administered an extra syringe of the drug. He had already given more of the stuff than he should have in the time frame that he had been working on the casualty, but hell, what did he have to lose? The guy was currently dead anyway. The idea of the drug was to try to stimulate a heart with an Asystole or "flatline" rhythm into Ventricular Fibrillation or "VF" rhythm that could be shocked by the defib. The electrical current that the machine pushed through the patient would actually stop the chaotic electrical impulses in the heart in the hope that it would re-start in normal sinus rhythm – "NSR".

He pumped the chest harder and faster than he ever had on any person before and after a minute or so, he noticed a change in the rhythm on the defibs screen – VF... shockable! He stopped compressions and manually set the shock box to analyse, and after the required twelve seconds, the indication to shock was given. Archie didn't waste any time pressing the button to put a charge of 150 joules through the heart. With his eyes firmly on the screen, he saw a change in rhythm that looked like NSR – it might not be, it could be PEA or Pulseless Electrical Activity, which presented very similar to the NSR. As quick as he could, he jammed two fingers into the patients' neck to feel for a carotid pulse. There it was. The steady bump against his finger-tips; he'd done it, he'd got him back. He was still unconscious, but he was alive, and right then that was all that mattered.

Several seconds after the heart restarted, the patient started to make respiratory effort and was trying to breathe on his own. Things were beginning to look up. Archie decided to leave the defib attached, as well as leave the ET tube and the cannula in place while he started to sort all the gear out and prepare to leave the area. By leaving those items in place gave him a better chance of getting straight to work on the patient should he "go off" again… die again. Often, people that have suffered a cardiac arrest and been successfully resuscitated would arrest again, and the rescuers would find themselves having to do the business over and over again. Before he started to clear all the stuff away, he just collapsed on to his back, breathing heavily for a couple of minutes as he tried to recuperate some of the spent energy.

As he lay there, Archie thought about what had happened through the evening, and the implications of it all hit him like a freight train. There would be a follow up to the crashed Lightship, and it didn't matter whether it was the aliens or the humans who actually came, he couldn't be there when they arrived. As the thought entered his mind, Archie also realised that he still had a fair bit of work to do before he could get away. For starters, he had to pack up the rest of the camp, which, fortunately, he had already started. He also had to give Blondie a proper looking over because he didn't *actually* know why he went into cardiac arrest. He had assumed it was because he'd drowned, but that might not be the case, and only a thorough secondary survey would give a better indication of any injuries that might have caused it. Whatever, laying there wasn't getting anything done, so he struggled to his feet and started dragging Blondie up the beach to the bivvy. There he would have a bit of light to help him look over the unconscious man.

Upon instigating the secondary survey, Archie got a closer look at the clothing that Blondie was wearing; it was a very quasi and futuristic, tight-fitting jumpsuit that seemed to mould to his body. Around his waist was a white, plastic-looking belt with several pouches. Using the shears from the medical pack, Archie started cutting all of the clothes off of the patient so that he could really see what he was dealing with. After all, you can't treat an injury if you can't see it. Once he had finished, he had a cursory glance along the length of the naked body laid out in front of him, where he found that there were no apparent injuries. That didn't mean there wasn't any, it just said they weren't visible. Not willing to take any chances, Archie started a full head to toe survey, and immediately found that there was a sizable lump on the back of the big man's head. There was no sign of external bleeding, which meant that right then, there was nothing Archie could do about it, so he continued the search for other injuries down the body. Finding nothing else to concern him, he started to pack everything away and run it all up to the van.

On one of his trips back to the camp to get more kit, he noticed that Blondie had started to come around and began moving. Archie knelt down next to him just as he started trying to pull the tube from his throat.

"Don't do that mate," Archie said as he took hold of the guy's big hand. "It'll really hurt. Hang on I'll take it out."

Blondie was trying to say something, as Archie deflated the cuff on the tube, but whatever the man was trying to say just sounded like gibberish. Pulling the tube out allowed for a cough and spluttering fit, along with a pleasant amount of vomit, but that was to be expected. Once he had finished coughing, the patient lay back down.

"Are you hurt mate?" Archie asked. "Do you speak English?"

"Yes, I speak... the tongue..." The reply was weak and raspy. "Where am I?"

"We're on a small beach. Your ship was attacked, and you crashed into the lake. I pulled you out – do you remember?"

"I... I think I... It's just flashes..." Blondie was clearly trying to make sense of what was happening. "You are Archie. We were sent here to con..." he slipped back into unconsciousness.

"Oi, wake up!" Archie shouted as he shook Blondies shoulders. "Wake the fuck up! How do you know my name?"

Getting no response, he put Blondie into the recovery position and made sure that his airway was secure before returning to packing the camp away. He thought about just leaving it all there and just throwing the big man into the back of the motor and getting out of there, but no sooner had he thought it, did he realise that his fingerprints were all over it – they would be on him straight away. No, he had to take it all with him. He had never busted down a fishing camp as fast as he was doing right now. He had to get a move on because he didn't know when the follow up would arrive. He basically just collapsed the tent and threw it into the back of the van, along with the rest of the stuff. Ten minutes later, as he chucked the last of the equipment into the vehicle, Archie started to think about how he would get Blondie up the bank. Could he use the equipment barrow to get him up? No, the slope was way too steep. That meant he'd have to carry the big man, he was already more tired than he had ever been in his life, and he really didn't relish the thought of having to pick the unconscious man up again.

On his last run up to the vehicle, Archie had started the engine so that he could get the heater going. It was cold out, *really* cold, he was cold, and he had been active for pretty much the last hour, which that meant that Blondie must be freezing. He hadn't checked, but he would have thought that the unconscious man's core body temperature must be lower than it should be. Preheating the van would go some way to rectifying the problem.

As he started back to get Blondie, Archie spotted one of the Arrowhead Darts coming towards them. It was heading straight for the bay he was in. He had to assume they knew there was a survivor from the crashed Lightship. He found himself frantically scanning the sky, hoping to see Blondies mates coming in to intercept them, but he was shit out of luck. He realised he was on his own as panic started to creep upon him. What was he going to do now? How would he get out of this? Should he grab the unconscious Blondie and try to drive away? No, that would never work, they'd just blast the shit out of him before he even got to the entrance to the lake. Speculation was getting him nowhere, so with a deep calming breath, he pulled the pistol from the waistband of his trousers and cocked the hammer back and ensured the safety was on before slipping back in place.

He ran down the bank and roughly tried to rouse Blondie, to no avail. Trying to wake him wasn't working. With every ounce of strength he could muster, he pulled the big man up into a firefighter's lift and got him on to his shoulders before moving to the van with as much speed as he could find. Trying to rush up the bank saw him slip and fall twice as the Dart flew over the beach. *Did they see us?* Archie thought as he pushed forward to the vehicle. All hope that the enemy had missed them were dashed as after about eight hundred yards, the Arrowhead turned around and started back towards the bay. Reaching the van, Archie bundled the big man inside. Once he shut the door, he made his way to the driver's side in a state of panic, only to again realise that trying to run was pointless...to even attempt it was suicide. His best hope would be to lure them out and take them on. Running back around the van, he opened the door he had thrown Blondie in and grabbed the survival bag before moving off of the road and finding a bush large enough to give him some decent cover. Getting in, he only hoped they would land and show themselves.

While he was waiting, he reached into the survival bag and pulled out the bowie knife that made up part of the emergency pack. *Fuck it, if I'm going to do this, I'm going to need the tools to do the job right!* He thought. This blade was a nasty bit of kit – literally, to be used in a survival situation, and Archie figured that this qualified as precisely that. This was the type of knife that could skin a fucking dinosaur.

He didn't have to wait long before they were overhead, where they just hovered for a minute or two before manoeuvring the Arrowhead in front of the van and started descending. Their positioning was perfect for Archie, as he was just behind it and to the right. He hoped this might give him the element of surprise.

As the vehicle came down, Archie felt the hair on his arms begin to stand on end, and as it got lower, he could hear a high-pitched whine that he assumed must have been the ship's engines. The electrical charge that he could feel seemed to worsen, and he felt like he had one of those joke shop wigs on his head. He even thought the hair on his arse was standing up.

The ship touched down on the dirt track in front of the van gently enough, but more importantly, only about fifteen feet away from Archie's position. The craft itself was nearly forty feet long, by twenty-five feet at its widest point, by twenty feet high at the rear that sloped down to form a sharp point at the front. At the rear of the vessel were four X-shaped wings that intersected at the back of the main body. The wing tips each held four engines that emitted a bright white light, that faded as the ship shut down. It was like a 3D model of a triangle. Its surface was like polished chrome and Archie could make out what appeared to be hieroglyphs etched into it.

The entrance to the ship came in the form of a loading ramp. No sooner had it opened than the most terrible smell assaulted Archie's nostrils. Through his time in the ambulance service, he had been around plenty of dead and decomposing bodies, and he had smelled some god-awful things, but this was far and away the worst thing to ever enter his nose. His eyes started to water as he fought back the almost overwhelming urge to vomit.

As the ramp touched the ground, he heard the pitter patter of tiny feet that reminded him of the sound that children made as they walked. This was soon followed by a heavy…no, *really* heavy footstep. The smell was still causing Archie's eyes to water, but wiping the fluid away, he saw that there were three Beings at the foot of the ramp. Two were small, almost child-like, if not for their bulbous heads – Greys. The third was huge. *It looks like… no, it can't be*. His mind struggled to accept what his eyes were showing him. In front of him was the largest… *reptile* he had ever seen. It was at least seven-foot-tall, thick set with a thick tail that must have stretched to over six feet. Its elongated head was wider than Archie's entire body. *Why couldn't they have all been the little guys?* He thought as he slowly pulled the pistol from his waistband. The lizard was going to be a problem for sure, but he didn't hold out much hope for the small ones – they'd be dead before they even knew what had hit them.

It was getting close to go time as the enemy started moving towards the van. The reptilian appeared to be giving orders to the Greys, which made sense. The big boy *had* to be the dominant species; Archie just couldn't see it being the other way around. When they got about half way between their ship and the van, he crept out of the bush and made his way to the rear of the ramp. Not wasting any time, he leaned out of the cover, lifted the pistol and aimed at the back of the lizards' head. He squeezed the trigger, and with a pop, the target fell face first to the dirt. Without waiting for a response from the other two, he ducked back behind the ramp and popped out the other side. Without hesitation, he fired two rounds into the big head of the Grey on the right, who crumbled to the ground as the large bulb on his shoulders disintegrated. Almost instantaneously, the second little alien started to fire some sort of beam weapon in return to the assault he had instigated. *Fuck, I thought they were unarmed*, he thought as he took cover. The sound of fizzling thuds hit the other side of the ramp as the Grey tried to find his mark.

Under the pressure of death if the beams hit him, Archie's mind started racing. How was he going to get out of this? His opponent had an excellent line on him no matter what he did, and he knew that if he stuck his head around the side of the ramp that was giving him cover, he was going to kop one to the face... game over. He had to put any thoughts of dying out of his mind as he made his decision. If he stayed where he was the little fucker would kill him. No, sitting tight wasn't an option. No more thinking, it was time to act. Archie leant out of the left side of the ramp and popped off two rounds before ducking back in to cover as fast as he could. He immediately leaned out of the other side and taking proper aim as he put two bullets right into the alien's face as it was still firing at the opposite side of the ramp. He was down; hell, they were all down.

Archie was leaning with his back against the ramp trying to catch his breath and thanking his lucky stars, thinking that he seemed to be a natural with the gun. It felt like an extension of his body. He had looked at his targets, lifted his arm and squeezed the trigger. Apart from the two rounds he'd used to draw the Greys attention to the wrong side of the ramp, he had managed to hit every target he aimed at. *And* he managed to not kill himself in the process. He decided that if he survived the night, he was going to buy a lottery ticket because clearly, his luck was in. For a few seconds, he sat there laughing.

The laughter didn't last long, as a large scaly hand reached around the ramp and grabbed him by the face. Archie's feet were flailing as he was pulled from his seated position and lifted into the air. The razor-sharp claws of the reptiles left hand dug deeply into Archie's face and head. Blood poured from the wounds as the aliens' grip got tighter. Kicking out with his feet, he couldn't gain any purchase. He brought the pistol up to the head of his attacker and fired repeatedly but got only clicks from the trigger In return. The weapon had jammed. The realisation that his prey had just tried to shoot him in the head again, *really* pissed the lizard off, he hissed and squeezed tighter as though he wanted to crush Archie's skull.

Archie felt the claws pop through the tissues of his head and start scraping on bone. The pain was unbearable as he realised that this was it, he was probably going to die, but he was far from giving up. Everything seemed to slow down as the adrenalin spiked in his system. His mind moved so fast that the world went into slow motion. Dropping the gun, he frantically reached for the knives. It felt like an eternity before finally, he found the grip of the bowie knife and pulled it from its holster. He jabbed it straight into the pit of his assailants left arm. The reaction was one of pure rage as the giant reptile bared his extremely sharp looking teeth and started hitting Archie to the body with his free hand. At the same time, the hand gripping his head got tighter.

All Archie could do was stab repeatedly at the enemy as fast as he possibly could. He knew he was doing damage because the blows that the reptile rained into Archie's side were getting harder, as though he felt he needed to put this pesky human down before he got really hurt. The hits had become too much for Archie to bare as he couldn't block any now. Initially, he'd been able to parry a few away, but now the punches were coming straight through his defences.

CRACK! The pain was immense and instant. Archie knew that he had broken at least one rib – probably several. Enough was enough. He had to get free, or he was a dead man. Bringing the knife over the top of the lizards left arm, he stabbed into the side of its cheek. When the blade was fully in, Archie pulled it directly towards him, opening up the creatures face. The injury that the move had caused had to really hurt the evil bastard. He repeated the process, but now he was stabbing at any part of the enemy's head, hoping for a lucky hit. He seemed to find it when he sunk the blade in behind a small hole that he assumed was the ear. The shrieking howl was enough to tell Archie that he'd hit the mark good and proper. He tried to withdraw the blade, but it was stuck fast.

The reptilian monster threw Archie away from him. Landing on his back and breathing through his arse, Archie couldn't get up fast enough to escape. The enemy was almost above him. Reaching for his fish knife, he managed to get a grip just as the lizard brought his big heavy foot back to give the floored human a good kicking. But he was too slow, Archie had him.

As the foot came through for the kick, Archie lunged forward and grabbed both legs. As he did so, he curled his body around them and in doing so gave the enemy less leverage to produce any more kicks. With the knife in hand, he stabbed up and into the groin area and twisted the handle. The blade went in easy as Archie found a soft spot. The hulking lizard arched his back and let out a deep roar that could have woken the dead. As he withdrew the knife, he ran the blade across the back of, what he presumed was the creatures right knee. He'd clearly cut the ligaments and tendons, as the reptile crumbled to the ground. Any thought of killing the human had disappeared, his own survival was now in doubt, and he started to crawl towards the ramp of his ship.

The creature was dead, and he knew it, but he continued to crawl away. Archie was always going to get to him before he got to the safety of the ship. Rising to his feet and grabbing the pistol, Archie removed the magazine and pulled the top slide back, releasing the stuck round and clearing the stoppage. Staggering toward the crawling monster, he replaced the clip and pushed it home. By the time he got to him, the lizard was at the foot of the ramp. The bowie knife was still sticking out of the side of his head, and there was a hole about two inches to the right of it. That must have been where Archie had shot him at the beginning of the firefight.

"Turn over you bastard," Archie growled with malice. He wanted to get a real good look at the thing that almost killed him.

The reptile did so, holding his hands up as if in pleading for the human not to kill him. *Fuck him*, Archie thought to himself. Pulling the top slide back, he aimed the weapon at the big scaly, horned head and fired. It took three rounds to finally put the creature down for good.

7

Fishing Lake

West Midlands

England

Surveying the scene around him, Archie couldn't believe what had happened. It had been mayhem with aerial dogfights, spaceships crashing into the lake, killing three aliens and two humans, and him, rescuing what he thought was an alien using a fucking rowboat. The boat! *What an idiot*! It still had the rifle in it. He could have done with using that just now, and maybe he wouldn't have these gaping holes in his head.

Before he went back to retrieve the rifle, there was something he had to do first. Walking over to each alien in turn, he lifted the pistol and shot them all twice in the head, just to be sure they weren't about to "jack-in-the-box" and surprise him again. After he'd shot the reptile, he put his foot against the things head, and pulled the knife free before he wiped the dark coloured blood on to its tunic. He cleaned the fish knife in the same way and holstered both on his belt.

With the adrenalin that had flooded his system subsiding, the pain in his head and face came to the fore. He was in absolute agony, with a burning sensation flowing through the wounds, as blood was ran down his face and dripped from his chin. He ran back to the van, and after having a rapid check on Blondies condition, he pulled out the med kit again. Opening a bag of saline, he poured it over his head and face in an attempt to clean the lacerations. The injuries burned even more as the fluid entered the gaping cuts, the runoff taking with it more blood.

Looking at himself in the vans side mirror, he saw the state of his face. He was smothered in bright red blood. Initially, he was shocked but quickly calmed down as he started sorting himself out. The head was filled with tiny veins and arteries and would invariably bleed a lot and generally make the casualty look like a shark had tried to eat their face when in fact there was really only a few small cuts. The injuries could be sorted out well enough, but the more significant concern was the possibility of contracting an infection from the dirty claws the creature had used to open him up.

The fluid alone wouldn't be enough to clean the deep scrapes that ran from his hairline down to his cheeks. He needed to clean it up properly, so taking a dressing from the bag, he unwrapped it and covered it in the saline before running it along the length of each bloody streak. He needed to treat the cuts with antiseptic, but he didn't have any in the kit. In a moment of madness, he wondered if the cream he used for the fish would work. *Fuck it, I haven't got anything else*, he thought as he reached in the door and got out the fish care kit. As he applied the potion to the open wounds, he noticed that the lacerations were worse than he had first thought, and he knew at once they needed to be stitched up. Archie was in no doubt that he was going to have extensive scarring. The cream hurt like crazy as he smothered his head with the stuff, but what else could he do? It wasn't like he could go to the Accident and Emergency Department and say he'd been attacked by a seven-foot alien lizard. They'd lock him up in a mental institution and throw away the key.

To make matters worse, the injuries to his chest had started to hurt as well, causing sharp pains as he breathed. The reptilian had definitely broken at least one, maybe two or three ribs. There was nothing he could do for that except self-administer morphine, but Archie knew that wasn't even an option. He needed to stay switched on, and morphine made you groggy, slowed the heart rate and dropped the blood pressure. It could also cause unconsciousness and respiratory arrest. No, he had to just man up and take it.

Once he had sorted his ailments out as best he could, he made his way down to the boat to retrieve the rifle. With blood, sweat and saline running into his eyes, he bent down to pick the weapon up, and as he touched it, he seemed to get that flash again, this time more detailed. He knew that in his hands, he was holding an M4 Carbine, it fired 5.56 calibre rounds, had a telescopic stock, and was capable of mounting an M203 grenade launcher to the underside of the barrel. The flash showed him exactly how to use and maintain it, but Archie hoped that he wouldn't need to do either. This instant upload or whatever it was, was really weirding him out. This was the second time he had experienced it, and he couldn't explain why it was happening.

As he turned away from the rowboat, he noticed a body floating in the water, it must have been the guy he had shot as he rappelled from the helicopter. Wading out to about waist deep, he grabbed the dead man by the scruff of the neck and dragged him to the beach. There he searched him, taking both of his weapons and pilfering all the ammo the man had on him. Running back to the van, he threw the wet rifle in the back, grabbed the thermal imaging camera and made his way to the driver's side. He had three weapons in the front with him; two pistols and the dry M4. It was time to get out of the area.

Putting the vehicle into first gear, Archie moved slowly along the dirt road towards the exit. He didn't want to draw any unwanted attention to himself, so he kept the van in low gear and wouldn't be turning the lights on until he got on to the main road. He was steering with his right hand while holding the thermal camera up to eye level with his left, without it, this short trip would have taken a lot longer. He could feel every little bump and rut the track had to offer. The van was tipping and bouncing all over the place as he edged his way closer to the exit. He knew that the vehicle's movements were being exaggerated by his heightened awareness, but it still felt as though he was driving over mountains when actually he was driving over stones.

Archie stopped the motor roughly a hundred yards from the gate, he needed to check that he wasn't driving into trouble. Handbrake on, he picked up the M4 and slipped the carry strap for the thermal camera over his head as he got out of the van. Moving off to the side so that he could parallel the road, he used any shrubs or bushes he could find as cover as he continued edging his way slowly to the gate and the main road beyond. His clothes were still soaking wet, and he was freezing, yet he was sweating at the same time.

Not wanting to go straight for the exit, Archie decided to move about fifteen yards to the right of it and come out through the treeline to get to the main road on the other side. If the coast was clear, he'd go back to the van and get the hell out of there.

When he emerged on the other side of the trees, Archie realised he was farther away from the entrance than he had anticipated. He moved back in to cover, and slowly made his way back towards it. It wasn't long before he heard something that stopped him in his tracks... voices, up ahead. Quietly, he raised the thermal camera to his eyes and turned it back on. After it had initialised, he began looking through the viewfinder to see two men carrying rifles. They were only about twenty feet away from his position and appeared to be talking. Very slowly, he got as low as he could and started to crawl quietly towards them.

Because they were carrying weapons, Archie knew they weren't out for an early morning stroll. Looking through the camera, he could see that the only option he had to get the van passed them, was to incapacitate them. He only hoped that he wouldn't have to kill them. The Karmic effects of what he'd already done were going to be a nightmare in the next life. This shit was really messing with his Zen.

He got to within ten feet of them and stopped, looked and listened. He couldn't quite catch the whole conversation, but he did hear one of them say, "Some fucking civilian is helping the Pleiadian."

Pleiadian? What the fuck is a Pleiadian? Archie thought to himself as he weighed up his options.

"The Draco War Lord is sending another crew in to wipe them out. ETA fifteen minutes," the other one said.

He knew he had to get a move on as he edged a bit closer. Once he got to within five feet, he stopped again and listened. But heard nothing more. Because they had said another crew were on the way, Archie decided that he didn't want to engage them with the firearms, that would be noisy. Equally, he realised that as much as he didn't want to, he didn't have a choice but to kill these guys. He sat there for a few seconds trying to figure out a means of subduing them both without either of them getting off a shot. Decision made, there was no other option; they were both going to have to die.

Laying the M4 and the camera gently on the grass, Archie prepared himself mentally for what he was about to do. It was really dark on the road, with virtually no light, but he could still see them with his naked eyes. He watched them closely as he slowly pulled the bowie knife from his belt. They were walking together, backwards and forwards across the opening to the dirt road. He sat stock still and held his breath as they made their way in his direction. Would they see him? What would they do if they did? Whatever. Archie would just have to be faster than them...

Nothing, they didn't spot him.

As they turned away, Archie made his move. Standing up from the bush he'd been hiding in, and with his right hand, he threw the knife at the man on the left, hitting him in the back of the neck. He knew straight away that it had severed his spinal cord because the soldier just dropped like a sack of shit, completely unable to stem his fall as his face hit the dirt with a sickening thud. In the same instant, Archie dived from cover and rolled forwards towards to the second man.

As the soldier turned to face his enemy, Archie was already coming out of the roll, slightly to his left. He was on him. Putting his left leg behind the man's, Archie used his forearm to smash him in the throat, making him fall backwards. As he was going down, Archie took hold of the guys left wrist and pulled up hard, forcing him to fall on to his right side. The instant the soldier hit the floor, Archie gave a swift, sharp kick to the centre of his back, making him arch. Then, still holding the left wrist, he forced his right hand into the front of the victim's elbow and rolled his hand over the top until it was folded under the forearm. Simultaneously, he'd knelt on to his victim's kidney and neck, respectively. Once the arm was rolled sufficiently, Archie straightened his back and partially stood up. This caused the bones in the wrist and forearm to shatter while at the same time dislocating the shoulder. The soldier screamed aloud, but it wasn't over as Archie pulled the arm out straight and snapped it the other way, across his right thigh, breaking even more bones. Throwing the shattered arm away in front of his body, Archie delivered a savage punch to the back of the man's jaw, breaking it instantly and turning his screams to a whimper.

Now that he was semi-conscious, Archie dragged him into the bushes, where he gave his victim another whack, putting him out cold. Then he made his way back to the dead man and pulled his knife from the guy's neck and cleaned the blade on his shirt, the body twitching as he did so. After dragging him into the trees, Archie searched them both and took anything that could be of use. By the time he had finished, he had pockets full of ammunition. He also took the radio from the soldier he'd knocked out, slipped it on to his waistband and put the earpiece in his left ear.

Once he had finished robbing the soldiers of their worldly possessions, he made his way back to his launching point to retrieve the thermal and the rifle. With these in hand, he moved out on to the road to open the gate so that he could drive the van straight through, but the sound of dogs barking stopped him in his tracks almost instantly. Looking through the thermal, he could see a dog patrol moving down the main road towards him. They were about two hundred and fifty yards away. Two dogs and two handlers. The mutts were going crazy. It was about to go off big time, and he knew it, as he ducked back into the bushes.

Standing firm in the trees, Archie watched through the thermal as the group started running in his direction. It was too late for him to run; he'd never make it to the van before the dogs would be on him. He naively hoped the animals had spotted a rabbit or something and were chasing that, but he also knew that was nothing more than just wishful thinking. As he watched, he silently begged for some kind of divine intervention to make them stop. But it wasn't to be. As soon as he saw the handlers release the dogs, he knew for sure that he couldn't sit it out, he was going to have to deal with them.

The thought of killing the dogs grated Archie like nothing he had ever experienced before. He loved animals, especially dogs. He'd grown up with a multitude of different pets, and this was the only time in his life that there wasn't a dog at home waiting for him to return. His last dog Zeus had died the year before, and Archie hadn't really got over it. The pain of Zeus' death still brought tears to his eyes every time he thought about it. At that moment, he wasn't sure if he could bring himself to end the lives of these animals hurtling towards him. But what else could he do? If he was going to survive the night, he had to kill them. Killing the soldiers, on the other hand, was a different matter entirely. They had made a choice to do what they do, whereas to the dogs, it was just a game. *Shit, I'm going to have to do it!* The stress caused his breathing rate to increase.

Going through his options, Archie came to the conclusion that he should continue to refrain from using the guns. Clearly, there were more soldiers around and using the firearms would only draw more attention to his presence. He knew the handlers hadn't called the situation in yet because he had the radio, nothing had come over the earpiece. The chances were that the handlers didn't even know for sure that he was there and were only reacting to the dog's behaviour. Quietly was the way to go.

Through the viewfinder of the thermal camera, Archie kept his eyes trained firmly on the dogs running along the road as he backed into a small clearing. He knew what he was going to do with the first animal. He had trained for it in his martial arts; in fact, he had trained to do it bare handed, but choking the mutt out was a long and painful death. As the first one lunged at him, he would drive the knife up through the lower jaw and into the brain, death would be almost instantaneous. Dealing with the second one carried too many variables that were dependant on the situation at that time, so planning for it was a waste of time. He'd have to deal with it as it happened. The mere thought of what he was about to do made his eyes well up with tears. He couldn't believe what was about to happen.

These dogs were big bastards, and he could hear their footsteps from a hundred yards away. Not long now and they would be on him. Archie readied himself. Fifty yards – thirty - at twenty yards, he had one last, quick look through the thermal to see where the handlers were and threw the camera to his right. The men were still over a hundred yards out. With the bowie knife in his right hand and the fish knife in the other, he put his left foot forward, standing side on; he was ready. The dog's heavy footfalls made it sound like a stampede of horses was coming at him. They hit the clearing - *Here we go!*

Nothing! They just stopped and looked at him, panting with their tongues hanging out of their mouths. They were beautiful animals. One was a German Shepherd whose fluffy tail was gently wagging from side to side. The other was the biggest Rottweiler Archie had ever seen. He couldn't do it; he couldn't bring himself to hurt these magnificent creatures. Holstering the blades, he got to his knees and raised his hands to his head, waiting for the handlers to come and arrest him.

The fluffy tail GSD licked his chops and trotted over to him. Preparing himself for the worst, he held his breath but was surprised when the dog rubbed against him as if he wanted stroking. The Rotty just stood there watching as Archie started petting his new friend. It was too much of a temptation for the big Rottweiler to resist, he wanted some love as well. The dog looked behind him, in the direction of the handlers and snarled, baring his huge teeth before walking over to get some strokes for himself. It was as though they were happy that they had found someone to show them some affection.

After a few seconds, Archie picked up the thermal again to see where the handlers were. They were about fifty yards out and closing. He knew they had to go, but he wondered how his new companions would react when he killed their owners. Maybe he should just kill the dogs anyway and be done with it. NO; soldiers, yes – dogs, no. Not unless he had absolutely no other choice.

"Sit," Archie said, trying his luck with the animals. To his astonishment, they did precisely what they were told. "Good boys," he added as he gave them both a quick pet.

When the handlers got to about twenty yards away, Archie replaced the thermal on the ground and pulled out his knives again. He wasn't going to mess around; he was going to throw both of the weapons at his attackers and finish it quickly. He didn't want to get into a physical with them, he wasn't sure what the dogs would do. Might they side with him or would they tear him to pieces? He just didn't know, and he wasn't prepared to take any chances.

Blades at the ready, he waited. He could hear the soldiers calling to the dogs, but they weren't listening, they just sat there looking up at Archie. The calls got louder as the handlers entered the bushes. They were only just in front of the clearing, and he was about to throw the first knife when the dogs both ran forward and set about mauling their handlers.

Archie couldn't believe what was happening. What happened to the loyalty of man's best friend? The screams the men were letting out were blood-curdling as the dog's teeth tore into them. He couldn't let it phase him, he had to do something before the cries drew the attention of any other patrols that might be nearby. Moving forward, he saw that one of them was trying to pull a pistol as the Rottweiler was tearing into his left arm. Archie knew that he couldn't let the man pull that weapon and from roughly ten yards away, he threw the knife. The blade buried itself deep into the handler's chest. The man seemed to die instantly.

Turning his attention to the second soldier, Archie saw that the German Shepherd had him by his neck and was trying to pull his throat out in an absolutely savage assault. He couldn't let the man die in such a manner. To his complete surprise, both dogs stopped what they were doing when Archie shouted "LEAVE" and came to sit by his side. "STAY," he said as he moved forward to check on the second Handler. The two animals didn't take their eyes off of him as they sat there growling. The man had some horrendous bite marks all over him, and he was whimpering in agony. Archie felt terrible for the guy, but not enough to jeopardise his own safety, so pulling the Beretta, he pointed it at the soldiers head and threatened to shoot him if he moved.

After ordering the man to lay on his front, Archie removed the sidearm from its holster on the prisoners right hip and threw it into the middle of the clearing. Then he used the guys own zip-tie plasti-cuffs to secure his hands behind his back as tight as he could before he rolled him on to his back and searched him properly. He had a silencer for the pistol in a pouch on his tactical vest which Archie stuffed into one of his own pockets. He removed the man's radio and knife and tossed them into the clearing. Once he had finished the search, he grabbed the back of the injured man's collar and dragged him to a nearby tree. He then took the plasti-cuffs from the dead soldier and used them to further bind the injured guy by forcing his feet back and tying them to his hands, around the trunk of a small tree. Once he was secure, Archie scoured the dead one.

He went for the obvious first, the pistol. The moment he touched it, he got the flash that told him everything he needed to know about the weapon. Hi-Power Browning with a thirteen-round clip. Making sure the safety was on, he threw it on to the pile in the middle of the clearing. Other than a radio and decent looking blade, there wasn't really anything else of interest. When he had finished, he took the stockpile of equipment that he had gathered and moved off into the bushes. There he removed the battery pack from the radios and put them into the same pocket that held the silencer. He then stripped the firing pins from the weapons and threw them as far as he could. He lobbed the soldier's knife as well.

Making his way back to the clearing, Archie stripped the dead guy of his jacket and put it over the other one. He didn't want the man to die of exposure. He wasn't worried about the soldier identifying him, he hadn't so much as looked at him throughout the whole ordeal. His eyes had been flicking between the pistol and the still growling dogs. At least if he was eventually caught, Archie could say that he only killed when he had no other choice. Not that he intended getting caught. Before leaving the man to his own devices, Archie ripped a length of clothing from the dead guys' shirt, making a gag out of it, and tied it tight around the soldier's mouth.

Using the thermal, he made sure the road was clear before he moved and opened the gate. Turning back toward the track, Archie noticed that the dogs were right there with him. Initially, he didn't know what to do with them.

"Fuck it; Come on then, you're on the firm," Archie said as he started making his way to the vehicle. "If I leave you here you're gonna get a lead injection."

With his new best friends in tow, he sprinted back to the van, it was time to get out of there.

8

Exit Of The Fishing Lake

West Midlands

England

Upon reaching the van, Archie threw the M4 and the thermal into the front and made his way to the side door. Inside, he felt Blondie's shoulder, he was freezing. He motioned for the dogs to get in, they complied by laying either side of the frozen man, as though they knew he needed warming up. Because he felt so cold himself, Archie suspected that the core body temperature of the unconscious form was probably on the dangerous side of low. He decided to open out the sleeping bag and lay it over both Blondie and the mutts in the hope that the animal's body heat would go some way to warming him up.

After doing all he could in the back of the van, Archie got into the driver's seat, wondering where he was going to go. Screw it; the where didn't matter. He just had to get away, deciding that he would only stop when he was clear before figuring out what to do. His immediate plan was one of necessity; get out of the area as quick as possible.

Slipping the van into gear, he made his way to the gate. The main road was actually a B-road, a country lane. The chances of any other vehicles being on the road at this time of night were slim. The only exception would be the ones that were actually looking for him. For that reason,

Archie decided that he wasn't going to stop at the gate to see if the way was clear; he was just going to drive straight out and turn right. What was the worst that could happen? It didn't matter if there was anything incoming or not, he wouldn't be stopping if he hit anything anyway. What was he going to do, stop and exchange insurance details? No, he just had to keep the wheels rolling, whatever the cost.

Looking through the thermal, Archie could see that the exit was still clear, so as planned, he drove straight out, turned right on to the road before flooring the accelerator. Travelling in the dark with no headlights was a risky business, but travelling at *speed* in the dark with no headlights was suicidal. With that in mind, he knew that he couldn't afford to draw any attention to himself with lights, he just had to get away as clean as possible.

As he was driving, Archie held the thermal above the steering wheel so that he could see where he was going. It wasn't perfect, but it was better than a slap in the face with a dead fish. Night vision goggles would have been better, but he was shit out of luck - none of the dead squaddies had been carrying any. If they had, then they would have been on his head, and his arm wouldn't be aching from the weight of the camera. His ribs felt like he was being stabbed with every breath he took, and his face was burning as though Satan was holding a burning pitch folk to his head.

The road was reasonably straight for long periods, but when he did have to turn, he could hear the fishing gear rolling and crashing about in the back. He just hoped it didn't hurt Blondie or the dogs. He couldn't slow down;

speed was of the essence. The soldiers at the gate had said that the ETA for the incoming Draco crew was fifteen minutes, and that was twenty minutes ago. Archie knew it wouldn't take them very long to figure out what had happened. He had to get a shift on. He wanted to get at least twenty miles away before he would even consider slowing down.

Flicking his eyes down to the clock, Archie saw it was approaching 04.30. He was shocked at what time it was. It didn't feel that late, or early, depending on what side of midnight you went to bed. But, time flies when you're having fun. Only, there was nothing fun about the events that had taken place.

Archie had been driving as fast as he safely could for about fifteen minutes when in the distance he saw something at the side of the road. Through the thermal, he thought he could make out a jeep with two heat signatures standing to the side of the road. *Shit, I can't just drive up to them*. He didn't know for sure, but he had a feeling that they were probably military. Slowly, Archie brought the van to a stop and noticed there was a large bush about twenty yards in front of the vehicle. *That will do nicely*, he thought as he pulled the van up as close to it as he could, hoping that it would provide a bit of cover. He nearly pulled right up, putting the front of the vehicle into it, but decided against the idea in case he needed to make a quick getaway.

Turning the engine off, he noticed the pain from his head again. It was getting worse, and it was beginning to itch like crazy. He wondered if it was because the wounds were scabbing up or if it was the onset of an allergy to the poxy fish cream. Whatever the cause, there was no time to worry about that now, he had to check that jeep out.

He wanted to make as little noise as possible, so when he got out of the van, he left the door open. Moving to the back, he opened the door to get the second M4, this one had a strap. Leaning in to pick up the rifle, he saw that the German Shepherd was laying tight to Blondie. Reaching under the sleeping bag, he could tell straight away that the unconscious man was significantly warmer. As he pulled away to close the door, the Rottweiler got up and made his way over. Something in the way he looked at Archie told him that the dog wanted to tag along. That bloody compulsion was back again, he knew he had to take him.

"Fuck it; you're on the team dog," he whispered as he motioned for the pooch to get out of the van. With that, he gently closed the door until it got to the latch then with a firm push, locked in place. Turning away, he saw that the dog was just sat next to him, looking up. Kneeling down, Archie stroked his head and whispered, "I can't keep calling you dog, so I'm going to name you Reg." He received a lick to the face in response. As he wiped the slime from his cheek, he couldn't help but smile. Of all the names he could have called the dog, Reg the Rottweiler was the only thing he could think of. As he silently checked the rifle, he hoped that Reg wouldn't give him away.

With the weapon ready, he slung it over his shoulder and across his back, before he pulled the Beretta from his waistband, checked the magazine and made sure it was ready for action. Safety on, he slipped it back into the front of his trousers. One last check told him that the blades were secure in their holsters. He was ready; well, as ready as he was ever going to be. Heading off into the trees, he noticed that Reg was at his left heel, moving in stride.

As quietly as possible, Archie edged his way towards the jeep. He was only about five yards into the treeline, but it was pitch dark and eerily silent. The only noise came from their breathing, their footfalls were surprisingly quiet. Archie was impressed with how Reg stalked his way forward as if he knew exactly what he was doing. He stuck to Archie's side as though he was attached by glue.

At around forty yards from the target, he remembered that he had the silencer for the pistol in his pocket. Stopping and dropping to one knee, he fitted it to the gun. Just as he finished screwing it on to the barrel, he heard a noise to his left. Reg turned in the direction and started baring his teeth before a low growl emanated from his throat. Peering hard into the darkness, Archie couldn't see a thing until he lifted the thermal back up to his eyes, but even then, he couldn't see anything out of the ordinary. He only saw the usual colours that made up the different heat signatures of various things like the ground and the trees. He had no doubt that the dog was on to something, but Archie couldn't see what it was.

As he panned the camera from left to right, he thought he saw a darker shadow move between the trees. At the same time, Reg became even more agitated. Archie realised that the thermal wasn't doing anything but light up his face, so he put it down. He was convinced there was something out there, but he still couldn't make anything out in the darkness. He didn't like it, the hair on the back of his neck stood to attention, and his intuition was screaming at him.

Archie had stayed in the same position for several minutes, trying to survey the area around him before he eventually decided that whatever had been in the trees was gone. He was just about to move off, in the direction of the jeep, when a big dark shadow broke from cover and started towards them. Reg went ballistic, barking, snarling, showing his teeth, but stayed at his new master's side. In a split second, Archie knew he'd been ambushed, and it dawned on him that the shadow was another giant reptile.

When the colossal lizard was about ten yards off, the dog went full bore and jumped up at it, but the creature just swatted him away as though he was nothing more than an annoying bug. Reg yelped as the big scaly arm hit him across the right flank. The blow sent the canine flying through the air, and he landed about eight feet to the left, whimpering.

Everything seemed to go into slow motion. The dog being hit and sent to the ground filled Archie with rage the likes of which he'd never known. Lifting the pistol, he started firing like mad. He was scoring hits with every shot, but this thing kept coming. The lizard was massive, at least eight feet tall, distinctly larger than the one he'd previously encountered. It was taking the rounds as though it was being shot with an air gun.

Realising the pistol had little effect, Archie started running back to the van. As he moved, he shoved the Beretta down the front of his shirt and pulled the M4 from his back. He could hear the thunderous footsteps as the reptile gained on him. He brought the rifle into his shoulder, stopped, turned and dropped to one. Through the sight, he lined up the shot. Selecting three round burst, he squeezed the trigger. The bullets seemed to rock the giant creature, but it kept coming. Another two blasts sent it stumbling forward. At the same time, Reg came from nowhere and locked his teeth around the lizard's neck and started yanking and tearing in a ferocious attack.

With the reptile on his knees and the dog ripping him a new one, the struggle was an almighty one, with slob and scales flying all over the place. Archie wanted to shoot the bastard, but he was too scared of hitting the Rottweiler to pull the trigger.

From the right, he heard the sound of rifle fire coming from the direction of the jeep, and the trees around him erupted as the rounds tore bark from the trunks. The soldiers had heard his gunfire and joined the fight. Facing the incoming, Archie flicked the switch to full auto and opened up. He couldn't really see what he was shooting at, he just wanted to get their heads down long enough for him to withdraw.

"REG LEAVE!" he shouted over the sound of gunfire. "COME!"

Archie turned back to the lizard, he watched the dog let go and start heading back to the van. With him out of the way, Archie emptied the rest of the magazine into the scaly bastard's chest and face. The reptile dropped on to his front, as the soldiers opened up again, their weapons spitting fire.

With the mag empty, he pulled it out as he ran towards the van. As he was moving, he reached down to the pocket on the side of his trouser leg for a fresh one. It wasn't easy reaching down while he was running. Eventually, he got a grip of one and slapped it in the slot, turned and fired. With the incoming getting heavier and heavier, Archie had to stop, fire, run – stop, fire, run, all the way back.

Before he got to the bush that hid the van, he moved out on to the tarmac of the carriageway. He fired as he ran across the road and dropped to the ground on the other side. As soon as he touched down, he quickly changed the mag and selected three round burst again.

"DOWN!" Reg took the order as he laid next to Archie.

He didn't have long to wait before the enemy came out of the treeline. They had no idea where he was and moved cautiously out on to the road as they began their search. They were looking through the sights that were mounted on the top of the weapons, the green glow around their eyes told Archie that they were using night vision.

The dogs panted breaths gave him away, causing the enemy to open fire. Rounds were pinging off the road and thudding into the dirt beside him. Keeping his head down as the lead flew, he knew he had to do something, but what? They had him pinned down. Without any thought of aiming, he let off two bursts. He knew they would drop to their knees or go prone, which might buy him a second or two. As he fired the second burst, he lifted his head. They were close, less than fifteen yards away, and directly in front of him.

"MOVE!" he shouted to the dog. Reg's movement drew their fire as he leapt forward at the same time, Archie got to one knee, weapon butt in the shoulder and fired. After hitting the guy to the left in the face, he turned his attention straight to the other one, but Reg got to him first and was happily tearing him a new arsehole.

"DON'T MOVE, DON'T YOU FUCKING MOVE!" Archie ordered as he moved forward to take control of the heavily bleeding soldier. Reg had done a proper number on the guy. The soldier laid face down with his arms spread out.

Not willing to take any chances, Archie smacked him straight in the back of the head with the rifle butt, forcing his face into the tarmac with a sickening pop. He went out cold. This was some serious shit. These guys appeared to be dressed differently from the others, their kit seemed more fitting, in that they were wearing full body armour with ceramic plates. There were pouches all over them, and they were wearing helmets that looked more suitable for a skateboarder or a rock climber. It occurred to Archie that these guys were probably some kind of Special Forces.

Robbing the two soldiers blind, he took every piece of ammunition they had, their rifles and their pistols. The weapons were the same as what he already had except that the guns had low light combi sights attached. He got the flicker again...this time telling him that the sight was an ACOG 4x32 scope, with dual illuminated crosshairs with a .223 Ballistic MOA RMR sight. In layman's terms that meant it had a Red dot sight for fast, close-range target acquisition that sat on top of a low light ACOG sight which was suited for more extended range. Two for the price of one. As well as the guns, he also had two types of grenade, a sting, and a fragmentation. He had found two of each, and the flicker told him that when detonated, the US M67 Frag grenade threw out shrapnel in all directions within its killing field, to a radius of 15 metres and could be thrown to a range of 30-40 metres -depending on how good your chucking arm was. The Sting was pretty much a stun grenade that threw out bits of rubber, designed to disorientate the enemy. Archie made a note not to be anywhere near either of them should he need to use them.

As he bent forward to pick up the last magazine, a blinding flash passed between his head and the ground, missing him by inches; so close that he could feel the heat that it radiated. Looking to his left Archie saw the reptilian emerging from the treeline. He thought he had killed the bastard; it must have been tougher than he gave it credit for.

Reg went for the attacker as Archie dived behind the unconscious soldier. Bolts of light flew above him as he tried to get as low as possible. He couldn't move, he was stuck; totally pinned down. He heard a loud yelp from the dog. Lifting the M4 over the makeshift barricade of the downed squaddie, Archie opened fire. He had no idea if he was hitting the enemy, but it felt good just to be fighting back.

The lizard's shots were flying over his head in quick succession, and they were getting closer. It wasn't long before energy bolts were hitting the man Archie was hiding behind. He had been firing back on full auto, and now there was nothing but clicks coming from his weapon, he was out of ammo. There was no way he could change the mag without taking a hit. Looking to his right, he could see that one of the other rifles was laying on the tarmac, about five feet away. It was so close, but not close enough; he just couldn't get to it without getting killed.

Come on Reg, get up, get up, He wasn't sure if he was thinking it or if he was shouting it; it didn't matter. He could hear the dog whimpering, and he knew that he was hurt. It was over. He was about to die. Looking into himself, he accepted the inevitability of it, as he heard the heavy footsteps coming towards him.

The bolts of energy were hitting all around him as the lizard drew closer. He waited for the end to come.

WHOOSH! This noise was different.

What the fuck was that?

Looking up, he saw that the enemy was still firing, but not at him. He was shooting toward the van. Flicking his eyes that way, he saw a big blond, naked man; half kneeling, half hanging on to the back of the vehicle, firing some kind of light weapon at the reptilian. Seizing the opportunity, Archie rolled to the side and grabbed the M4 next to him. At the same time, he heard the snarling barks from the German Shepherd as it ran at the enemy.

The lizard's attention was firmly on Blondie and the dog. Archie got to one knee and fired on full auto, emptying the entire clip into him. The massive reptile dropped to his knees, as Archie slotted home a fresh mag. A quick look towards the van told him that Blondie was on the ground, not knowing if he'd been hit or not, Archie turned his attention back to the enemy, he wasn't going to make the same mistake twice. Making every bullet count, he switched back to three round burst and unloaded another mag, only stopping when the dog got in the way and attacked. By that time the lizard was down anyway.

With the dog ripping into the creature's throat, Archie dropped the M4 and picked up one of the pistols from the floor. Moving forward, he ordered the dog to leave, and from no more than three feet away, he put five rounds directly into the things scaly face. He was definitely down this time. Moving closer, he shot another three bullets into the thing's skull, just to be on the safe side.

The lizard was finished, so Archie made towards the van. Blondie was lying face down, moaning and groaning. Turning him on to his back and checking him over, there were no signs of injury, he must have just passed out. Dragging him to the rear of the van, Archie noticed something that looked like a remote control for a television laying on the floor. It must have been a weapon of some kind. He realised that he hadn't actually searched the man after rescuing him. He never actually checked to see what the little pouches contained when he had cut his clothes off, then again, Archie had been too busy trying to save his life.

Getting to the rear of the van, Archie heaved as hard as he could as he lifted the heavy bastard into the back door. Once inside, he replaced the sleeping bag over the top. Afterwards, he picked up the device from the ground and started to make his way back towards the area of the fight. There were twelve buttons on the little machine and a small screen centred around a large circular switch. Then it hit him, the flicker; it was a weapon, but not only that, it had other functions as well. It was also a diagnostic and healing tool. For the first time since receiving the flicker, he never got any information on how to use it. He knew what it was but not how it worked. Not that it would have mattered anyway, he wasn't about to stick it in his pocket. No, he was going to leave it with Blondie. After all, he had just saved Archie's arse with it, and he might have to do it again.

Arriving back at the site of the battle, he made his way straight to the dog. The German Shepherd was whining as he stood over the Rottweiler who was lying flat on the ground. There was a massive gash along his left flank. The blow he took must have been huge, he was hurt bad, but there was no way Archie was about to leave him behind. Picking him up was no easy task, he seemed to weigh as much as Blondie. Struggling, he lifted Reg up, he staggered back to the vehicle.

Reaching the back of the van, he slid the big dog inside and covered him up. When he turned around, the German Shepherd was looking up at him, so he did the same as he did with Reg.

"Your name is going to be Kaiser from now on mate," he said as he stroked the animals head and receiving a face full of slob in return.

It was time to collect the equipment and get out of there while he still could. With Kaiser at his side, he ran back into the tree line to find and retrieve the thermal camera. Fortuitously, when Archie dropped it to the ground, he'd left it on. That meant the screen was still lit, making it that much easier to find. As he picked it up, he noticed that there was a dead reptilian in the vicinity. It was the one that had initially attacked him, which meant there had been two. *Thank god for that*, he thought as he realised that they weren't as hard to kill as he'd first thought.

From there he moved out on to the road and made his way back to the dead soldiers. He picked up the remaining pistol and stuffed it down the front of his shirt, then slung the two rifles across his back. He changed the mag on the third one, made it ready and left it on the ground. He was going to return for the grenades, and he wanted to leave some firepower in place for when he came back. Try as he might, he just couldn't get anything else in his pockets.

With all the kit stowed in the vehicle, he went back to the dead soldiers for the last time and dragged them off the road. The guy that he had knocked out was well and truly dead; the reptilians weapons fire had really done a number on him. The energy bolts had gone through the man's body armour like hot piss through snow. That dirty bastard had wanted Archie dead so desperately that he had killed one of his own allies to get at him.

Having stashed the bodies in the treeline, Archie struggled to pull the lizard to the front of the van. It had occurred to him that he had been trying to shoot them in the head to destroy its brain, or centre mass, going for the heart. But in reality, he had no idea of the creature's anatomy or where the heart would be located. So, for the first time since leaving the lake, he turned the headlights on, he wanted to see the thing up close.

Once the area was illuminated, he opened his attacker's tunic. Standing over him, he pulled out his bowie, bent down and started cutting the reptiles chest open. The skin was really tough, and the scales were making the job more difficult. *His skin would make a lovely handbag*, he thought as he sliced a straight line down the middle of the chest. From that point, he cut two lines out towards the sides.

With the skin open, he set about jabbing through the dense bones that made up the creature's rib cage. Ironically, this brought Archie's attention back to his own rib pain. Once he had detached a section either side of the chest, he started forcing the blade through what would have been the sternum. It wasn't a straightforward action; he had to push in and withdraw the knife repeatedly to achieve, what amounted to a dot to dot line. Then he forced the blade through to join the dots together until it all fell apart. With the chest hanging free, he opened the rib cage out as though it was a book to expose the reptile's innards. The smell was horrendous, and Archie found himself gagging several times.

Moving the contents about, he couldn't find anything that even remotely looked like a heart. After a few minutes, he noticed a black plate located to the upper right, just under the site where a human's collar bone would be situated. Tapping it with the point of the blade, the plate seemed as though it was as hard as steel.

It was protecting something; Archie was sure of it. But he just couldn't penetrate it. *If I can't get through it, I'll go around it*, he thought as he held the knife flat and slipped the blade under the edge of the plate and into the softer tissue beneath it. He felt like he was back at school dissecting a frog, albeit a massive one. Once the knife was properly in, he started cutting until he could lift one side away. He never removed it completely, just enough to get it out of the way. Lifting up the free side of the plate, Archie found a dirty greenish black lump. That was it... the heart. Confirmation came when Archie pushed the tip of his knife into it. Giving it a little squeeze, he watched as the horrible dark viscous fluid seeped out of the hole. With the heart found, he now knew where to shoot.

There was one more thing he needed to do before leaving. Replacing the plate and putting the rib cage and skin back into position, he stood up and pulled the silenced pistol. Taking aim, he fired at the plated area. Then he pulled the skin back and had a look to see if the round had penetrated through to the heart; it hadn't. He did the same with the unsilenced pistol, but that ended with the same result. *Fuck it*, he thought as he took aim with the M4 and pulled the trigger. Green shit splattered everywhere. Bingo! Now he knew where he had to hit them. Headshots with the handguns and the heart with the rifles.

With his knowledge of alien anatomy updated, Archie dragged the giant science experiment off the road and into the trees. After he had a last look around to make sure he got all of his kit together, he got into the van and turned the lights off. He waited a minute or so to let his eyes begin to adjust to the darkness before he moved the vehicle up to the jeep and stopped. Predictively, he found the keys in the sun visor, before driving the thing straight into the treeline. When he was far enough to be hidden from the road, he stopped and turned the engine off and wiped his fingerprints off the steering wheel. Now that everything was hidden from sight, he made his way back to the van and checked the speedo. He had travelled nearly twenty-two miles from the lake, but that was irrelevant now because he had just had another firefight. Which meant that he had to reset the getaway counter. The time was 05.45, and it would be daylight soon. He had to get a move on.

9

Undisclosed Location

The Midlands

England

After driving for about thirty miles, Archie noticed a light emanating from the hole in the bulkhead that separated the front from the rear of the van. Looking back, he saw that Blondie was sitting upright.

Other than the odd helicopter in the distance heading towards the area of the lake, there had been no sign of pursuit. Deciding to pull over to find out what was happening in the back, Archie found a road off the main. It was a dirt track that was lined with overhanging trees, he guessed that it was an access road for some farmer to get his tractor to his fields.

Once he had found a particularly well-hidden area, he stopped the van and made his way to the back door. Because he didn't know what to expect, he pulled out the pistol and flicked off the safety. Opening the door, he found Blondie was sat crossed legged, leaning forward over Reg. He was using the remote control thing to shine a green beam of light onto the dog's injuries. Archie just stood there watching in awe as the light pulled the Rottweilers wounds together.

"You will not need that," Blondie said, flicking his eyes to the gun.

"What are you doing to the dog?" Archie asked with his eyes firmly on the green light.

"I am sealing his wounds," replied Blondie. "When I am finished, he will no longer feel any pain. It will be as though he was never injured."

"I appreciate that thank you," Archie said, pausing for a moment. "Now if you don't mind, I want to know who the fuck you are and how you know my name?" It was a demand, not a question. He wanted answers. He had been *Compelled* to kill a lot of people throughout the night to keep this guy alive, and now he wanted to know why.

"All in good time, Archie. For now, I will heal this animal. He is important, as is the other one. There are no accidents in the Universal Laws. These animals are here to aid you," he said in an accent that was somewhat reminiscent of being Nordic in origin.

"Listen, I have no idea what you're talking about. I want to know how you know about me. How do you know my name? What is going on, and why am I involved?" Archie's tone was harsher than he'd intended, but he didn't know how much time they had before they were found. It was beginning to get light, and he could see that although he'd parked under the overhanging trees, there wasn't much in the way of foliage on the branches and that made him concerned about the amount of cover they could really provide once the sun was fully up.

"In time I will tell you what you require. We are safe for now," Blondie said, using his eyes he motioned to the cover above. He made the statement as a matter of fact, as though he knew something that Archie didn't.

Knowing he wasn't going to get any answers just yet, Archie decided to have a walk up the track. Leaving the van with Kaiser watching him intently, he made his way farther up the dirt road, where, after around fifty yards or so, he found a small path that led deeper into the trees. It was just about wide enough to get the vehicle in, and the cover was apparently better, so he made the decision to move in. If they were going to be there a while, he might as well try to hide a bit better.

As he got back to the van, Blondie must have finished treating Reg. The big dog jumped out of the vehicle, ran straight to him and started rubbing against his leg. The animal was so excited that the stump of his docked tail was wagging so fast that it made his arse wobble. As Archie knelt down to pet the Rotty, Kaiser jumped out of the side door and ran at him so quickly that the force knocked him over. Both dog's set about licking his face with such vigour that anyone passing would have thought they were trying to eat him. Archie was absolutely smothered in slob, but he loved it. They were his dog's now, and he already loved them.

When the tongue mauling died down, Archie picked himself up and noticed that Blondie was standing beside the van, stark bollock naked. He needed clothes. Pulling the clothing bag from the kit, he knew that none of his threads would actually fit the big man properly. The best he could manage was the waterproof waders that he used when he would return a fish to the water. They weren't going to be perfect, but they had adjustable braces. They would be better than nothing, and if nothing else, they would cover that tree branch of a knob that hung between the guy's legs. Things were bad enough without that flying around.

"Here put this on," Archie said as he passed over the waders and a fleece-lined jacket. "I'm sure you didn't come all this way across the Galaxy to show off your gizmo."

He then dug out a dry set of clothes for himself and got changed. Once he was dressed, he started transferring the ammunition. He felt like some sort of action hero from a film as he stuffed the pockets full of magazines and grenades. When they were ready, he got everyone back in the van, jumped in the driver's seat and moved the vehicle off the track and on to the pathway between the trees.

When Archie was happy that he was in as much cover as he was going to get, he stopped the vehicle, and turned off the engine, before making his way to the rear doors and letting the dog's out again. While they wandered around for a sniff and a shit, Archie made sure all of the rifles had a fresh mag and were ready to fire. With the safeties on, he did the same with the pistols. As he was doing so, it occurred to him that Blondie might know why he was getting the flicker that told him how to use the weapons.

"Do you know why I keep getting information downloaded to my brain on how to use a weapon?" he asked, before adding. "It happens every time I touch a new gun or grenade. It's like I already know how to use it, but I've never fired or even held a real gun in my life."

"It is… complicated. I am uncertain if your consciousness is ready to accept this information yet, but I will try to explain. In human terms, it is what you call an upload, and it is sent by the consciousness of the Light to aid you in your mission. It will only happen as and when you need it." Blondie spoke in a soft tone, knowing that what he was about to say next could completely shatter a person's world view. "Archie, you are not what you think you are… *You* are one of *us.*"

One of them? Archie stopped what he was doing and looked at the big man. "What do you mean, one of you?" he asked.

"I am Pleiadian. I come from the planet Erra which is situated in the Pleiades star cluster, where we have colonised several Systems. Everything Earth humans have been told about extra-terrestrial life is a lie. There are many species of what you call aliens. Most are a part of a Galactic Alliance that is ruled through consent by the Great Council of Light," he spoke clearly. "The Council is made up of many species that are elected by the Alliance Senate, similar to how the Governments of Earth are perceived to be made. They write the Galactic Laws that are obeyed throughout the Galaxy. One of the first laws is the non-interference law; that means that no species can interfere in the development of an undeveloped world - a planet such as Earth would fall into that category." Blondie took a seat in the doorway of the van before continuing. "We, the Pleiadians, believe there is something very wrong here on this planet. We monitor the development of certain worlds, and we believe that the Draconian Empire has infiltrated your governments to influence the development of the human race. We have long suspected Draco involvement here but have been unable to provide the necessary proof to enable the Council to act."

"Hold on, Blondie. What do you mean? I have no idea what you're talking about," said Archie, clearly confused.

"We believe that the Draconians; the reptilians, have infiltrated the people who truly run the planet. I say *truly* because the real rulers are *not* the elected politicians. There are secret societies which make the real decisions, and the elected are simply the face of puppets put in place to keep the real decision makers secret from the civilian population. There are beings from other worlds... the Draco, that control these societies that rule the world, which by extension means that the *Draco* rule the world. They are controlling everything, from government, religious and financial systems, to the entertainment industry. Everything; including the weather, they run it all. By being in control of these systems, the Draconian's have control of humanity."

Archie had done a bit of research into the worlds secret societies, so some of this made a little bit of sense. However, his studies had been limited, to say the least. At the time he felt that there wasn't anything he could about the cabals that ran the governments, so he had focused most of his time into the things he could change or effect; like the spirituality and the UFO thing. After all, it didn't take much to go into a field and look into the night sky for freaky lights, whereas taking on the establishment would be suicidal.

"I think I might need a history lesson here, mate," he said. "My knowledge of the Masons is limited."

"I will try to explain. The Masonic Knights of Dark Light have been around since antiquity but on the Earth date of May 1st, 1776, a Professor who went by the code name Brother Spartacus, along with four others, founded the Order of the Illuminati. They aimed to use ancient esoteric mysticism to bring the world out of the darkness of slavery and into the light, thereby allowing freedom for all mankind. They were going to infiltrate all elements of government to achieve their goal. They were becoming more and more successful as they beat back the Masons, who had used the same mysticism for their own ends of power and wealth. That is, until the year 1784, when they were met by a contingent of Draconian's who, after performing human sacrifices on children, forced the group to join with the Masons and submit to the reptilians will and use the influential positions attained by both of the Societies to carry out Draconian deeds."

"Wait, wait... okay, I've heard of both of these groups," Archie said. "Didn't the Illuminati get discovered because one of their couriers got struck by lightning and was found to have their manual or something? And didn't they die out shortly after?"

"Ah, so you are familiar with them. Good. Yes, but no," Blondie replied. "They never died out. That was nothing more than an illusionary smoke screen to ensure they remained hidden from the population. The manual that was found actually planned for the implementation of the French Revolution, which was designed to remove the government of the time and replace it with Illuminati members. When this all came to light, the organisation had to go deeper underground because they were being hunted across the globe and anyone who was found to be a part of the group was executed. There are truths among the lies of history. The lightning that struck the courier down wasn't lightning at all." The Pleiadian thought for a moment before continuing. "This all happened at a time when we had sent a scout ship to perform routine analysis of the planet and its inhabitants. The ship detected energy signatures beyond what the human population could have generated at that time of development. The ships Traton, or to you, the Captain sent a communications drone back to Erra, but unfortunately, it was severely damaged. The only real intelligence we could ascertain from it was that the ship had encountered a hostile species that were not of the world's inhabitants and they had taken measures to prevent the alien influence. We have cross-referenced what we got from the drone with Earth history and came to believe that the lightning strike on the courier was, in fact, a beam weapon from our scout ship. Fired in an effort to prevent any further alien interference. There were no storms detected for that area on our long-range telescopes or scanning equipment. The scout ship never returned home. We assume it was destroyed during the encounter. The last thing we got from the drone was the Traton saying to start the Earth Born Project. That alone meant that something was seriously wrong on Earth."

Sadly, after what Archie had seen during the night, it was evident that the reptiles were working with human defence forces. This was beginning to look bad... *really* bad.

Blondie continued. "The Illuminati Masonic governments of the world signed a treaty with the Draconians. The humans wanted technological advances in exchange for both animal and human abductions; apparently, the Draco wanted to study them. The humans who signed this treaty thought they could limit and control what the reptiles could do on the planet. They were wrong, and now there is nothing they can do to change it. Eventually, the governments would come to realise that the *study* was never part of the reptilian agenda. The Draco is a mighty warrior race. Far too powerful for humans to challenge."

"Okay, I'll buy that for a minute, but how do I fit into all this? I was born in London, I didn't arrive in any spaceships," Archie said.

"You are Pleiadian, Archie. Albeit in consciousness only. Before you were born into this incarnation, you were a Pleiadian. Specifically, High Traton of the Armies of Tardra, equivalent to the rank of General in human terms. Tardra is the Pleiadian military world. The Earth Born Project was designed to transfer consciousness from one of us into a human foetus that would have otherwise been stillborn. You chose this... it is your mission. When you began your way through the spiritual path as an Earthman, your consciousness opened to the Light, and that was our signal to make contact with you and remind you of your task."

"What the fuck have you been smoking? Are you on drugs?" Archie couldn't believe what he was hearing. The mere prospect of there being any truth in what he was being told was outrageous.

"Just think about it for a moment," Blondie said calmly. "There have been things that you have always known. You knew the name of your wife, long before you met her. You even knew from which area of the city she would originate. You have been compelled into various practices. You frequently experience the phenomena known as déjà vu. These experiences are not a coincidence. There are no coincidences in the Universal Laws. You have always felt that you were here for a reason. Open your heart and mind and think about it."

Archie sat there, dumbstruck. He didn't know what to say. The Pleiadian was right on all counts. He'd never been able to explain it, but he did know his wife's name before meeting her, and he knew the area from which she would live. In fact, everything that had been said was true. Even the bit about feeling like he had been put on earth for a reason, although, he'd always suspected that might just have been an ego thing.

Blondie went on to talk about Pleiadian life and culture, and as he was speaking, Archie was shocked to realise that he could not only picture but understand it as well. He felt like he was being reminded of something he already knew rather than hearing it for the first time. Blondie said that all Pleiadians, although individuals, were connected through consciousness. Their life spans were over a thousand years. They were a peaceful race that abided by the Galactic Laws rigidly, and they took the defiance of those rules seriously; particularly the Non-

Interference Law. Infringement of this Law could mean death for the individual perpetrator or severe economic or military sanctions for any species responsible. This Law wasn't just limited to undeveloped worlds but all worlds within the Galactic Alliance.

There is no crime in Pleiadian society, to even think about it would be to commit it. There is no monetary system; there is no need for such a system as the needs of all the people were catered for as a fundamental right. They have their own governing council, similar to that of the Galactic Council, that would govern the entire race of all seven worlds they had colonised within the Pleiades star cluster. Every decision that the council made had to be for the betterment of the species as a whole.

Each planet that makes up Pleiadian civilisation has its own purpose, such as education, where the people spend their early lives. They put great importance on each person knowing who and what they are. They learn about galactic history and their place within it. Information and education are open to all, and there are no limits on what subject or how long a person can study. They learn a multitude of skills and practices that can, if they wish, lead to what they eventually do within society. Everything that they learn is for the benefit of the entire race.

There is a planet solely to produce goods for whatever is needed throughout the system; everything from ships, food, clothing, and electrical appliances. In fact, all production is created there, with the exception of weaponry and military vehicles. Tardra is the only planet within the cluster that deals with anything military. There, all strategic and security issues are prioritised and dealt with. This includes a specialist department that provides a contingent of Pleiadian military vehicles and personnel to the Galactic Alliance Security Forces, where they enforce the Laws throughout the entire Galaxy. Although, if the Pleiadian Council doesn't sanction a particular action to be taken by the Galactic Alliance, they do not allow their forces to be involved. It's the same choice for all member species.

The whole conversation was becoming too much for Archie to take in, which must have been evident because, after about an hour of talking, Blondie suggested that they stop so that Archie could digest the information he had received.

While he was thinking over what he had been told, Archie started to get the cooking equipment together, hunger had hit him like a bullet to the gut. He filled two pots with water and put them on the ground for the dogs. As he reached into the van for the camping stove, Blondie asked him what had happened to the rest of his crew. One thing Archie learned from his time in the ambulance service was to not beat about the bush when giving bad news. You shouldn't say to a bereaved family member *"they're gone"* or *"they're not with us anymore"* because this could lead to confusion, and provoke a response like, *"where have they gone"* or *"who are they with then"*. No, you told them outright.

"Sorry mate, they're all dead," Archie said. "You were the only survivor."

"Okay, thank you," Blondie replied calmly. He accepted the news remarkably well, considering all of his friends were dead and he was marooned on an alien world.

"You seemed to take that fairly well, mate." Archie was probing.

"For us, death is only physical. Our bodies die, but our consciousness joins that of the Light Elders. But if a Pleiadian is caught violating the Universal Laws, they are executed; their consciousness is wiped from existence. Although this never happens nowadays. But general death is viewed more as though the person is moving on to a higher plain of existence, is usually celebrated."

This was all very interesting, but Archie started feeling ill. Sitting down on a fallen tree stump, he noticed that the wounds on his head had begun to really hurt. His vision started spinning as if he was drunk. He couldn't figure out what was happening to him, and after a few minutes, he started having difficulty breathing, he couldn't seem to catch his breath.

Blondie was still talking, but all Archie could hear was the sound that came from an audio file or video being played too slow. He stopped trying to listen, he was getting worse, and it wasn't long before the dog's noticed something was wrong with him. They both started barking in his direction, which drew Blondies attention to the struggling human.

Kneeling down next to the stricken man, the Pleiadian was asking what was wrong, but Archie couldn't answer, he couldn't talk, his speech was eluding him. Finally, he collapsed face first to the ground. Blondie rolled him onto his back and pulled out the remote control and shined some sort of light over Archie's entire his body, from head to toe.

"How did you get these wounds?" the Pleiadian asked. Archie couldn't answer. "Were you attacked by a reptilian?"

All Archie could do was nod his head slightly. He was in trouble, and he knew it. The pain was indescribable. It wasn't just in his head either, his entire body felt like it was on fire.

"You should have told me the instant I awoke. The Draconian warrior has a neurotoxic venom that it secretes into its victim. You will need to be still," he said as he looked at the remote intently. "I am surprised you are still alive. The toxin is deep in your system, and I will need to remove it. This will hurt. In fact, it will be excruciating. I will have to draw it from the tissues and circulatory system, back through the entry wounds."

At that point in time, Archie didn't give a shit what the Pleiadian did to him. For all he cared right then, Blondie could have shoved a tree branch up his arse if it meant it would take the pain away. He just wanted it to stop as soon as possible, and if it wouldn't stop, he'd prefer to be dead; it was that bad. Far beyond anything he had ever experienced before.

Blondie fiddled with the remote before holding it above Archie's head. The thing emitted a light blue beam towards his wounds. The pain was instantly excruciating; so bad that he couldn't keep from shouting. It felt like a thick, viscous fluid was being sucked through his veins and out of the gaping holes in his face and head. It wasn't long before Archie started convulsing. He had no idea how long it lasted, but it felt like hours.

Eventually, the seizure started to ease, along with the pain. His vision came back, and the world stopped spinning. Whatever Blondie had done, seemed to have done the trick. His breathing returned to normal, but his head was thumping. When it was all over, he just lay breathing heavily as he tried to recover.

Several minutes passed before the Pleiadian used the remote to scan Archie again. Reading the results, he announced that the venom had been removed and it was time to close the wounds. He held the remote over each gash in turn. The beam was back to green, and the skin on Archie's head felt as though it was being stretched as the wounds were pulled together. It didn't hurt, but it was one of the weirdest feelings he had ever experienced.

When the Pleiadian was finished, Archie sat up and put his hands to his head. He could feel that the holes were gone. He stayed there for a few more minutes before he made his way over to the vans wing mirror and had a look at himself. He looked like a tramp, with dried blood and mud caked all over his face. The only consolation was that at least he didn't look like a tramp with dirty great holes in his head.

He needed a brew. Getting the stove fired up, he put the kettle on, his hands were still shaking as he made them both a cup of orange and lotus flower green tea. His body was still in shock from what had happened, and he was freezing cold. Looking over at the Pleiadian, he said that they should stay put until nightfall, it just seemed too risky to leave beforehand - that, and he knew he was in no condition to drive.

While he had the stove out, he decided to get some food on the go. Plain noodles were the order of the day. They both tucked into the grub as though it was their last meal. For all Archie knew, it might well be. Once they had finished, the dog's started sniffing about, they were hungry too. But like any regular predator angler, he hadn't brought any dog food, but he did have a few tins of chilli.

"Fuck it; that'll have to do boys," he said as he put the pots down on the ground. He was surprised at how much they both seemed to enjoy the spicy mince. There was a downside though. Within twenty minutes of eating it, their arses started cracking like thunder. It made Archie laugh to see Blondie screw his face up as the whiff hit him. In the end, the big Pleiadian was laughing as the horrendous smelling fog engulfed the area.

After he had cleaned and put the camping equipment away, Archie came over really tired. The events of the previous night and the venom removal had caught up with him. He needed to get his head down for a while. Pulling the bed chair from the back of the van, he positioned it next to the side door and lay down. Although he was dead tired, sleep didn't come easy. The sensation reminded him of trying to have a kip when he was on the ambulances; you couldn't quite get off to sleep because you had one eye and one ear open all the time, listening in case a job came in. This was a similar feeling, albeit here he wasn't waiting for an emergency call, he was waiting to be attacked.

After a two-hour power nap, Archie awoke to feel somewhat refreshed, his headache had cleared, and he was able to think better. He sat on the bed and run his fingers over his head, feeling where the wounds had been, and a question popped into his head.

"Why didn't I get the same flicker when I picked up your remote-control thing?" he asked, turning to Blondie. "With every weapon I picked up, I got a... well, a full set of instructions – what it was, how to use it, that sort of thing. But with your thing, I kind of knew what it was, but I never got anything about how to use it."

"That's because you already know how to use it," Blondie replied. "You just don't remember at the moment, but in time, as your consciousness awakens fully, your memories will return to you. Believe it or not, you have used this tool on many occasions. There is much you do not remember, but you will."

Was he talking bollocks, or was he telling the truth? Archie wasn't sure, but he felt like he was edging towards believing it was all true. Then again, how did he know he wasn't being manipulated by another hostile alien race to carry out *their* bidding. He needed to keep an open mind on the whole thing. The only thing he was sure of right now was that he had that fucking *compulsion* to help the Pleiadian... for now. Although that didn't mean Archie was going to be a slave to any alien race. His spiritual path and philosophies had opened his mind to the reality of possibilities of a different nature, but his mind wasn't so open that his brains would spill out. If he found out that the Pleiadian had got one over on him, Blondie wasn't going to make it off this planet. Because of the spiritualism, Archie hadn't killed so much as a bug for the past couple of years, but throughout the past twenty-four hours, he had killed several people to save this alien. So, in for a penny, in for a pound; if he found out that Blondie had tricked him, Archie would kill him.

Feeling the need to meditate on this, Archie took himself off into the forest, about fifteen yards, sat down and began a session of contemplation. It would only be a short sitting, and he merely focused on trusting the Pleiadian. The guiding light gave him the answer – *YES...* trust him, for now anyway.

10

Undisclosed Location

Midlands

England

After about an hour of contemplating his predicament, Archie felt a large hand on his shoulder. Blondie didn't speak, but Archie could hear him, the Pleiadian was using telepathy to communicate. He was told to look forward and into a tree, where he saw a beautiful looking owl staring back at him. It didn't move a muscle, it just watched. As impressive as the sight was, something didn't feel right. Looking to the ground and about five yards to the right of the same tree, was a deer stag. Again, a lovely looking animal with big antlers. It was stood stock still, also staring at them.

"What do you see?" Blondie's voice was in his mind. Archie gave the answer; an owl and a deer. "Look again," he said. All Archie could see was the animals he'd already described.

"We need to go now," Blondie said aloud as he took his hand away from Archie's shoulder. "It isn't safe here anymore."

What did he mean it wasn't safe? Because of a deer and an owl? Archie didn't understand, and he was confused as they made their way back to the van. It was all a bit cryptic.

"You look, but you are not seeing Archie," Blondie said as they walked. "Open your mind, and you will see what is right in front of you."

"Listen, Blondie, you're too vague. How is a bird and a deer a risk to us? What's the owl gonna do – fucking peck me to death?" Archie said sarcastically.

"They are not what they might appear to be. If you look, you will see that the deer is moving towards us. This isn't normal; wild deer have a natural fear of man, yet this one has not. Ask yourself, why?"

"Mate, you've lost me here. I've got no bloody idea what you're on about." Archie still wasn't getting it.

When they got back to the vehicle, Archie turned back to see that the owl had silently moved to a closer tree, still watching them intently. As he stared at it something strange happened; for a split second, it seemed to change shape before changing back to the bird. *That's not right*, Archie thought. He looked at the deer to see if the same thing happened, but it stayed a deer.

He turned to Blondie to tell him what he had seen, when the Pleiadian put his hand onto his shoulder and gave him the thought talk again. *"You saw something beyond the image of an owl. Do not say anything. Just be ready to pick up your weapon."*

As he received the thought, Archie's mind caught up with what he saw, and he realised that the image he saw in place of the owl was that of a Grey. Looking back to the deer, he saw something that his mind just couldn't comprehend. Slowly, he reached down for the M4. At the same time there was an almighty roar from the direction of the deer. Bolts of energy started hitting the ground around them as the Grey opened fire from the tree.

Snatching up the rifle, Archie returned fire into the tree. The dogs went at the deer as Blondie pulled out his little remote and blasted beams of energy at the animal on the ground. The deer wasn't a deer anymore; it was the biggest reptile Archie had ever seen. So far, the only Draco he had encountered had been bipedal, but this thing in front of them was a giant quadruped. It was far bigger than anything that walked the Earth. A massive triangular looking head, with what looked like an armour-plated halo that extended from the neck and circled around the entire skull. It had three large horns; one on its snout and two either side of its head. The thing was snarling, showing off its massive shark like – saliva covered teeth. It had a body like that of a rhinoceros, albeit with large scales, and its tail that must have been at least ten-foot long. In all, the creature was a whopping twenty-five foot in length. It reminded Archie of a picture he'd seen of a Stegosaurus. It hissed like a snake in between roaring like a lion. The thing was getting properly pissed off as Blondie hit it over and over again with the remote. It was so transfixed on getting to and killing the Pleiadian that it didn't notice the dogs until they were tearing into its hind legs.

Archie tried to keep his attention firmly on the Grey in the tree as he repeatedly fired three round bursts, pulling the trigger in quick succession. His shots didn't hit, but the weight of fire was enough to make the little bastard jump through the branches to get away. He lost sight of it after the third tree.

Archie's attention was drawn to the giant lizard as it charged forward. He changed the magazine and flicked the weapon to full auto. Taking a good aim, he fired at the things head. Blondie was still shooting his little ray gun remote and along with Archie, was hitting the thing consistently, but the animal kept coming as though it was being hit with rain rather than weapons fire. The only thing slowing it down was the dogs hanging onto its legs.

"Have you got that fucking thing on stun? Fucking kill it!" Archie shouted. He couldn't believe that the Pleiadian's super advanced weapon had no effect and he was beginning to panic as he heard the thudding of its footsteps getting closer. It was trying to kick the dogs off, but they weren't giving up that easily as they latched back on. They wouldn't be able to keep it from getting to its targets. *Fuck this*, Archie thought as he pulled the pin.

"KAISER, REG – LEAVE, COME!" he shouted. "BLONDIE, GET DOWN!"

Both the dogs and Blondie did as they were told as Archie threw the grenade. He aimed at tossing it just in front of the dragon. The instant it left his hand, he ducked behind the fallen tree that he'd been using for cover. The dull thud followed by the squealing roar told him that the grenade had hit the mark. Lifting his head over the makeshift barricade, he saw that the big reptile was down, its front legs removed from its body, leaving only bleeding pulpy stumps. At the same time, energy bolts began hitting the ground behind him.

Turning on his haunches, Archie saw that there were now two Greys shooting at him. One was in the tree above the van, and the other was on the ground next to the tree trunk. Bringing the M4 into his shoulder, he dropped the grounded enemy with three to the chest. Blondie took care of the other one with a blast from the remote. It fell from the branch and started moaning as it hit the dirt.

Rising to his feet, Archie took aim as he moved forward to the Grey he had shot. It looked dead, but he made sure it wasn't going to surprise him by putting two more rounds into its head, which exploded like a manky watermelon. As he started to make his way to the injured one, Blondie called over, saying not to kill it. He thought the Pleiadian had gone soft. *No thanks, Blondie...* Archie was definitely going to be putting three in the little shit's face.

"Do not kill the Reticulan," Blondie said, firmer this time. "It is vital." Archie took the word Reticulan to mean the Grey. Big bollocks seemed very insistent that he didn't kill it.

"You had better have a fucking good explanation, Blondie," he said, not sure what the Pleiadian was up to. It didn't matter, Archie had to make sure that they were safe while the big man did whatever it was he was going to do, so made his way over to the big reptile.

The thing was horrible. It had substantial armour-plated scales all over its body. No wonder they struggled to put it down. The teeth were like serrated knives and were covered with drool. There were multiple bullet holes in its head and chest. Its front legs had been blown off and were

152

pumping out a thick, green viscous fluid, yet it still tried to get to him. He had trouble comprehending the amount of damage this thing had taken, but not only was it still alive, but it was also still trying to kill him. *Fuck it, it doesn't matter*, he thought as he put the muzzle of the rifle to the side of its head and pulled the trigger. The bullet did nothing but piss it off worse, and it started scrambling even more, to get to him. This was one nasty, horrible bastard. Keeping the single round fire selected, Archie kept firing until the creature was dead. It took seven shots in the same place, at point blank range. He couldn't help but be impressed, even though he was fearful of meeting another one.

Archie made his way back to Blondie, who was kneeling over the Reticulan, with his hand gripping the Greys large head. The Pleiadian was mumbling under something his breath, but Archie couldn't make out what he was saying. Looking into the Pleiadians face, Archie saw that the big man had his eyes closed as he concentrated on what he was doing - whatever that was. For a few minutes, he just stood there watching until the dogs drew his attention away, they were sniffing around the giant lizard. He instinctively called them away and put them back in the van, he didn't want them licking the thing in case it carried the same venom as the warriors. With Blondie occupied, Archie started to pack away what little equipment they had out in preparation for a quick departure. As soon as the big man was finished, they were hitting the road. The light was beginning to fade, and Archie was feeling edgy – *really edgy*.

It felt like an eternity before the Pleiadian stood up and started walking back to the vehicle. After three or four paces, he stopped, turned back to the Grey, lifted the remote, and fired four bright red beams into it. The little creature disintegrated. Whatever Blondie needed from it, he'd got and no longer needed it alive.

"Did you get what you wanted?" Archie asked as Blondie arrived at the van.

"We need to go," he replied. "I will explain as we travel."

Blondie got into the passenger side as Archie made his way around the back after shutting the side door. As he turned the corner to the rear of the van, he was hit, smack in the face, making him drop onto his back, dazed. He had barely landed before he was picked up from the floor. He struggled to figure out what was going on. Hearing the hiss, he knew exactly what was happening... Draconian. Through tear-filled eyes, Archie could see that this one wasn't as large as the others he had encountered so far, and when this realisation hit him, he started raining punches on the creature anywhere he could land them. He reached out with blow after blow to his assailants' head and body. The lizard had his hands around Archie's throat and was squeezing hard. The human struggled to get air into his lungs; the thing was trying to strangle the life out of him.

It didn't take long before it dawned on Archie that punching wasn't going to cut the mustard. Hand to hand wouldn't be enough, he needed a weapon. Pulling the fish knife from its sheath, he tried to jab it into the reptiles' face, but as he brought it over the creatures left arm, some sort of spiny hood shot out from around its neck, hitting the blade and knocking it out of Archie's hand.

He could feel his life beginning to slip away as his vision started closing in. He was desperately trying to reach for the pistol or the bowie knife, but he couldn't get a grip of either. Panic was well and truly on him. The only weapon he had left was his fingers. As a last gasp effort to escape the lizards' death grip, Archie plunged his thumbs into the orbits of the creatures' eyes and scooped the things right from their sockets.

The reptile dropped Archie to the ground and started to run into the trees. Pulling himself to his feet and breathing heavily, he watched as the overgrown gecko ran straight into the trunk of a large tree, knocking him on to his arse. Before the Draconian could get up, Archie pulled the pistol from the front of his trousers and shot him twice; once in the left leg and once to the back of his head, causing the lizard to fall forward against the tree.

Upon hearing the shots, Blondie got jumped out of the van and rushed to the vehicles rear to see what was happening. By this time, Archie was right behind the enemy with his gun pointed at the back of the Draconians head. BANG! It was over, but that didn't stop him putting another two rounds into the thing before he walked away.

"What happened?" Blondie asked.

"What the fuck does it look like?" Archie replied, still breathing heavily. "Come on, we need to get out of here," he said as he made his way to the driver's side and got in.

11

Unknown Road

Midlands

England

They had been driving for about fifteen minutes, and Archie had spent the time thinking over the last fight, particularly the giant reptile. It was like the sort of thing you'd see in a film. He was genuinely shocked. No, that wasn't the correct description for what he felt... scared by it, was more accurate. He believed that although it wanted to kill him, this thing intended to eat him afterwards. *Fuck that for a game of soldiers*, he thought. He was beginning to wish that he'd cut the thing open to see if he could find a way to kill it in case he came up against another one, but that was just wishful thinking. In reality, there just wasn't the time for such a luxury. To do so would waste precious driving time, and they needed to get away.

"Blondie, what was that big thing back there?" he asked. "It was like some sort of dragon."

"Dragons are creatures of Earth legend and myth," the Pleiadian began, "however in the void, such things are no myth; they are all too real. Extremely dangerous. They are called Dracoderos, and they are a subservient subspecies of the Draco..."

"How do we kill them?" Archie asked, cutting him off.

"As you saw, even my weapon - the remote, as you call it, did little to harm it. There are no rules…" sighed Blondie. "We must kill it any way we can. It was a good thing you had that explosive device. Otherwise, we would have probably been its meal for the day. I suggest you try to save any more explosives for use against any Deros we might encounter." He took a breath before adding, "My name isn't Blondie, it's Garindanasther. Do you not remember me, Archie?"

"How would I remember you?" Archie snorted. "You're from another fucking world mate." *I've met some fucking weirdos before, but this is getting out of hand*, he thought as he glanced over at the Pleiadian.

"I was hoping that some of your memories might have started to return upon hearing my name. Remember you're not entirely human. You are Pleiadian of mind, and we used to work together before you took this mission to earth."

"Enough!" Archie snapped. He was stressed out enough without these wild claims making things worse. "I'm not convinced of anything. In fact, right now, to me, you're talking bollocks! You say that the 'Plei-adi-ans' follow a strict non-interference policy on other planets, yet you're here on Earth. Your other ship shot down two helicopters, killing the crews, and you say that I was *installed* here on some secret mission. How the hell does that fall into the category of non-interference? It seems to me that you're talking shit, Garandararar – fuck it, I can't even say your name, so I'm sticking with Blondie. Tell me what the fuck is going on and tell me, *now!*" Archie was pissed off. It all seemed too much, too fantastical to believe. He wanted answers, he wanted the truth, and he wanted it now.

"We truly do have a non-interference policy, and we do stick to it rigidly. The punishments for breaching this law are what I have already told you. In fact, everything I have told is true. The information that we got from the drone in 1784 told us that we needed to begin the Earth Born Project... we did. You are just one of the thousands to have taken part. You may not remember it, but it *is* true. We believe that the Draconian's are part of a larger Confederation of negative Beings that have embedded agents within humanity's institutions. Of this, we are sure. About fifty Earth years ago, we noticed a large build-up of Draconian military hardware, massing within their home system. This could mean only one thing; they were preparing to invade, but their target was unknown. We were fearful that the target planet could have been Earth, so we increased the Earth Born Project to what it is today. We originally incarnated only a select few personnel for purposes of information gathering - the messengers - but it became apparent that this wasn't enough. Therefore, it was decided that we would increase the project to include, what would be a fighting force planetside in case the need arose. It appears that it has..."

"But isn't this Earth Born Project a form of interference?" Archie asked.

"Yes and no." Blondie continued, "Every Being has the right to choose a reincarnation - if they have the ability that is. So, choosing incarnation on Earth is fine, but the problem comes with how the reincarnation was carried out. We didn't want to interfere with the *natural* cycle of human life, so we chose to incarnate into babies that would otherwise have been stillborn. We used a technological transfer of consciousness to achieve this. So, in that respect, we may have broken the rules." Blondie paused for a moment, thinking, before continuing. "Maybe the term incarnation is inaccurate. Although, it could be argued that we broke no rules because humanity is children of the Pleiades - ancient descendants, if you will."

Archie thought for a second before asking, "What do you mean humans are the children of the Pleiades?"

"A colony was established here a millennia ago, but contact was broken when the colonials decided to form their own world, apart from us. Once we realised that there was a possibility that the Draco was going to invade, we reviewed and amended our policy and found a way around the Laws." Blondie took a deep breath and sighed. "That said, we need to seek a permissive order to engage humans and was instructed to contact and protect you at all costs. But if a human force was to get the upper hand over one of our ships that had nothing to do with your protection, that ship is expected to try to escape or allow its destruction."

"You mentioned messengers, what do they do exactly?" Archie asked, ignoring the last part of Blondie's statement because flattering comments could easily be used to manipulate the recipient. He feeling like this was all getting a bit heavy, and he started to wonder if maybe ignorance might have been bliss.

"They were put in place to gather information and pass it back to the Council. However, there are two types of messenger. The second has another mission. They are to *channel* information directly through consciousness and pass it to the planet's population through various means. The messages they receive, regard the spiritual awakening of the human race. If you look around the world, you will see uprising after uprising. This is the awakening, but sadly, most of the people taking part in these movements do not know what they are rising against. They haven't opened their minds sufficiently enough to understand what they are doing or why. They think that the enemy is other humans, and where that is true to a point, they are totally missing the *real* enemy. I am not just talking about the Draco either. They need to understand that it's the *systems* that control the masse's that also need to be changed. Many have simply jumped on the bandwagon, as you say."

Archie couldn't argue. Through his Ufology research, he had seen that there were many so-called channelers throughout the globe who were putting forth theories regarding alien spiritual enlightenment, most of which, he put down to be a complete load of bollocks... hippy shit. But he also couldn't disagree with the uprising stuff either; it was happening worldwide, including America, the Middle East, and even Britain was experiencing protests and sit-ins. To top it off, the Government forces that were sent in to deal with these protesters were extremely heavy-handed, outright violent in most cases, and were clearly the instigators of the resulting conflicts. Things had gotten to the point where several Arabian countries had found themselves fighting civil wars and invasions from other nations. In the UK and America, protests that were designed to be peaceful, ended in violence as the police started beating the crap out of anyone in the area, turning the whole thing into a riot and then having the news agencies report it as such. When, in fact, the civil unrest was due to the protesters having to defend themselves against police brutality. Blondie was finally beginning to make some sense. *But then again, he only has to watch any news channel to know what is happening on Earth,* he reminded himself, sceptically.

"Along with the Channelers, there are another group of intelligence agents." The Pleiadian paused before continuing. "They are unaware of what they are. They are in positions of authority, such as government, industry, and military, where they learn matters of secrecy. We tap into their consciousness as they sleep and retrieve the information."

"Wow, that's a bit strong, mate," Archie replied. "You're basically robbing them of their memories."

"No, it is not like that, at all. These people, like you, knew that they could eventually be in a position of power and we would take the information in this manner," Blondie said as though it was a matter of fact. "We don't actually erase their memories; we simply retrieve the information and leave their memories intact."

Archie was stunned. "Wait, you can actually choose where to put these spies, knowing they would find their way to a position of leadership or power?"

"To a point, yes," Blondie replied. "Although it does not work quite like that. We incarnate a Pleiadian consciousness into a foetus that is to be born into a family of high standing that will likely end up in a position of power. As the child grows, we influence their lives to take certain paths. This way, most incarnations will find themselves in the right place at the right time." He paused for a moment. "The persistent inbreeding within the elites' bloodlines make the process of finding a suitable foetus, that will otherwise die, relatively easy."

As he digested the information, Archie found himself being impressed, that they could do any of this. "Let's say I believe you, why was I protected?" He was intrigued as to why the Pleiadians would circumvent their laws for his protection.

"I am not entirely sure. I was told that we were to make contact and remind you of who you truly are."

"Come on, mate. You must know more than that." Archie wasn't buying it.

"I only know that you were of high military standing before this incarnation and that the Council views your position here as invaluable. I believe that it was hoped that you would regain your memories soon after contact. However, there have been many instances where memory recall has been stunted or failed completely. I only hope this isn't what transpires here." Blondie's words seemed sincere, but Archie wasn't sure.

"Honestly, that sounds like a get out clause to me," Archie said. He didn't disbelieve, but he didn't believe either.

"I am aware of how things may appear, but I have no reason to lie about anything," was all Blondie could say.

The conversation went back and forth for some time, but nothing more really come out. Either the big man was telling the truth, or he was an accomplished bullshitter. After the talking died down, Archie concentrated on driving. Flicking his eyes to the clock, he noticed they had been on the road for roughly four hours and were well into the night. They had covered a little over a hundred and twenty miles from the lake; not bad going. It wasn't long before they started to hit sporadic traffic as they passed through built-up areas. Birmingham was the goal, London after that. Getting into the cities meant they would have more protection - from the reptilians at least. It wasn't as though they could just start blasting them with energy weapons and chasing them through the streets in spaceships in full view of the public.

Archie asked why Blondie hadn't wanted to kill the Grey during the last fight. Apparently, he had read its mind; by all accounts, the Pleiadian was some sort of telepath that could not only talk through mind speak, but take information as well. According to Blondie, the team that had ambushed them in the forest were a scouting crew, kept secret from their human counterparts. For some reason, the aliens wanted the whereabouts of Archie, and the big man kept from the humans. It appeared that the fight was initiated before the team reported their position. Hopefully, they would be safe for a while.

"Where are we going?" Blondie asked.

"My place. There are a few things I need," Archie replied. "Why; have you got somewhere you need to be?"

"I have. The circle of the stones. It is a place of rendezvous in the case of accidents."

"Is there a timescale for this meeting?"

"Not specifically, no. The Lightships assigned for rescue will return to the area until I am either retrieved or dead. Their proximity to the planet will allow their consciousness to detect the severed connection to mine. That way, they will know of my death, should it happen. The larger problem is that the longer I am planetside, the greater the chance of capture or death." There was urgency but no panic in Blondies voice. "What do you wish to get from your abode?"

"Things," was all Archie was prepared to say. He wasn't sure how Blondie would feel if he was to tell him the truth. The reality was, he was going to pick up the weapons he was most proficient in. Blades of various sizes. The Katana; a single-edged sword, approximately 90cm long. His Wakizashi; another single-edged short sword, 60cm long. Last but certainly not least, the Tanto; a single-edged knife of around 12 inches long. He had trained extensively with the smaller of these weapons over the years, but he never thought he would ever contemplate using them for real. Much of his training had been in the form of self-defence from bladed attack during Ju-Jitsu, but he did take part in limited Bushido classes. He was no Samurai, but he could throw a sword about quite efficiently. It was extreme to consider that these blades could be of any use in the modern day, but then again, he never thought he'd be fighting giant lizards either. The weapons were silent and deadly. They may also come in handy if they ran into another Dracoderos; the energy and ballistic weapons didn't do much to it, but maybe with a sword...

To get to Archie's place safely, he would need to take a few precautions. He wasn't about to rock up to his front door, in case the van had been spotted by the enemy. No, he'd make contact with a couple of people first. He wasn't going to use his own mobile phone though; he'd have to stop off and buy a throwaway. The trouble was, it was far too late for any shops to be open at this time of night. He was going to have to wait until the morning and then he could indulge in a bit of retail therapy. In the meantime, Archie would get them to the Cathedral at Litchfield and park up for the rest of the night.

Roughly forty-five minutes later, Archie pulled into the car park and stopped under a tree. As he turned the engine off, he asked Blondie what the Circle of the Stones were. The Pleiadian said that they were megalithic structures placed around the globe. Built upon the convergence of Ley lines, they enhanced spiritual energies, that could, if you knew how to use them, tap into the Universal Energy and Spiritual Consciousness.

"What are you on about?" Archie asked incredulously.

"It is true. At these places, the Electromagnetic and Spiritual energies are potent. They are the planets Chakra's, and there is a Lightship around these sites most nights."

"Are you talking about Stonehenge?" Archie had been wondering what the Pleiadian was talking about, but the mention of megalithic structures and circle of stones; could it be the famous landmark?

"Yes, I believe there is one that has been given that title," he replied, "but there are many situated around the world. There is one at Avebury, in Wiltshire, Ayres Rock – Australia, Bimini – Florida, and Machu Pichu in the Andes, to name but a few. We will need to get to either of the local circles for my retrieval. Even if there are no Lightships in the vicinity, my consciousness will be magnified to the extent that I will be able to make contact."

Although the information was fantastic to hear, Archie wasn't too happy. These places were nowhere near where he wanted to go as he realised he wouldn't be going home just yet. He just hoped the people he needed help from would be able to come out of London when he needed them to.

As he was sitting there mulling over everything that he had been told, a worrying thought popped into Archie's head. "Going back to what you said about the Pleiadian Agents and being able to tap into their minds as you need to, does that mean you lot can do the same to me?"

"No. Any Pleiad who did not sanction such an action before their incarnation cannot be read in that manner. This is for the general security of their individual tasks as well as the overall mission. We can only assist those agents by *giving* information, not taking it."

"Oh, right," Archie said as nonchalantly as possible. He didn't relish the prospect of anyone being able to read his mind, and he wouldn't be giving permission for such a thing any time soon. With everything that had happened so far, he could still be helping the wrong side. Even though he didn't believe that was the case, he wanted to be careful. For all he knew, it could be the Pleiadians that were the invaders and the Draco that were the ones trying to save Earth. Although that was a possibility, he didn't believe that either.

Now that they had settled down after the fights and the long drive, it was time to get some shut eye, Archie was knackered. As he started to doze off, he thought about the day ahead. For the first time since this all started, he had a plan. He knew what he was going to do, but he was going to keep it to himself, Blondie would just have to tag along.

12

Litchfield

Midlands

England

He awoke with a new lease on life. Everything that Archie had been told seemed to make sense during his dream state. It was like a giant jigsaw puzzle that suddenly all fell into place, with the picture becoming more transparent. He wondered if his mind had been messed with to make him think that it was all true. *Fuck it, I've got my plan, and I'm sticking to it*, he thought. *First things first; phones.*

The shopping centre was on Bakers Lane, Litchfield. Pulling into the parking space, he counted what money he had on him, £600 would be more than enough for what he needed. Going into the mall, he made his way straight to the first mobile phone shop and looked at the pay as you go section. He picked up two of the crappiest mobiles and made his way over to the kiosk to pay. The salesman behind the counter gave him a quizzical look as though he was mad, a look that said *what do you need two of the same phones for?*

"It's the twins birthday mate," Archie said with a smile.

"I wondered why you had two. I'm guessing it's their first phones. We're doing a special offer on these fifteen-pound monthly contract; you get the Noki..."

Archie held his hand up to interrupt the guy. "No thanks, mate. They can't be trusted to stay within the minutes and texts. This gives us more control," he said. He was all smiles, but really, he was thinking, *Fucking salesman are the same everywhere – pain in the arse – who needs them?*

With the first two phones bought, the next stop was the supermarket to get some freeze-dried noodles and dog food. Archie didn't want or need the noodles, but he wanted the carrier bag they would come in so that he could put the mobile phones into it. Suspicion would be raised when he went into the second phone shop and bought another two handsets, while already having two from another store in his possession. Hiding the first set would negate that problem altogether. The idea was that he would have four phones that he could bin when he'd finished with them.

After getting the second set of phones, Archie made his way towards the van, trying to look as nonchalant as possible, but it was difficult. He was paranoid, feeling like everyone was watching him. As he thought about it, he realised people probably *were* watching him. After all, he was wearing manky old fishing clothes and a baseball cap with a hood over the top. There was nothing he could do about his appearance, he just had to put the thoughts aside and get a move on.

As he made his way through the shopping centre, he flicked his eyes up to see where he was and noticed a Martial Arts shop. *Sod it, I'm going to have a look and see what they've got*, he thought as he walked towards the store. Going inside, he felt like he'd gone to heaven. The walls were lined with every conceivable weapon relating to the Art and Sport of fighting. Mooching about, he saw a cheap Katana and next to it was a Tanto...cheap, in that they were knockoffs, rather than genuine. *That'll do*, he thought. They wouldn't be anywhere near as good as his own but buying them would mean that he wouldn't have to go all the way home to get his. Their quality was poor in comparison to his own, but he figured they'd do a job. As he walked back to the van, Archie wondered if he was just lucky in spotting the martial arts shop, or whether this was some sort of synchronicity at play. The answer didn't really matter, he was just thankful that something was going his way.

Getting back to the van £400 poorer, Archie put two of the phones on charge using the cigarette lighters. When he was finished, he checked the fuel gauge and realised that he needed to get petrol. Finding a garage wasn't an issue, and paid with cash after filling the tank. From there, he was going to get on to the M1 motorway, towards London. He wasn't going into the city, but he needed to be there or there about for the next part of his plan.

They had been on the road for about another hour or so, and the journey itself was non-eventful. That was good, it meant there had been no attempts to apprehend or kill them. As they neared the town of Crick, Archie pulled off the motorway. It was time to make a phone call.

Taking the first two mobiles off charge, he replaced them with the second two. Pulling out his own phone, he went through the contacts list until he found the number he wanted and punched it into the new phone. The other end of the line rang as he waited for an answer that didn't come. It seemed as though the recipient was letting it ring off the hook. It was now nearly 2 pm, and the chances were the lazy bastard was still in bed. Archie was going to keep ringing until his call got answered.

"Allo?" the voice was croaky.

"All right, Joey? Wakey wakey!"

"Fuckin 'ell, is that you Arch?"

"Yep and I'm in a big pile of shit," Archie said. "I need your help, mate."

"Fuck it. Give me a minute," Joe said before adding, "I was at it last night, you woke me up. I'll ring you back on this number in a couple." That was it; he put the phone down.

Joey was Archie's cousin, and by day he was supposed to be a very gifted mechanic, but the rest of the time he was a career criminal. His leading enterprises involved armed robbery; turning over banks and post offices, as well as ringing stolen cars. Occasionally, he'd move a bit of weed but never dealt in anything that could hurt people. Even during his stick up's, he made sure that no one ever got hurt or injured in any way. Well, apart from maybe the odd slap, after all, no body's perfect. The man was an absolute diamond, and Archie trusted him more than anyone, other than his own brother. Joe had substantial underworld connections that could sometimes come in handy. If you wanted it, he could get it. When he said he was "at it", it meant that he'd been up to something dodgy.

Less than five minutes later, the shitty little pay as you go started ringing. The number wasn't Joe's. Archie answered but said nothing.

"Right you dopey fucker, what you got yourself in to?" It was him... *thank god for that*.

"Is this line safe?" Archie asked.

"Of course it fucking is," Joe said in his thick cockney accent. "What do you take me for? Now, what's wrong?"

"I can't tell you everything over the blower mate, but I need you to go round my brothers and get him to come with you. I need you to meet me at Watford Gap services. Bring everything you need to remove all the ID tags from my van," Archie said.

"Okay, that's no problem, but I don't need Jeff to hold my hand to sort a motor out." Joe sounded insulted.

"I know that you muppet. You need him to drive the new van that you're going to bring for me."

"What new van? Has it gotta be hooky, or can it be straight?" Typically, Joe was already thinking ahead.

"Straight, but untraceable to us in any way," Archie replied. "I can't get pulled by the old bill, mate. You'll see what's going on when you get here."

"Yeah, no worries sunshine. What do I tell Jeff? You know what he's like." He had a point. Jeff could be a bit of a dopey fucker sometimes, and he needed an explanation for everything. Where Joe knew when to ask questions and when not to, Jeff didn't. There were times when Archie wondered if Jeff needed instructions on how to wipe his arse.

"Either tell him the truth as you know it or make something up," Archie said. "One more thing, Joe, only ring me on this number if you need me. Same goes for Jeff. And neither of you use your own phones."

"No probs, this ain't my first rodeo," Joe said. "Consider it done. I just gotta get rid of this skirt, and I'll be on my way. See ya later." As he put the phone down, Archie could hear him telling some girl she had to leave.

As he sat there thinking about what to do next, Archie considered phoning home, but after a moment's contemplation, he thought better of it. There was no need to run that risk; Lucy wouldn't know to keep shtum, and Archie wasn't sure if he'd been identified yet. Well, at least he didn't know if he had at least, but it wasn't worth taking the chance on her mobile or their home phones being bugged. Joey and Jeff could pass any messages on later. For now, it was better to be safe than sorry.

All he had to do now was wait. It would take a couple of hours for the guy's to get things sorted out and make it to the meeting spot. Archie decided to find a little fishing spot. He didn't intend to actually fish, but it was more for appearances. It looked weird for two men to be sat in a van doing nothing for hours. At least if they were beside a lake, they would look like they had a reason to be there. Perusing the map, Archie found a fishery off of the A428.

That'll do nicely. Even better, he'd fished there with Joe several years earlier. Hopefully his cousin would remember it.

The lakes were only about twenty minutes' drive away. It wasn't long before Archie was pulling the van on to the dirt road that led to the water. He stopped the vehicle under the trees and made his way to the hut where he would have to pay for the day tickets. Going inside, he was greeted by an apparently pleasant chap who was sat behind a desk, watching T.V.

"Hello mate, I was on my way home from a fishing session, and my van has pretty much conked out on me. Is there any chance I can wet a line while I wait for my mate to come and recover the motor?" Archie said. "He's coming from London, and I've got a load of time to kill."

"Well," the man said, and instantly, Archie knew he was in for a story. "This is a syndicate lake – members only ya see. We don't do day tickets cos blokes take the piss, ya nah. They turn up here with their leadcore and barbed hooks and damage our stock." As he was droning on in his northern accent, Archie was thinking, *a simple yes or no will do, I don't need your fucking life story!*

"I don't use any of that, mate," Archie replied. "I'm a simple free running, ejectable lead kind of guy; barbless hooks, clean mats, and nets. *And* I carry a fish care kit. I won't be damaging your fish. In fact, they'll probably go back in better condition than what they came out." Archie wanted to tell the man to piss off, but he needed to play nice.

"I tell ya what. If you show me ya gear so that I'm sure you're on the level, I'll let ya fish for fifty poound," he said.

"You're on pal," Archie replied as he pulled the money out of his wallet. *Fifty-fucking-quid. Cheeky bastard is taking the piss! But at least we'll be "oout" of the way, even if it is daylight robbery!*

As they walked back to the van, the site manager was giving a history lesson regarding the lake. Archie knew the guy was speaking English, but the accent was so thick, he might as well have been talking Japanese. It was one of those situations where you just nod, smile and hope he wasn't asking you a question. The only thing that he did understand was that the lake was empty - no one else was fishing today. That suited Archie's needs perfectly. While the thieving bastard was chatting away, Archie was looking around for security cameras; fortunately, there weren't any. For a split second, he thought about getting Joey to have one of his mates rob the place, to get his fifty *"poounds"* back.

Arriving at the vehicle, he noticed that Blondie had hidden the weaponry under the seats while Archie was getting robbed. After showing the thief his fishing gear, and got the okay to fish, he pulled out a rod and clipped a lead onto the line before casting out about forty yards. It didn't even have a hook on it, let alone any bait. He wasn't really here to fish, he just had to look the part. He thought that was probably why he was so pissed off about the money. One rod no hook – fifty fucking quid!

There was nothing left to do, but sit about, eat noodles and wait for Joey and Jeff to turn up. The dogs had a runaround, having a sniff and a shit while he and Blondie munched on some grub. As he was eating, a few questions arose in Archie's mind.

"What will the Alliance do with the intelligence they get, Blondie?" he asked. "Will there be a war or something?"

"I do not think so," the Pleiadian replied. "They will probably watch from afar while they investigate the claims of wrongdoing. I have a feeling that they will hope that humanity will rise from its current paradigm into a new one by the raising of consciousness, and in doing so, be able to stand with the Light against any foreign interference."

Archie snorted a laugh before speaking. "Are you joking, mate? There is no way humanity is going to do that. You're talking about everyone helping everyone else; doing things for the greater good. Look around, mate. The only thing the human race is interested in is self-gain, nothing more." He hated saying it, but it was true.

Blondie thought for a moment. "No. it *is* possible, Archie. Aeons ago, the Pleiadian society was pretty much the same as humanity is now, and we found a way to change. We had to because not only were we destroying ourselves, but we were constantly attacked by the Draconians. You see, our species did not originate in the Pleiades. We were from a star system called Lyra. But we were forced to evacuate when our home world was annihilated by the reptilians. For a while, we were nomadic

177

refugees, searching the Galaxy for a new home. Some of us settled on Erra, while others found different planets within the cluster. Some had temporarily settled on Earth until their new homeworlds had been terraformed, at which point most left. It was a time in Earths early history and the natives were cave dwellers - Neanderthal, I think you call them."

Blondie took a moment before continuing. "It was during this period that the Pleiadian colonists altered the DNA of the early humans to advance the evolution of the species. I should say that this was a long time before the Alliance and the non-interference laws. That is why your scientists *never have* and never *will* find the so-called *missing link*. They haven't discovered it because there isn't one. The apparent evolution of humanity was a direct result of genetic manipulation."

Archie listened intently, and what he had just been told slipped in line with something that he'd always thought; *human evolutionary advancement* had *to be something to do with alien interference.*

Blondie continued. "In time the colonists built a magnificent city, which is known in human mythology as Atlantis. The philosopher, Plato, wrote of its demise, saying it was destroyed in one day and one night and was shrouded in smoke and fire as it fell into the sea. This description is almost correct, except that it did not fall into the sea and disappear; it lifted into the sky. The entire city was built using a multitude of Pleiadian ships that were interconnected to allow the whole thing to ascend into space as and when it was required to. The reason Plato wrote the description the way that he did, was because the entire event was beyond his conception of reality, and he assumed the city had been destroyed and fell into the ocean. Back then, our ships used a completely different drive system, similar to conventional engines that humans use now. Several hundred Pleiadians stayed behind. To them, this was their home.

"At no time did any of the colonists reveal who or what they truly were to the humans." He continued. "This would have been disastrous in many ways. For example, biologically, we are the same as humans, yet by some, we would have been revered as gods; as humanity's creators. This could not be allowed. There are no gods – only the Prime Creation, which is responsible for the creation of all things. Another reason is that some of the indigenous humans may have felt threatened by our presence, which could have led to war - both in terms of with each other and with us."

Archie finally felt like he was starting to get somewhere. Atlantis, the missing link, this was a conversation that he enjoyed, and it went on and on. Revelation after revelation. The history of the Mayan's and the Aztec's, right through to the Pyramids. Which were primarily built as ancient gathering sites for off-world visitors - a kind of refuelling station of spiritual energy. He actually felt like he was learning something; something that archaeologists, historians, and scientists alike had been working on for their entire lives but still had no clue as to the real answers that he now had. *Who needs a PhD when you've got a Pleiadian?* The subject went on to

Religion and only confirmed what Archie had already believed.

"Religion is nothing more than a control mechanism, designed to keep the masses in line by forcing them to live in fear of a wrathful and vengeful deity. Throughout history, Religious texts have been written and rewritten to suit the needs for control for that particular period. If we look at artefacts such as the Holy Grail or the Arc of the Covenant, for example, you need to understand that they are nothing more than metaphoric props, designed and used to hide the truth of the divine. The Knights Templar, upon occupying Temple Mount, searched for both the Grail and the Arc but found nothing but their *own* Divinity. That *is*, they realised the truth; that Divine order does not come from the heavens - it is within ourselves and always has been. This is why mainstream religious sects ordered the hunting down and slaughter of the Templar Order over the following centuries, so that the truth would only be known to the elite. In this way, they could continue their control of the people by making them *search the heavens* for the Divine, safe in the knowledge that they would never, ever achieve such divinity because they would be looking in the wrong place. This gave rise, initially, to what is now known as the Secret Societies; they know the truth, and they use it to gain ever-increasing amounts of power, wealth, and control of the planet's population."

"So, why are there so many different religions?" Archie asked with interest.

"To put it simply, Divide and Conquer. This religion will say, *this is the truth*, which creates a faction of

180

believers, while a different religion will say, *no, this is the truth*, which creates another faction of believers. Then, in turn, their individual beliefs are used to set one against the other, which *can* and often *does* lead to war. While that is happening, the only faction that is truly growing in power, are the heads of the religions and their secret societies. All the while, the different factions are killing each other in the name of their supposed God. It is a very clever ruse, but it can only work if the belief systems are upheld. If they fall, then the entire religious system falls." Blondie paused for a moment. "The best way to keep it going is to create fear within the population. So, for example, one religion will say that a person has to live their life *this* way to gain access to heaven at the point of death, and if that person doesn't live *that way*, they will go to hell. All religions say the same thing, in one way or another. While at the same time, they will say that their God is all forgiving and even say that God will absolve a person's sins at their funeral. How can that be? If they have lived a life of sin and never repented, why would this so-called God absolve their sins when the price for such a lifestyle should be that they go to hell? It makes a mockery of the *live your life this way* decree. It is all utterly contradictory and hypocritical. They have created a *better be safe than sorry* mentality. *Thou shalt not kill*... unless it's in the name of *our* God. It really is obvious to anyone awake."

Archie wasn't, and has never been a member of the God squad, so he had to think hard about what he had just been told. He had never believed in God, ever. Especially after some of the things he had seen while serving with the ambulance service. The truth is that those experiences only helped to sway him away from religion. Though, he was desperately trying to find an argument to counter what Blondie had just said – if for no other reason than to play devil's advocate, but he was completely stumped. He had no rebuttal to give because everything that he had been told made perfect sense to him. He was sure that there would be a bible basher out there who would try to put up a fight, but that person wasn't him.

Archie moved the conversation to a different subject and asked about the Secret Societies. He had a basic understanding, but that was it; basic. He wanted to know more. What are they doing? Why are they doing it? How are they doing it? He had questions that needed answers.

"From the intelligence we managed to get from the drone," Blondie started, "it was apparent that the Illuminati was initially set up for the purposes of good, to put an end to the darkness of slavery and deprivation that had engulfed the human race. They were making great strides in achieving their goal when the Draco first appeared. Even after their capitulation to the reptilians, they tried to warn of impending disasters and false flag events. They did it through, what has now become known in conspiracy circles, as Predictive Programming; they would have an article published in newspapers or magazines, that would relate to the upcoming event. It was subtle, it couldn't be obvious. They couldn't just say, *"this is going to happen on this date"*. They had to do it in such a way as it could be construed as fiction or fact. They still do it now, but not with the same intent. Now they do it as a means of showing off their power to their reptilian overlords while rubbing it in the faces of the masses. Their intentions have changed over the past century or so. They no longer try to warn of the events, but rather celebrate them"

"But how?" Archie asked. "How do they do this?"

"A good way to put it would be... Problem, Reaction, Solution." Blondie paused for a moment's thought before speaking again. "They create a problem, let's say, a false flag terrorist event; that's the Problem. Then they await the public's Reaction, which will be to call out for the government to protect them, usually by any means necessary, even if it includes breaching civil rights and privacy laws. Then they provide the Solution; Laws and Rules that will gain the Secret Society even more power and greater control over the population.

"You need to remember that this has nothing to do with money; they own the worlds banking systems and could print all the money they want. This is about control and power. Nothing more. They need to control the people of Earth to stay in line with the orders to their Draconian masters. This New World Order that the puppets of Earth's governments are trying to push through is actually a Draconian decree. No Planet or race of Beings can enter the Galactic Alliance without being a unified world. By forcing Earth into the one world government, they have the option to promote the acceptance of the human race into the Alliance; a human race that *they* control. That gives them another ally in Alliance matters. Albeit, a forced ally, but an ally nonetheless."

Archie chewed on that information for a few minutes. It all made sense. He had long suspected that the current drive for anti-terrorism laws was really a way for the elites to gain more control. Be it by tapping phone lines and internet communications, to putting innocent people into prisons. Hell, even prisons were a for-profit business nowadays. If you were a conspiracy theorist who was close to the truth, the elite would know everything about your life, and they could use that information to discredit or even imprison you to keep you quiet. He had watched plenty of supposed terrorist attacks on the news and saw that the narrative being portrayed didn't line up with what he was seeing. He'd seen the injuries being shown on TV that didn't even look real. They looked as though they were faked. And every time one of these events took place, a new law would be proposed, one that took another little bit of freedom away from the people. Maybe, just maybe, the Pleiadian was telling the truth.

"You mention the banking system, I've heard that it's rigged, is that true?" Archie had seen several documentaries showing how the system was doomed to fail but he couldn't remember the details.

"It is as you say, rigged. Governments do not own the money that is in circulation. Actually, we shouldn't use the term money at all; the notes are no more than Promissory, rather than actual money. It even says so on the note itself. Although the banks state they are Nationalised, they are not. They are in point of fact, private corporations, who loan currency to their respective governments, but they do it with interest that can never be repaid."

"Wait, what do you mean, can't be repaid?"

"Okay, so we'll keep the sum small, but you'll get the idea. The government needs to use currency to run their country, so they go to the British bank and ask for a loan. The bank says fine here is one million pounds, but in three years you need to repay the loan with two hundred thousand pound interest. The government agree and takes the loan. Now, three years pass and the bank calls in the debt, so the government tries to get the million back from circulation, but they can't, and even if they could, it wouldn't matter, because how can they pay the interest?"

"Well, they... can't." It dawned on him. "The two hundred thousand pounds never existed, so it could never be paid back."

"Precisely. Now the government borrows more currency to not only repay the interest on the original loan but also to keep enough in circulation to run the country. Do you see? They have created a system whereby they cause an ever-increasing amount of debt. It's fixed in such a way that the banking elite can, and often do cause planned economic crashes as and when they need to by pushing up interest and inflation rates." Blondie paused. "That means that by these banks being in control of a nation's currency, they control that nation. It's also worth noting that approximately 98 per cent of the world's banks are owned by only a handful of families. They conspire with elites from other industries and the world's royalty to formulate the plans for humanity."

The conversation had been interesting, but it was getting heavy again. The pair had been talking for hours, and it had started to get dark as day gave way to night. It

185

was time to have a break and digest it all over a brew. As Archie finished pouring the tea, a car pulled up on the other side of the road, next to the van. It was the thieving site manager. Archie got up to meet him before he could get out of his car. The driver's window opened, and the thief said that he was going home for the night and that he was leaving the gate unlocked so that Archie and Blondie could stay until their pick up arrived. The only proviso was that they had to shut up shop when they left. With that, the man was on his merry way… fifty quid richer.

13

Fishing Lake

A428, Between Birmingham and Luton

England

The crappy phone started ringing at about 6.45pm. Archie looked at the display and saw that it was the same number that Joey had used earlier. He answered but said nothing.

"Allo?" it was Jeff.

"All right, Jeff, where are you?" he asked.

"We're about two miles from the services." Jeff's tone made it was clear that he was nervous.

"Okay, mate. Good," Archie said. "Don't bother pulling in. I want you to meet me just outside the town of Crick. To be precise, a fishing lake, just off the A428. There's a dirt road on the left a few hundred yards out of town. I'm down there. I think Joe knows where it is, we fished there a few years ago."

"Yeah got it Arch. Joey's following just behind me. He's got another phone; he'll give you the number when we get to you" he said.

"Okay, mate, see you in about half an hour," Archie said before hanging up.

Twenty minutes later, Archie heard the sound of cars moving up the track. They had arrived quicker than he'd expected. Having told Blondie to stay put, he grabbed the two cameras, got out of the van and made his way to meet the new arrivals. As he walked towards the vehicles, he noticed that Jeff was driving a people carrier and Joe was in a dirty old mini-van.

"All right chaps?" Archie asked in greeting. "Thanks for coming."

Joey's reply was short and to the point. "No worries. Now, what have you done you dickhead?"

Archie indicated for them to get into the people carrier and proceeded to explain the events of the last couple of days. Jeff didn't seem to have any problems believing what he was being told, but Joey wasn't having any of it. Archie understood the difference in opinion, after all, Jeff had experienced a UFO sighting, whereas Joe hadn't.

"Fuck off" he exclaimed, "I wasn't born yesterday. Have you been smoking crack? LSD? Charlie? It's too much Charlie, ain't it?" Archie nearly laughed as Joey added. "And who's the big fucker in your van?"

"Here, look at this; pictures and film of the initial UFO sighting," Archie said as he started the playback. "And *he* is one of *them,*" he added as the video showed a Lightship flitting around the night sky.

They both sat there in total amazement as they watched the footage. Their jaws hung so wide open that Archie thought he might have to close their mouths for them. When the video finished for the second time, he showed them the stills photographs.

"Fucking 'ell, Arch," Jeff was the first to speak. "What were you thinking? What are you going to do?"

"I'm going to get the geezer to Avebury Henge so that his people can pick him up" Archie began, "but there's more to it than that. He says that I'm, one of them - that I have been incarnated into this body, and put on Earth, and that I have some sort of secret mission." He said, pulling a face of disbelief. Saying it out loud seemed to make it sound even worse than it did in his head. He continued. "Honestly, I don't know what to think about it, though. There are things that he has said that I *know* are true, but I can't seem to remember it all."

Joe was looking at Archie as though he had lost the plot... gone mental. "Are you sure you've not been on LSD?"

"No, mate," he said before continuing. "It gets weirder. Every time I touch a gun, I get this... flash of schematics, or instructions. The next thing I know, all the information a person needs to effectively operate and use the weapon is in my head."

"Like what?" Jeff asked. "What sort of weapons are you talking about?"

"Well, for starters, there's this," Archie said, handing over the silenced Beretta, "and these." He pulled out the grenades from his pockets. "There are also four M4 Carbines under the front seat of the van."

"Shit," Jeff muttered as he looked over the pistol.

"What do you need from us?" asked Joe, with the, *what the fuck are you on about,* look gone entirely from his face as he eyed the gun. The appearance of the weapons had removed all doubt from Joey's mind. There was no-way Archie could have got hold of a gun, he wouldn't even know how to get one.

"First off, I need you to take my motor closer to home and strip it of everything that can ID it to me; license plate, VIN number, Serial numbers, and all that shit. Then I want you to burn it. I don't know if it's been made or not, but I'm not taking any chances. After that, I want you to get round to my place and tell Lucy what's going on, show her the video. Give her this pay as you go phone and tell her I'll phone her later from the number I used to ring you. Also, one last thing, before you leave here, get my fishing gear into the mini-van; I know that hasn't been made and I see no reason to burn that. Cost me a fucking fortune!"

"None of that should be a problem, Arch, but then what? Are we supposed to go home and forget about it or what?" Joey was in with both feet, doubt entirely gone from his mind, and he was already looking forward to planning for the next phase. Archie guessed that the weapons were the thing that had changed his cousin's mind. After all, this was the UK; you couldn't just walk into a shop and buy that shit, and you certainly wouldn't find it discarded in the street.

"No, I want you to make your way to Avebury in case it all goes wrong," Archie said. He'd been planning this since last night and had a good idea of what he wanted.

"I'm going to give you both a rifle and a pistol, just in case. Also, just so that you're in no doubt; the government is in on it – they're working with the reptiles, so be careful, don't get stopped by the police whatever happens."

The look on their faces confirmed to Archie that they both acknowledged the severity of the situation. "Well, I guess we had better meet the big fella then," Jeff said as he opened the car door to get out.

As they approached the van, Archie motioned for Blondie to get out and meet them at the front of vehicle. Jeff and Joe both stopped dead in their tracks as they clapped eyes on the Pleiadian. Initially, Archie thought it was due to the size of the man... he *was* big, but he was wrong, that wasn't it.

"Hello Jeffery, hello Joseph." Blondie seemed to know them. The two men just stood there with their mouths agape again.

"How the hell do you know them?" Archie asked, eyes flicking between his relatives and the alien.

"They too were incarnated here, in the same manner as yourself. I knew you all before the commencement of your missions here on Earth," he said in his usual low, slightly accented tone. It came as no real shock to Archie, but to the other two...

"So how do you two know him?" Archie posed the question to his dumbstruck family, before turning back to Blondie. "And why didn't you tell me about this earlier?"

"Until now, it wasn't relevant to our situation," Blondie stated as a matter of fact.

"Dreams…" Joey said.

"He's been appearing in my dreams," Jeff added.

"For the past two years, I and certain others have been trying to encourage certain Earth Born to awaken and find their own spirituality. There are others that you know, who are of the same origin."

"Who?" Archie could feel his blood beginning to boil, he was far from happy about this revelation. "Who are you talking about?"

"There are many, too many to name them all. But I will give you the names of several." Blondie was feeling Archie's anger, and the Pleiadian didn't think this was the right time for this particular conversation, but he also knew it was going to happen anyway. "Joseph and Jeffery, you know about, your wife and children, and the friend you call Jason."

"Lucy and the kids?" Archie had to cool his rage. Biting his lip wasn't cutting the mustard right now. "What the fuck have they got to do with this?" He knew his voice was getting louder as the red mist began to cloud his vision. Putting himself in harm's way was one thing but, putting his family in harm's way was… beyond reason.

"All were put here for specific reasons, all of which relate directly to your mission. When the time is right, their true origin will be revealed to them. I do not know all the answers that you seek. However, I do know that *you* chose the team that surrounds you. I was left behind to be a part of the liaison and awakening group; whoever that person was, had to be someone you knew well. *You* decided that it should be me for the reason of familiarity upon the revelation of the truth." Blondie spoke quietly, measured, knowing that the wrong word could push Archie's rage over the edge, and he'd end up with a bullet to the brain.

"And what about my kids?" Archie said, virtually through gritted teeth. "What have they got to do with any of this?

"Nothing. You wanted them close, nothing more. They are safe, Archie. They always will be. We have a fleet permanently in phase on standby, ready to extract them in the event of a full invasion." The sincerity was evident in Blondie's voice.

"Are you having a fucking laugh?" Although he could see that the Pleiadian meant what he had said, Archie had a problem accepting there was a fleet standing by to pick up his kids. "How can you say that? When your ship was shot down, I never saw any fleet of ships coming to save your arse... I fucking did!"

"Yes, I see your meaning. However, that was a completely different scenario. While the Pleiadian mission is of a covert nature, I am expendable. If or when that situation changes to a full-scale invasion, everything will change, and direct intervention measures will be employed to remove all agents and messengers from the planet by every means necessary. Where possible, no-one will be left behind."

Archie liked the no-man left behind part. "So your people *will* intervene?" he asked.

"Until the Alliance or our Council sanction military or security operations, we will only act in the capacity to extract our own people. After that..." Blondie's speech trailed off.

That bit, Archie didn't like. "Okay, let me get this straight. You rescue your own, and fuck everyone else. That about right?"

"I am sorry, Archie, but I do not make the decisions. I simply follow the orders I am given," Blondie said, resigned to the fact that he wouldn't - *couldn't* change the mind of the Earth Born.

"You sound like a typical manager. *It's not my fault – I just do what I'm told,*" he said sarcastically, looking at his two relatives as he shook his head. "You know, that's what the fucking Nazi's said – they were just following orders – like *that* could absolve them of their crimes."

"I am no manager," Blondie said, "in fact, you are the team leader here."

"Wait, what? So, you have to follow my lead, my orders?" Archie asked after a moment's contemplation.

"Yes. I can only guide you, I cannot make decisions for you," Blondie replied. "I will do as you command. With that in mind, I still need to get off of the planet. You are all at serious risk of compromise all the time I remain here."

For a moment, Archie stood there, thinking. The distant sound of rota blades snapped him out of it. It was time to switch on and get this plan moving forward.

"Right, you two get to work. Joey, you get started on removing the vans ID, and Jeff, start getting all my gear – except the big holdall – into that one" Archie said pointing to the shit heap of a mini-van.

"Yeah, no probs, but I've got more questions for the big man," Archie could see that Joey's mind was working overtime. "Where do Jeff and I fit into all this? I mean, what are we supposed to do?" It was a fair question.

"To start with, you both need to start working on your own spiritualism and begin to open your third eye. Until then, you will be of little use in the early part of the mission. Once your minds are open, you will begin to receive the knowledge necessary for the tasks ahead. You must both continue with your respective lines of work. Jeff, monitor the status of the health system. We believe that something is wrong within it, but we cannot ascertain what the problem is. We hope that your position will render us some intelligence. Pass that information on to Archie." That kind of made sense. As a hospital porter, Jeff had access to areas that would generally be very difficult to gain entry to.

Looking a bit confused, Jeff asked, "What am I looking for?"

"Anything out of the ordinary. Particularly within the accident department and the mortuary." Blondie's tone was low, and his speech was deliberate. "Joe, you need to keep working within the underworld. There you have a network of contacts and access to things that may be required later."

"Are we all satisfied?" Archie was anxious to crack on.

"No, not really," Jeff said with a smile on his face as he started to make his way to the back of the van. "I was hoping for a ride in a flying fucking saucer."

"You Twat, Jeff. I thought you were serious for a second." Archie couldn't keep the grin from his face either.

"What the fuck?" Jeff shouted in a panic as he opened the back door and fell on his arse.

"Meet Kaiser and Reg," Archie said between belly laughs. "Sorry, I forgot to mention them."

"Yeah, you did, didn't you? Fucking idiot – I nearly shit myself!" The laughter grew. Even Blondie was pissing himself as Jeff fell victim to a severe slob attack.

14

Fishing Lake

Between Birmingham and Luton

England

Midnight

Everything was ready to go. Joey knew his stuff alright. Archie was surprised at how quickly his cousin had gotten the van prepared for torching. As he was standing there, memories of their childhood came flooding back. He could clearly remember the three of them over the field working on a shitty little mini motorbike that they had decided to build. Jeff was the planner - the designer, and he was reading the plans while Joey put in to practice what was being said – he was the builder. Basically, the thing was made from two bicycle frames welded together with a small lawn mower engine bolted under the seat. It was a fantastic bit of engineering for three kids under the age of ten. Archie's role in the escapade was test pilot. The bike worked perfectly until he tried to jump over a ditch, where, upon landing, the frame welds disintegrated, sending him over the handlebars, and causing him to land headfirst on to a rock. Four hours, and twelve stitches later, the pit-crew and pilot were back home, patting each other on the back for a job well done. The three boys were as thick as thieves. As the memory passed through his mind, it brought a huge smile to Archie's face.

"It's ready, Arch." Joeys voice brought him out of his reminiscing. "Are you sure you want it burnt?"

"Yeah, there's no choice, Joe," Archie replied in a solemn tone. He liked the van more than any other vehicle he had owned, but he just couldn't take the chance on it. "If it's found burnt out, and it's been made, I'm hoping the police will think it had been stolen. Listen, once you've sorted the motor out, get round to my place and give Lucy a rundown of what's going on, and get her to report the motor stolen in the morning. Flip me a text message once you have given her the phone, and I'll ring her. One more thing, take the dogs with you as well... the kids will love it."

Jeff looked at Archie with a frown. "The kids might love it, but Lucy will do her nut."

"Don't worry about that; just don't take them in until after I've spoken to her," Archie said with a smile as he thought of how Lucy would react to two big dogs turning up at the front door.

Just before they were about to go their separate ways, Archie went over the plan again. Everyone was in agreement - everyone except for Blondie. "It is not wise that they join us at the Stones," he said. "There is a strong possibility that we will find ourselves engaged in combat, and they do not have the knowledge or skills required for such an event. I fear they will not survive." Pausing, he looked around the small circle of men. "It would be better for them to begin their spiritual work as soon as possible. This way, when the time is right for them to be involved in military operations, hopefully, they will have opened their consciousness enough that they will be ready. Or at least, they will be open to receiving the information they will need, as you have, Archie. However, the decision remains yours."

Before Archie could answer, Jeff spoke up. "Nah, fuck that!" he said with a scowl. "If it's going to get naughty, then we need to be there. Archie's my brother, and he can't do this on his own."

"Slow down, Jeff. I think he could be right," Archie said thoughtfully. "Without my martial arts training and the *information flashes*, I don't think I could have done what I have. Honestly, I think I'd be dead. Besides, if something happens to me, I need you two to look after Lucy and the kids."

After a few minutes of discussion, Archie had made his decision - they wouldn't meet up at Avebury. So, with that in mind, he also decided to keep all of the rifles and only give the two men a pistol each. He showed them how to use the weapons and gave them an extra magazine each.

It was time to leave, and after saying their goodbyes and good lucks, they made their way out of the fishery. Archie hoped that by this time tomorrow, Blondie would be on his way home, and he would be sleeping in his own bed.

As the crow flies, it was only about 70 miles or so to Avebury, and at this time of night, it wouldn't take long to get there. Driving along the A346, Archie decided to put the radio on to see if any news reports related to what he was experiencing, but the station was playing some shit old country music.

Looking over at the Pleiadian, he saw that the man had just as bad a taste in music as he did hairstyles as he sat there tapping his foot and swaying his head to the tune.

"Are you sure we were friends before my reincarnation?" Archie asked with a smile. "Look at you bopping away to this shit; no friend of mine would like this crap."

As the Pleiadian grinned at the Earth Born, the music was cut away, and a news flash caused the alien's appreciation of the tunes to evaporate in an instant.

"The small town of Avebury, in Wiltshire has had to be evacuated for a second night running amid fears of a large gas leak. Emergency Services are working alongside the Gas Board to rectify the situation. It is thought that a mains pipe that supplies the entire county, had suffered a serious rupture earlier in the week has failed again after being repaired..."

"Gas leak my arse. It sounds like they have the area well secured. We could be in for a bit of a bundle," Archie said as he glanced over to Blondie.

"Indeed, it does. I think you mean fight?" The Pleiadian replied with the slightest look of confusion on his face.

Archie laughed and replied. "Yeah, mate. That is exactly what I mean... fight. Sorry, maybe I need to start speaking the queens English."

Turning the people carrier onto the A4, he pulled into a layby and checked the map. He didn't want to just drive into town knowing there was a welcoming committee waiting for them. From what he could see, the small village seemed to be flanked pretty much on all sides by fields. Two roads ran through the place, which intersected more or less, right in the centre of town. At that moment, they were stopped just South East of the target area.

The route that Archie was originally going to take was along the A4, to the small town of West Kennett. From there he was going to travel North onto the B4003, cross over a small junction, onto the A4361 and drive straight into the village of Avebury. But this way was not an option anymore, not with an ambush waiting for them. A new plan was needed.

Studying the map, he noticed that the road which led into the town from the East was called Green Street; this had to be an Oman. Archie's beloved football team used to have, until a few years ago, their stadium on the road called Green Street, in Upton Park, East London. He had plenty of good memories of that place, and again wondered if this was synchronicity at work. It didn't matter. *That* was their route in, but he wasn't just going to drive in.

Archie decided to drive along the A4 and turn right onto what looked like a dirt road, which was probably five or six hundred yards before the town of West Kennett and

201

head North. He would stay on the road for approximately three-quarters of a mile before ditching the motor and walking across the field until they got to Green Street. From there they would have to wing it and see what happened.

He had his plan, now it was time to double check he had all of his shit in order. There was no point rushing headlong into trouble and finding out that you were missing something vital. Besides, he had a bit of time to kill anyway; he wasn't going to move until he had spoken to home, and he couldn't do that until Jeff and Joey had done their part. In the meantime, he'd check, double-check, and re-check the kit over again.

Having sorted out the equipment he'd be taking, he decided it was time to move the motor onto the dirt road. Headlights off, thermal up, he started towards West Kennett. When he located the track on the right, he pulled the vehicle onto it and stopped after about a mile. That left about a hundred and fifty yards, cross country, to Green Street.

He found the waiting to be nerve-racking as he sat there thinking about what might be in store for them. His heartbeat was banging so hard, that it felt like someone was playing the drums inside his rib cage; he wouldn't have minded so much, but whoever the drummer was, they were shit. He was sweating like a pig, and he had that sense of foreboding again. It was going to kick off, and he knew it.

Archie knew that they needed to see around them, but it was absolutely pitch dark outside. He had the thermal, which was doing a job, but he was concerned that it wouldn't pick up the reptiles. After all, it didn't last night.

"I have a weapon," Blondie said as Archie passed him an M4 rifle.

"I know. It's not for shooting, it's for looking through. Look through the night sight and keep an eye out for those lizards," he replied. "This thing didn't pick up their body heat the other night, and if it weren't for Reg, I would have been brown bread."

The Pleiadian threw him a quizzical look. "Brown bread?"

"It's slang for dead, mate," Archie laughed. "Fucking come on son, get with the programme."

The big man snorted a laugh and started looking through rifles sight. A moment later, he spoke. "Thermal Imaging will not always detect the heat signatures of the Draco. They are cold-blooded and have excellent camouflage abilities. They have a naturally low body temperature, but they are also extremely good at hiding it."

As Blondie finished talking, Archie thought, *Well, that's just fucking great – I've got a thermal camera that can't pick up lizard heat*. Cynicism aside, it did explain why he only saw a glimmer of a shadow when he got jumped. From then on, he kept switching from the thermal to the rifle. Even though the immediate area seemed quiet, he couldn't help being jumpy, and as the phone suddenly started ringing, he nearly shit himself. He looked at the time, it was 3.48am, he answered the call but didn't say anything.

"Archie?" it was Lucy.

"Watcha babe."

"What's going on? Are you all right?" She asked, concern evident in her voice.

"Yeah, I'm fine. I'm guessing Jeff and Joe have told you what's happened?" He asked.

"Yes, but is this some sort of joke? Are they taking the piss or what?"

"No Luv, it's not a joke. Did they show you the video?"

"Yes, but I don't know what to make of it all." There was fear and confusion laced in her tone.

"Well, right now, all you really need to know is that it's all true. Listen, I need you to report my van stolen in the morning...do it at about 10 o'clock. It's important, alright?"

"Yeah, okay. What are you going to do?" Lucy asked, with concern.

"I'm going to get this big blond bastard back to his people," Archie replied, looking over at Blondie with a grin on his face.

"Be careful, make sure you come home safe, okay?" Lucy was apparently more than nervous, she was outright scared, and he didn't blame her - so was he.

"Of course, I will. That goes without saying. Oh, by the way, Jeff's got a couple of dogs for you. They both saved my arse a couple of times, and I couldn't just leave them behind. So, now they're ours." Archie tried to slip that little gem into the conversation and get her off the phone quickly, "Look, I have to go. Put Jeff on. Love you, see you soon."

"DOGS! What bloody dogs?" Shit, he thought he'd got away with it.

"Don't worry, they're lovely. Now put Jeff on. See ya later."

"We'll talk about this when you get home – bloody dogs! Here's your brother. Now he's saying we've got fucking dogs!" she said as she handed the phone over to Jeff.

"All right Arch? I told ya she wouldn't be happy with the dog's mate," he said with a little chuckle.

"Yeah, don't worry about that. Is the van sorted?" Archie asked.

"Yeah, it's done. It brightened up the local pikey's night as well. They all gathered around to warm their grubby little hands up."

"Okay, nice one. Right, I'm gonna go. I want to get this done while it's still dark. See ya later," Archie said just before hanging up.

Pulling out the map and showing Blondie where they were and where they were going, he tried to make sure that the Pleiadian knew what was what. Which by the, *Don't take me for a prick,* look that the alien had on his face, made it pretty obvious he understood.

"Right, you big blonde turd sniffer, let's do this," Archie said with a chuckle as he got out of the vehicle. It was time to get going.

15

Avebury

Wiltshire

England

It was windy, and there were spots of rain coming down as they moved through the treeline, into the field. Archie hoped that the weather would get worse to help cover their approach to the village. Every ten or fifteen yards he stopped, got to one knee and had a good look about. So far he'd seen nothing, not even the village. It wasn't long before the rain started getting heavier as they made their way forward. This was good news, as it would make it harder to be seen. Stealth was an excellent ally right now. But at the same time it was a double-edged sword, not only did the weather hide them from the enemy, but it also made it more difficult for them to spot the opposition who were almost certainly lying in wait. *Fuck it, there's nothing I can do about it*, Archie thought as he moved on.

The trek through the field was hard going; the terrain was a nightmare, with bumps and mounds everywhere, and the mud was thick and slippery underfoot. Combined with the wind and rain, it was a job just to keep upright. Archie was trying hard to move tactically, but what the hell did he know about tactics? Nothing, that's what. All he could do was find a bit of cover, get in it, and have a look around, before moving on.

About forty minutes later, the pair found themselves hiding in a bush, approximately fifty yards from Green Street. It was time to stop, take stock of the surroundings, and assess the situation.

"Do you know how to get back to the vehicle if this goes wrong?" He needed to be sure that the Pleiadian knew the escape route.

"I do," Blondie replied as Archie placed the equipment bag next to him.

"Good. Wait here a minute, I'll have a look up the road and see what I can see. Don't shoot anything unless you absolutely have to." Archie wasn't asking, he was telling. The way he saw it was that if someone needed to be killed, it needed to be done quietly... where possible anyway. He just hoped that nobody was going to have to die at all, especially them. "When I give you the signal, I want you to move up to my position, and make sure you bring the bag with you."

As he started moving out of the bush, he noticed that Blondie was sliding the shoulder strap of the holdall across his back. *Good, I don't want him leaving that behind*. He moved forward really slowly, deliberately placing each foot purposefully. It was hard going, but he didn't want to fall flat on his face and compromise himself now, not after such an ordeal to get this far. Every ten yards or so, he would stop, take a knee, and look around. It took almost twenty minutes for him to finally get to the road. Once there, he just sat quietly in the treeline for a few minutes; for two reasons, one – to catch his breath, and two – to tune in to this environment. He was just about to move out onto the road when the wind brought with it a god-awful smell. His heart rate soared as he realised that he knew that whiff. He wasn't alone.

Slowly, he brought the thermal up to his eye and cupped his hand around the viewfinder. Pointing the lens upwind, to the east, and where he assumed the smell was coming from, a quick flick of the on switch, and there they were; two Greys. *What was it Blondie called them? Reticulans, was it?* These two were different though; at about five and a half, perhaps, six feet tall they were larger than the two he'd previously encountered. Size didn't matter when you were getting striped up by a samurai sword. Large people died just as well as small people.

After a quick check in both directions to ensure they were alone, Archie turned the camera off and put it down next to the M4. These were going to be silent kills; he just hoped the cheap Katana was up to the job.

Searching the ground around him, he found a small rock and took it in his left hand. His right hand held the short sword, his heart rate went up as he held his breath and waited. As the enemy passed his position, he threw the stone into the trees on the opposite side of the road, hoping the aliens would turn to face the noise. When they did, he knew it was time to start chopping.

The enemy stood about four feet apart from each other as they looked for the cause of the noise in the trees. Archie sneaked out of his hiding place, and after three steps, he found himself directly behind the Grey to the left of the pair. With a single swipe of the Katana, the bulbous head of the alien left its body and fell to the ground. In the same movement, Archie pivoted on his right foot, spinning towards the second Grey, who had been alerted by the thud of his comrades' head hitting the floor. It started to bring his right hand up, but it was too late as Archie's blade made easy work of taking the appendage clean off. The alien began to raise its other arm over his abdomen, and as it did so, the belly began to glow, as though it was generating energy. Archie was still swirling the sword, bringing it back over, and taking off the aliens other hand above the wrist. The glow vanished instantly, as the Grey dropped to its knees. The realisation of imminent death caused him to try to scramble away, but it wasn't going to happen. One final swipe and it was over, another head was rolling along the road.

Not a bad buy, that, Archie thought as he cleaned off the blade of the sword and looked over the scene. Without wasting any time, he dragged the bodies off the road and into the treeline. Once he had recovered the M4 and the thermal, he motioned for Blondie to move up and join him. He couldn't help but be amused as he watched the Pleiadian run, squat, run, squat as he tried to find cover on his way forward. He looked like a giant, demented rabbit.

"I smell Reticulans," Blondie whispered as he reached the trees. Archie gave him a nod, and Blondie's eyes followed the direction, where he saw the two decapitated bodies. "That is wrong on many levels," he said as he realised that Archie had stuffed the fingers from the severed hands into the small nasal cavities of the dead Greys.

"I thought you'd like that," Archie whispered back. "Come on, follow me."

They moved out of cover and crossed the road and entered the trees opposite. Slowly, they started heading towards the village, but they had only travelled about fifty feet before the world around them seemed to erupt. Tracer and laser fire were flying all around them, and Archie could hear shouts of commands from enemy soldiers as well as hisses and roars from... something - reptilians, he presumed.

"Return fire!" Archie shouted.

The night sights were a godsend as he opened up on the enemy. He dropped two almost straight away. He noticed that Blondie wasn't messing around either, as he picked his shots. The trouble was, his aim was crap with the rifle. He would run out of ammunition quickly, and Archie didn't have time to fuck about trying to feed him magazines.

"Use your remote thingy," Archie shouted, "but don't lose the rifle. Sling it over your back." It made sense for the Pleiadian to use the weapon that he was most familiar with.

"You take the humans, and I will take the Draco," Blondie called back as he dumped the holdall and started blasting away with the remote.

The incoming rounds were stitching the ground and tree trunks. Mud was being kicked up, and leaves were falling all around them. Archie was getting smothered in crap. BANG! He found himself flying through the air. He landed on the grass verge beside the road. Shaking himself out of his daze, he realised he hadn't been shot, but rather that he had been hit by a person or an animal. There, a Dracoderos; another one of those dragon things! *Shit! Shit! Shit! Where's the rifle? Where's the rifle?* He couldn't find it, and the massive animal was almost on him. There was nothing else to do but pull out the Tanto as it lunged at him.

He forced the blade up and through the underside of its jaw and kept pushing. The animal pulled away, but Archie kept stabbing and withdrawing. He was panicking, badly; stab, pull, repeat. Eventually, the creature fell onto its side, but its legs were still trying to run, and Archie wasn't sure if it was the animals' death throes or if it was still trying to kill him. Whatever the case, it was about to die. Archie brought the blade to its neck and started slicing, almost severing its head before it finally stopped moving. *I'm not on the fucking menu!*

The rate of incoming fire increased, bringing Archie back to the present as the situation around him intensified. Jumping back into the cover of the trees, he found the M4. Picking it up, he shouldered the weapon, and started firing again. Another one down, change the mag, fire…

It was evident the pair were not going to be able to fight through the enemy lines, and the cover they were in was pitiful. They needed a way out, but Archie was still in panic mode. He slowed his breathing from rapid, shallow breaths to long deep ones and felt calmer almost immediately. While Blondie provided covering fire, Archie picked up the thermal and looked around to see if he could get a better picture of the battlefield. The human enemy was still about seventy – maybe a hundred yards away, it was hard to tell through the imager. But it seemed as though the distance was far enough to buy them a little bit of time, providing they could keep up the covering fire. Looking to the right, into the field, Archie noticed a jeep that looked as though it had a machine gun turret on the roof. *That'll do!*

"Give me your rifle," he shouted to Blondie, who was dropping the Draconians like they were fish in a barrel as he fired like a man possessed. When he handed the weapon over, Archie changed the mag and set it to full auto and laid it next to the Pleiadian. "Use this too - fire both weapons. Don't worry too much about hitting anything – just create a distraction. I'm going for that jeep."

Through the sight, Archie could see that there were two soldiers in the vehicle; one on the turret, and one in the driver's seat. Picking his shot carefully, he dropped the driver with ease. He slid the Katana down the back of his jacket, and moved back up the treeline, about thirty yards in the general direction from which they had come. There was a small ditch that ran around the circumference of the Henge that would give him a bit of cover on his approach to the jeep.

Blondie opened up with both weapons, immediately drawing the attention of the jeeps gunner, who started firing into the trees where the Pleiadian was hidden. Slowly, carefully, Archie belly crawled over the crest of the ditch and lined the gunner up in his sights. The weight of fire he was putting into the treeline where Blondie was creating the distraction was massive, and Archie could tell that either the big man was hit, or he had his head down because his fire had slowed to nothing. As the shooting from the jeep continued, Archie took the shot; single fire, one round, in the guy's face. He knew he had finished him as he slumped over the back of the turret.

Scrambling to his feet, he started running towards the vehicle. He got to within about twenty feet, when he heard a roar coming from his right. Turning to face it, he had to dive out of the way as the thing ran straight for him. It was another Dracoderos, only this one was bigger, much bigger, and it looked nastier, with huge saliva covered teeth and massive horns with ridges on its head. It looked like a cross between a rhinoceros and a dinosaur – *Rhinosaur!*

Getting to his feet, he realised that the M4 had got caught around his back, so he reached over his shoulder and gripped the handle of the Katana and pulled it out, still in its scabbard. Drawing the sword out of the covering revealed its shiny, razor sharp blade. No sooner had he completed the manoeuvre, did the Rhinosaur start galloping towards him.

Don't get it wrong! Don't get it wrong! He thought as the thundering footsteps got closer and closer. Archie could hear it snorting as it breathed. It seemed to take forever for the thing to get to him, but in reality, it took no more than a second or two before it lunged, with its jaws extended to take a bite. In the same instant, Archie sidestepped, turned the blade so that the sharp side faced the sky, and lifted it upward aggressively into the underside of the animals' neck as it passed. The moment he felt contact, Archie pulled the blade towards him, slicing deep and hard into its throat. In the same movement, he pivoted away as though he was a bullfighter, and as the blade came free, he dived into a rolling break-fall away from it.

Coming to his feet, he turned and faced the creature, it was bleeding heavily, but it wasn't finished. Archie held the sword high and waited for the next opportunity to strike. The wait wasn't a long one, as the Rhinosaur charged him again. This time it was closer, and within a few steps, it was on him. Archie sidestepped again, this time to the left, and brought the blade down across the back of its neck. The creature slumped to the ground; its spinal cord severed. It was down, but not yet dead. The thing was still breathing through the blood-filled blade slits in its throat, but at least the only thing it could move now, was its mouth and jaws - it wasn't going anywhere.

Slipping the sword back into its scabbard after flicking off the blood, he returned his attention to the jeep. The stench of death was awful as he opened the door; the aroma of shit and blood filled the air within the confines of the vehicle. Getting in, Archie realised there wasn't a turret at all, the gunner had been standing through the sunroof firing a machine gun. As he pulled the dead guy back into the car, he noticed there was a weapon wedged between the driver's legs. Touching it gave him the flash; H & K 417, 7.62mm, 20inch barrel with sound moderator or silencer, folding bipod, 20 round magazine, and telescopic night sight. *I'll have that*, he thought as he searched the driver for spare mags.

Now that he had pulled the gunner into the vehicle, he searched him as well, taking his FN 5.56mm Minimi Light Machine Gun, LMG. The ammunition for this weapon was box fed. 13.7inch barrel, collapsible stock, with a standard NATO night sight. At 700-850 rounds per minute, this thing could deliver some serious firepower. He took the two additional boxes of ammo as well.

After lightening the jeeps load of anything that could be of use, Archie got out and realised that the fighting had stopped. He initially hoped that Blondie had won the day, but it became evident that he was gravely mistaken. Looking through the scope of the 417, he could see that a particularly large Draconian was holding the Pleiadian in the air by his neck, as though the Pleiadian was some kind of trophy.

Archie felt panic, threatening to overwhelm him as he looked around. He was desperately trying to figure out what to do. If they had Blondie, they would find him soon after. He had to do something, and quickly. Looking back at the jeep, he noticed that the ground sloped downward and away behind the vehicle. That gave him an idea. He set up LMG next to the back wheel and started watching what was going on through the scope.

The reptile was still lifting the Pleiadian by the neck and was shaking him, as though he was trying to throttle him. At the same time, four other Draconians emerged from their hiding place and moved in towards them. From the right, human soldiers did the same thing, although they were running.

"HE'S OURS, HE'S OURS – PUT HIM DOWN DRACONIAN!" One of the humans ordered as he moved up to the reptile.

"NO HUMAN – THIS CREATURE IS MINE!" The lizard wanted his prize badly and wasn't about to give him up so easily.

"FUCK OFF – put him down, NOW!" This human was clearly in charge, and he wasn't taking no for an answer. "We have our orders. He is coming with us for interrogation."

"NOOO! I care not for your orders… he is *MINE*!" The relationship between these two factions wasn't good; that suited Archie, it might work in his favour.

The Draco were all snarling as the human force stepped forward, surrounding the reptiles and lifting their weapons. The human commander was saying something, but Archie couldn't make out what. It looked to him as though there could be trouble between the two groups, so he flicked the safety off on the LMG and waited. This was going to end badly for everyone that stood around the Pleiadian. If they didn't kill each other, Archie would do it for them.

"Fucking put him down now you scaly bastard! I will not…" The human never got to finish his sentence as the Draconian sideswiped him with his free hand.

In the same instant, the Draco warriors opened up on their human counterparts. It became a free for all, as both sides started shooting at each other. After a moment, Archie opened up with the Minimi LMG, but the problem was, he couldn't quite get the accuracy to hit the lizard holding Blondie. He quickly switched to the 417... POP, POP. He hit reptile right in the side of the head with two rounds in quick succession. It didn't kill him, but it was enough for him to drop the Pleiadian. Blondie was running back to the treeline before his feet even touched the ground. Archie switched back to the LMG to cover his retreat and opened up on full auto. The rate of fire being spat from the LMG was immense as Archie poured lead into the maelstrom.

He knew that the big man was back in position when the light blasts started shooting out and into the melee as the two factions tried to kill each other. For several moments the humans and the Draco were so focused on each other that they didn't realise there was a third faction putting rounds into both groups. However, it didn't take long for them to figure out that another party was taking advantage of their lack of discipline and started to turn their attention to Archie and the Pleiadian.

The enemy's targeting of Archie was excellent – they knew exactly where he was, and their rounds were thudding into the ground around him and pinging off of the jeep. He knew that he couldn't stay where he was. Staying as low to the ground as he could, he started pushing himself backwards, down the small gradient to the back of the vehicle. That shielded him from the incoming fire. Facing the enemy position from there, he made his way left using the incline for cover until he reached the Rhinosaur. The thing still wasn't dead and had enough energy left in him to snarl and try to turn its head for a bite. Archie pulled the Tanto from his pocket and stuck it through the chin and straight into its brain and twisted the blade, hard. He had to repeat the action three times before the thing would finally succumb to its injuries.

Back at the treeline, Blondie was still at it, blasting away like crazy as Archie got himself into a good firing position. He switched back to the 417 and started popping off rounds at the human ranks. They hadn't realised that he had moved and were still shooting at the jeep. It only took a few minutes to finish them off, but it felt like the firefight had been raging for hours.

Archie got to his feet and ran back to the ditch before making his way back to the treeline, where Blondie had retaken his position, just as the Pleiadian took down the last of the Draconian's. The look on the big man's face made Archie laugh aloud.

"Welcome to Earth big boy," he said as he dived into cover.

"Honestly, I thought we were dead men," Blondie said through panted breaths. "I thought you had been killed and I was going to be food for the Dracoderos."

"Not tonight, mate." Archie was displaying bravado. It was his way of dealing with stressful situations. He would either laugh at a problem or brush it off as no big thing. This method had allowed him to keep his head while others lost theirs countless times. "They need to seriously up their game if they're going to take us out!" He couldn't help himself as he continued laughing at the *We're gonna die* look on Blondie's face.

At that moment, there was an almighty clap of thunder from above that caused Archie to look up. He saw the clouds flickering with lightning… deep purple lightning. He'd never seen anything like it before.

"Look at that!" Archie exclaimed.

"We need to go… now!" Blondie said sternly. "NOW, ARCHIE – NOW!"

Archie wondered what the Pleiadian was getting all excited about until he saw the underside of a sizeable Draconian Dart breaching through the cloud cover. It was vastly larger than the ones he had seen at the lake. On the ground, he spotted more soldiers coming through the field. *Oh, so that's why he's all worked up!*

"Fuck it, come on, let's get out of here; back the way we came," Archie said, realising there was nothing else they could do but run.

The weight he was carrying was an absolute nightmare, and as they ran East through the field, Archie was breathing through his arse – and not for the first time in the last few days. He struggled to keep his footing in the slick mud and kept falling and stumbling. *This is bollocks*, he thought as he muddled on. The only consolation he saw was that the journey back to the people carrier was a lot faster without the need to be tactical, they just had to get out of the area – sharpish!

He wanted to stop and catch his breath so badly that the only thing that kept him going was the knowledge that the enemy was so close behind, and they were not best pleased that Archie and his Pleiadian friend had killed their comrades. He also knew that stopping now would only serve to increase the likelihood of being spotted by the alien ship. No, they couldn't stop and fight, they had to get away while they still could.

After finally making it back to the motor and throwing the gear inside, Archie looked up to see that the massive ship was holding station, just inside the cloud. Jumping into the driver's seat, he asked Blondie what it was.

"It is a Draconian Battle Cruiser," he said. "Very, very dangerous. The general rule is that; if you have any doubt of being able to destroy it, you do not instigate a fight with it."

"Battle Cruiser – check - don't fuck with it – check. Now shut the fucking door and let's go!" Archie said, spinning the wheel to full lock and turning the vehicle around, heading back the way they had come, before flooring the pedal.

16

Avebury

Wiltshire

England

"Sorry you couldn't get back to your people, mate," Archie spoke loudly, to be heard over the noise of the screaming engine, as he pushed the accelerator to the floor.

"It is not your fault, Archie. In fact, I am just glad we made it out alive. I honestly thought you had been killed. Besides, there was no way we could have fought them all off while we waited for pick up. To even attempt it would have been suicidal," Blondie replied.

"What now?" asked Archie.

"We must go to the other Circle," Blondie said.

"What, Stonehenge?"

"Yes, the one that is South from here." Blondie paused for a moment before continuing. "The Spiritual energy at Avebury boosted my consciousness enough to allow for a telepathic link to a phased Beam ship that had been awaiting our arrival."

"Whoa, whoa, whoa, there was one of your ships there?" Archie wasn't best pleased with the revelation. "Why didn't they help us?"

"They would have been destroyed. You saw the Battle Cruiser. It didn't just turn up when it did; it was there the whole time. It only revealed itself as a show of force - probably to encourage us to surrender. There is no chance a single Beam ship could win in a fight against it. It was better to make contact and arrange another rendezvous point. That is why we must go to the other Circle."

The engine was screaming as Archie drove like a mad man. Hitting the T junction at the end of the track, he swung the vehicle right onto the A4. He knew that Stonehenge was directly South of their current location and about fifteen miles as the crow flies. They would be there in no time. He just had to keep heading South until he hit the A303 and head West, take the right fork onto the A344, and the Stones would come up on the Left. Or alternatively, stay on the A303, and they would come up on the right, but that would mean they would have a longer trek across the field to get to them. *Fuck it, we'll take the shorter walk.*

"Okay, so what happens if we get to the Stones to find more enemy are waiting for us? I mean, it must be pretty obvious to them where we're heading. What if there's another Cruiser there?" Archie was naturally concerned about the ship.

"Things are being prepared for that eventuality," Blondie replied, but he didn't elaborate any further.

"I hope you're right, mate, or we're dead men."

The roads were pretty much all winding country lanes, which suited Archie down to the ground. He had trained extensively on this kind of driving through the Ambulance Service, and any pursuer would have to be going some to catch them. Using the system of car control, he was taking the sweeping bends at 70 – 80 mph, doing so with ease. If there was one thing he was *really* good at, it was throwing a motor about at speed. In his younger days, he'd even been offered a job as a getaway driver for one of Joey's crews, which he'd politely declined.

Blondie was a terrible back seat driver. He was gripping the dashboard and pushing his feet into the footwell so hard that Archie thought he was trying to do a Barney Rubble and stop the vehicle with his great big feet.

"Relax, you doughnut," Archie said, laughing at the Pleiadian's terrified look. "I *can* drive. I just want to put as much distance between them and us as possible."

Archie's amusement vanished in an instant as he heard the distant sound of rota blades again. He was *really* beginning to hate those things. Looking out of the window, he saw it approaching from the right. The road they were travelling on had forced them to go East, and he hoped that was the direction that the helicopter would report them heading in, rather than the Southerly direction they needed to go in. The closer it got, the more obvious it became that the jig was up, they had been found. The firearms they had weren't enough to bring it down.

"How powerful is your laser thingy?" Archie asked over the noise. "Can it bring down that helicopter?"

"Yes, but I am forbidden to harm humans. That is why I wanted you to engage them during the fight." Blondie's voice was solemn, as though he knew the statement would piss the Earth Born off.

As they got to another T junction, Archie slammed on the brakes and brought the vehicle to a stop. "What the fuck are you talking about? Can't harm humans? They're going to *KILL* us!" he shouted.

"I cannot do I..." Blondie started to reply, but Archie cut him off.

"Set the thing up and give it here. You might not be able to kill people, but I fucking can," he exclaimed as he got out of the car.

As he got to the passenger side door, Blondie opened it and handed the remote to Archie and showed him what button to press. The Pleiadian's words were ringing in his ears, *"Don't miss – it uses a lot of energy and takes several minutes to recharge."*

I won't fucking miss, he thought as he ran to the side of the road and hid in a bush. Within seconds, the helicopter was hovering just to the South, no more than fifty feet away. From his hidey hole, Archie took aim through the holographic sights that popped up from the screen and pressed the button; the weapons discharge was unexpected and threw him backwards. He landed on his bruised arse... again! As he picked himself up, there was a massive explosion as the chopper impacted the ground and was engulfed in a fireball.

"Good shot," Blondie said as Archie got back into the driver's seat. "Though, I am surprised that you actually hit it," he added as the remote landed on his lap.

"So am I, but fuck it, it's done. Now let's double back to the right, and we'll be heading South again" Archie replied, as he hit the accelerator causing Blondie to resume his, *Brace for impact* position. This brought another smile to Archie's face.

The clock said it was fast approaching 7 am, it would be daybreak soon, they could already see the sky getting lighter in the East. Archie was starting to doubt the plan, but the optimist in him was saying that daylight would hinder the enemy as well as them. They'd just have to wait and see what happens.

As Archie turned onto the A345, compulsion told him to slow the vehicle right down. This was the road that would lead them to the roundabout, from which they would take the A303 to Stonehenge. As he approached the junction, they saw that the traffic was beginning to build up. He tried to blend in with the other motorists, but around three hundred yards from the roundabout, traffic slowed to a crawl and eventually came to a stop. He was torn between getting out of the car to have a look up the road, or whether to stay put. Getting out might give them away if there was a roadblock up ahead, but not getting out might leave them severely limited in what action they could take if there were some sort of checkpoint. In the end, he just hopped out and had a look; the risk in not knowing what was ahead was just too high.

"Bollocks! There's a military roadblock up there," he said after getting back in. "We won't get through without a fight."

"That is not good news," Blondie replied, clearly disappointed. "What do you think we should do."

"Well. We're not turning around," Archie said with confidence. "We've got somewhere to be, and we're going to get there, one way or another."

The map told him that there was nowhere else to go. It was evident that taking any other route would be pointless, there would be checkpoints on all access roads around the Henge, so they might as well front this one out. There was nothing else for it.

"We're going to run into these roadblocks no matter what way we go." Archie started before pausing for a moment, he knew that Blondie wasn't going to like the new plan, but there was no other choice. "We're going to have to fight our way through, mate. They would have closed off the 303 in both directions around the Stones, so logically, there should be two checkpoints North and South of the roundabout. If you look at the junction, there are a load of trees, and big bushes that block the view to the South. That should give us enough cover to hit the Northern roadblock without the other one seeing us. Then we'll go through thc junction and hit the second checkpoint. We'll have to do this as quietly as possible, but once we're through, it's just a case of staying on the 303 to the Stones. What do you think?"

"I am not sure about this, Archie," he said. "It sounds like a lot of people are going to die."

"I really can't see any other way, Blondie. It doesn't matter what way we go, someone is going to die, and as long as it's not you or me, I'm good with it. At least if we do it here, they can't bring in the Draco because of all the civilians." Archie was racking his brains, but he just couldn't find another way. "Are you still going on about killing humans? If it comes to it, I'll do this on my own, but this *is* the way forward. Anyway, what happened to protecting me at all costs?"

"That order stood until contact with you was made. Now that it has, the order has been rescinded, and I am expendable, remember?" Blondie replied.

"Well, I can see your logic, but it's rubbish. There's another way to look at it; what's the point of keeping me alive just until the point of contact? I *am* about to put us into a situation that could see us both killed so contact would have been a complete waste of time. So you might as well have a say in its outcome. Besides, you said earlier that you have to follow my orders and *my* orders are simple – keep us both alive by any means necessary. So that there is no confusion here, I'll be specific – kill any human that needs to be killed so that we don't die – end of story. You can't get in trouble with the Council if I told you to kill, because their orders are for you to follow *my* orders. So, man the fuck up and do what I tell you to do."

Blondie's face told Archie that he wasn't happy, but he seemed to get it. "I do not think that the Council will find that acceptable."

"I don't care what the Council thinks. If you're right about why I'm involved, then they sanctioned my being here for a good reason, and with that, they have to accept that I will decide what is appropriate to accomplish the mission and ensure its security. Which, by the way, could be severely compromised all the time you're on the ground. Furthermore, if they *really* have a problem with it all, then they will have to pull me out. You can also tell them that I will *not* accept any form of punishment that they might decide to place on you either." Archie was serious; if this was all true, then he meant what he'd said. To place blame at Blondie's door was unacceptable.

Since rescuing him from the crashed ship, Blondie had been emphasising Archie's importance to the Pleiadian mission on Earth, and now the human was going to use it in his favour. To Archie, it was apparent that they were going to have to fight their way to the Stones, but he couldn't do it alone; he needed Blondie to be able to kill people to achieve their goal.

"No one has ever defied the Council of Light, Archie." Blondie had real concern in his voice.

"Well, I don't like saying it, but I think it's about time someone did," he replied. "But if you think about it, I'm not actually defying them, I'm just doing what needs to be done to complete this part of the mission, and that is to get you home" he paused for a moment before speaking again. "Sometimes, we need to make sacrifices, and they will have to accept that this is part of my mission decision-making process, and if they can't accept it, then that's their problem. They'll have to pull me out and start again. And we both know that could take another forty-odd year's for the incarnation to come to fruition and by the looks of things, that'll be too late."

Blondie sat there in silence as he digested what the Earth Born had said, and while he did, Archie was planning how to deal with the checkpoint up ahead. Whatever he chose to do, he would have to be fast in doing it, as well as quiet. For the next ten minutes or so, he just watched the soldiers, noting their movements, their numbers, their reactions to the cars that approached, and their attitudes.

They certainly looked the part, in their military BDU's, but they also looked overconfident. Though, there were probably a lot of people who would ooze confidence while wearing Battle Dress Uniforms, carrying rifles and stopping cars. The soldiers were chatting and joking as they waived cars East. Archie felt that they were not the same breed of soldier that he had encountered so far. *No, definitely not specialists*, he thought. They looked like regular squaddies, and he would have been surprised if these guys had any idea what they were really here for or what had happened over the last few days. If he had to bet, he would lay money that they didn't even have any live ammunition in their weapons. Two guys were working the traffic and another two leaning against the jeep that was parked across the road that made up the checkpoint.

"Well?" he asked the Pleiadian. He had a plan but needed to know where he stood with Blondie.

"I will follow your commands," he replied solemnly. It was clear that the Pleiadian didn't like the idea of killing humans, but he was also resigned to the fact that there was no other way.

"Good. I've got an idea. All you have to do is be ready to react just in case I'm not quick enough, but by the look of this lot, I don't think it'll be a problem," Archie said as Blondie nodded.

Before moving the vehicle forward, he checked that the pistol was good to go and that the silencer was in place. Then he laid the map across his lap and slid the fish knife between its pages. He was ready, he just had to wait for a line of traffic to build up at the checkpoint. He hoped that when he initiated the contact, the people in the cars would panic and start running around, looking for cover, or even better, try to drive through the roadblock...the more confusion, the better.

Several minutes passed before a small convoy of three cars passed them, Archie knew it was time as he pulled in behind the last vehicle. He drove slowly and deliberately as he psyched himself up. His mind raced as he thought about what lay in store; *What if this? What if that?* He tried to calm himself as he realised that the answers to his what if's would be answered no matter how much he obsessed over the questions. He put it all aside as he pulled up to the small line of traffic and stopped the car, he needed to be in the moment, and not thinking of anything else.

As the soldier started talking through the drivers' window of the first car in line, Archie got out with the map in his right hand, his fingertips between the pages, holding the base of the knife's handle. His heart rate went through the roof as he started walking towards the front of the traffic. When he got to the second car back, he slipped in behind it and moved to the curb, heading towards the second squaddie, who wasn't paying any attention whatsoever.

"Yeah, we're doing an exercise, that's why the road's closed." Archie heard the soldier say to the driver, as he got to the back of the first car. At the same time, he felt the *Compulsion* not to initiate the contact. He didn't know why, but his intuition was screaming at him again. He followed the guidance and approached the squaddie on the curb with a big friendly smile on his face.

"Hello mate. What's going on?" Archie asked politely.

"Exercise." The minute the guy opened his mouth, Archie knew that the man was pissed off.

"You don't seem too pleased about it." Archie was using his best conversational tone.

"We're not, mate. They dragged us out of bed at 3am for this. Where do you need to get to?" Although the soldier was pissed off, he was still trying to be helpful. *Shame I might have to put a bullet in your head*, Archie thought.

"We were going to have a look at the Heritage site, up the road there, but it looks like that's out of the question now," he answered in a friendly way. "I guess we'll find a café, have some grub and go home."

"Yeah, sorry. The site is shut for the day. I don't even know why we're here; we can't even do anything around

232

the place anyway, it's protected land. This is nothing but a waste of time." The guy spoke in a tone that made it clear he wasn't a happy camper.

As the squaddie continued to moan, Archie was looking around to see if he could figure out why he had been *Compelled* to refrain from instigating the firefight. There, just on the other side of the jeep... Smithy. Archie couldn't believe his eyes. Jason Smith had been one of Archie's closest friends right up until the man joined the Army twenty years ago. According to Blondie, he was also an Earth Born Pleiadian. They had kept in touch over the years, but with work and family commitments, they weren't as close as they once were. The last time Archie had seen Jason was at least four years ago when he was just about to leave the Army. *Wait, I thought he left...*

Was this synchronicity again, or was it just coincidence? No, it wasn't a coincidence – it couldn't have been. This was all happening for a reason. Jason's eyes locked onto Archie's, it was clear that he had recognised his old friend, but Archie gave a quick shake of his head as if to say, *You don't know me*. Smith got the message and gave the slightest of nods in return.

The difference between Jason and the other soldiers was as clear as day. If not by the clothes they wore but by the way they carried themselves. The others were wearing the standard military garb, while Jason was wearing blue jeans, a black T-shirt, and trainers; then there was the high-powered pistol he had strapped to his leg, that was definitely not standard issue, and neither was the short-barreled rifle in his hands. Archie had known for a long time that his friend had gone into the Special Forces, but he had never expected to see him at work. *Wasn't it against the law to deploy the military in combat roles on the streets of the UK outside of war?* He couldn't remember, and it didn't matter.

"Okay, Dave I'll deal with this," Jase said to the soldier as he approached.

Archie turned his back to the motor and started walking back towards the people carrier as Jason fell into stride alongside him.

"What the fuck are you doing here?" Archie asked, "I thought you were out."

"I got a call from my old C.O saying I had been recalled. This is no exercise, we're really on a terrorist job," he said before adding. "Anyway, what the fuck are *you* doing here?"

"You're not going to believe it, mate, but I'm the one you're looking for," Archie said quietly.

Jason stopped dead, "What? Why?"

"It's a long story, but suffice to say, I'm in the shit. I can tell you it has nothing to do with terrorism." Archie hesitated and debated whether he should tell the truth. "I was on a fishing trip, saw a few ufos. One crashed, I rescued the alien, and now the government and you won't believe this, but the government and their *own* alien cronies are hunting us down. There's a lot more to it, but I haven't got time to explain."

Jason studied Archie's face before saying, "You don't look stoned, have you been drinking?" He apparently thought Archie might have lost his mind. *Why does everyone think I'm stoned whenever I tell them what's going on?* Archie thought before answering his own question. *Probably because of my misspent youth.* After all, he had been a party animal before life caught up with him.

"It's all true, Jase... all of it. Come to the motor, I'll show you something."

As they were walking, Archie heard a rustle in the treeline next to the road. Quietly, he asked Jason if there were any of his mob hiding nearby.

"Yeah," he said in a low voice. "Three blokes from my old unit." They wouldn't have heard what the pair had been saying, but it made Archie feel uneasy knowing that armed men were sitting in the bushes watching them.

"Come to the drivers' side." Archie didn't want to take any chances that they might be overheard. Opening the door to the car, he introduced Jason to the Pleiadian and explained that he was the *alien* that he had rescued from the ship.

"Fuck off, Arch. You're having me on," Jason exclaimed. Archie couldn't blame him; he wouldn't have believed him either.

Looking at Blondie, Archie asked the big man if he could do the same telepathy thing on Jason.

"Okay, then do it," Archie said as Blondie nodded. Turning to his friend, he said, "Shake his hand, Jase. But keep any thoughts you might get inside your head - don't speak aloud." As their hands touched, Blondie took a firm grip, and Archie knew his old friend got the message, as he looked blankly at him.

"What was that?" he said, trying to keep his voice low. "How did you do that?"

After Blondie gave him a quick explanation of the telepathy, Archie started quizzing Jason on the checkpoint; what was the troop numbers, their strength, their level of training, and where they were actually positioned; was their numbers what he could actually see or were there more in the bushes?

"Why?" Jason asked, knowing he didn't want the answer.

"Because I think I'm going to have to kill them to get to the Henge."

"I had a feeling you were going to say that..." Jason thought for a moment, then continued. "I've got some good friends in those trees. We've been through a lot together. I can't just let you kill, them, Arch."

"I can't promise anything, but I will say this; if I can subdue them in a nonlethal way, then I will, but if I have to do it... another way, then..." Archie trailed off, knowing he was pushing his luck, but at the same time, he knew that lying about it might cause his friend to turn his allegiance away from him. He wanted Jason onside, now and in the future, and lying could jeopardise his integrity, so he left the words hanging.

"I'm not sure, but for now, we'll see how it goes," Jason said. He knew that Archie was in the top tier when it came to martial arts and was more than likely to be far better in unarmed combat than even his friends from the unit. He just hoped that Archie didn't have to take them out properly, he wasn't sure he could allow that to happen.

17

Amesbury

Wiltshire

England

"Pretend to be looking at that," Archie re-holstered the knife before passing the map to Blondie. Turning, he said to his old friend, "Go into the treeline and distract your guys. Keep their attention on you, I'll come in from the North and take them from behind, but I'll tell you now, Jase, I'm not fucking about when we have to deal with the checkpoint. We need to get through it fast, and we don't have time to piss about playing nice."

Jason nodded as he started moving towards the treeline. Archie began to walk to the back of the car and shouted back to Blondie that he was just going for a piss in the bushes before they left; all for show of course. He made his way about fifty yards to the North and slipped into the trees.

As he moved slowly forward, Archie was hoping that Jason would do a decent job of distracting his three mates. They were Special Forces, and that meant that they were going to be as hard as nails, and if he didn't do his bit right, he would have to kill them. Archie just couldn't take the chance of any of them getting a round off and alerting the other soldiers in the area.

His heart started pounding as he was stalking through the scrub. The beat in his ears got louder as he found himself getting closer to their position. At about ten yards away, he stopped and slowly squatted down. He could hear them talking as he readied himself for the conflict to come.

"I told you, Smith, the orders are bollocks, mate. We've done plenty of Counter Terrorist jobs and never has anything like this shit happened before. I just don't think that we're here for the reasons we've been told. Something else is going on. Where are the CT team? Where are they? Why call us back? We've all been out for years now... it's unheard of." Archie had no idea who was talking, but two things were crystal clear. One, whoever the speaker was, was talking to Jason. And two, they weren't convinced they had been told the truth.

"Listen, I think you're right, but there's nothing we can do about it. You know what the Regiment are like, you're never really out." This time Archie could tell that the other voice belonged to Jason.

Archie used the distraction of the conversation to start moving forward again. Easing his way closer to the group as quietly and as slowly as he could. Through the shrubs, he could see that they were all squatting down, and the only one facing his direction was his old friend. Jason had done his bit, now it was Archie's turn.

As he edged closer to the men, he held the bowie knife in his right hand, so that the blade was lined back along his forearm. SNAP! A twig broke under his foot, causing the three men to turn around. They saw him instantly.

He had gotten himself into a position that was directly behind the guy in the middle, and as the man tried to bring his weapon up, Archie lunged forward, driving the base of the knife's handle into the man's shoulder, feeling the crunch from the fracture as his collar bone collapsed. He fell backwards and as he did Archie used the momentum to put the sole of his left foot into the face of the guy to the left, knocking him unconscious. He then brought the base of the knife away from the first man's shoulder and forced it into his temple, instantly silencing him. Turning to the last soldier, Archie realised he was too late. The guy had his pistol pointed at his face.

"NO! Drop it Steve – Drop it… NOW!" Jason had his weapon aimed at his comrade. "I'm not fucking around! I know this guy."

"What the fuck is going on here, Smith?" Steve wasn't having any of it as he held firm, weapon steadily pointed at Archie's head.

Slowly the three men started getting to their feet. If Steve were a foot closer, Archie would have had him, but this guy was in the zone; far too switched on to make that kind of mistake.

"He's an old school friend, Steve," Jase said. "I've known him since we were three years old, he's okay."

"O-fucking-kay? Are you taking the piss?" Steve wasn't convinced. "He's just dropped two of the hardest men I've ever met. What the fuck is going on?"

"It's complicated, but I'll tell you this, he's no terrorist. He was in the wrong place at the wrong time, and he ended up with information that... well, let's just say that the government don't want it to get out, and they'll kill to keep it secret. He needs help. They're hunting him down." Jason thought for a moment before speaking again. "Think about it, mate. You said yourself, we were called back under strange circumstances. Well, this is why." Jason paused for a moment. "The rest of the Regiment is probably sitting in ambush, waiting for him at Stonehenge and like us, they'll just follow the orders they're given. And I'll guarantee you this, nobody within the unit will know what he knows."

"Oh yeah? What do you know then, son?" Steve asked Archie, pistol still pointing at his head.

"I know that if he weren't here," Archie said nodding towards Jason, "you three would be dead. *He* told me not to kill you all. But now I'm wondering if that was a good idea. I also know that all this is about information control. I have knowledge that will completely destroy the paradigm that we live in. The world's governments, religions, power elites, and a whole host of other institutions have been forcing us all into living controlled lives..."

"What are you talking about, you fucking prick?" Steve said, jabbing his weapon at Archie as if to emphasise his point.

"Aliens," Archie said, hoping to draw his opponent closer.

Steve took the bait and stepped forward. "What the fuck is he talking about, Smith?" he said. "Is he on drugs?"

"No, I'm afraid not. It looks like he's telling the truth, mate," Jason replied as he kept his own weapon aimed at the back of his friends head. "Come on, Steve put it down and listen."

Archie could see the dilemma Jason was in; on the one hand, he had his longest friend in a position where if he didn't help him, he would probably be killed by government forces, and on the other hand, he might have to kill another one of his best friends to keep the first alive.

"Listen, Steve, I rescued a benevolent alien from a crashed ship, that was shot down by a malevolent race of aliens. This race, the Draco, has been forcing the world's governments to work for them since at least the 1800s. They have to silence me and kill the Pleiadian that I'm trying to save so that they can keep their dirty little secret. This really *is* about information control." Archie took a moment to let Steve digest what he had said, before continuing. "The species that I am helping are trying to guide humanity out of this shit. I honestly don't fully know what the powers that be are doing in all this, but I do know that for the past three days, I've been hunted like a fucking dog for helping someone in an emergency. Come on, even you can see that's not right."

Steve took another step closer; it was his first and last mistake. With his left hand, Archie swiped the barrel of the weapon to the right and turned it back in the direction of his opponent in a wrist lock that forced the weapons release from Steve's grip. In the same movement, Archie smashed the palm of his right hand into Steve's face, putting him on his arse.

"Sorry, Steve, but I had to do that. I couldn't take the chance that you wouldn't kill me." Archie said as he squatted down in front of the shocked soldier. "Everything I've told you is true - every word of it. Now if you stay still and play the game, everything will work out for you, and you'll walk away from this intact, but if you make a move on either of us, I'll kill you without hesitation."

Standing back up, Archie pulled the silenced pistol from his waistband and pointed it at Steve as he moved back several feet. "What do you want to do now?" he asked Jason. "Do you want to come with us or what?"

It was the first time he'd ever seen Jason suffering from indecisiveness, and if the situation weren't so dangerous, he would have taken the piss out of his old friend and slaughtered him with laughter and ridicule. "I can't really see any choice. I think I have to come, but what about him?" Jase nodded down at Steve.

"You tell me what kind of man he is?" Archie asked. "Can he be trusted?"

"Honestly, he's a good bloke and an even better soldier," Jason started. "I really think that once he sees what's really going on, he'll side with us. I think we should take him with us."

Archie thought about it for a moment. He hadn't even contemplated the prospect of taking Steve along;

he'd only been thinking about whether or not to put a bullet in his head.

"What do you think, Steve? Do you want me to knock you out and leave you here with your mates, or do you want to come with us and wake up to what's really going on in the world?" Archie asked, trying to gauge the soldiers' reactions.

Steve was clearly thinking about the situation, and after a moment or so gave his answer. "I've said from the moment I got back to Hereford that something was off – it just didn't feel right. The orders were all wrong. Nothing made sense. There was no paperwork for the recall, and we were kept away from the regulars. That shit is unheard of. So, now I think that maybe, just maybe you might be on to something. But, *aliens*? That bit, I'm struggling with, but I *would* like to find out the truth, so yeah, I'm in."

"Okay, fine, but be warned, it's going to get messy. A lot of your old mates *are* going to try to kill us," Archie said, trying to put things into perspective.

"I'm in; if it's them or me? It's going to be them," Steve said without hesitation. Archie wasn't sure where the soldiers' loyalty would be when the rounds started flying, but nothing ventured, nothing gained. He would make sure that Steve wouldn't get a weapon until he'd seen the Draco first. Once that had happened, the man would have no doubt about Archie's honesty.

After giving Steve a proper search, and tying the two unconscious men up, they made their way back the people carrier. Archie was amused to see that Blondie was still looking at the map book, trying unsuccessfully, to look inconspicuous. He looked as guilty as hell. Archie made his way to the passenger side and told the Pleiadian to get in the back with Steve. Jason took the front passenger seat, and Archie got in behind the wheel.

The new plan was simple; drive up to the checkpoint, Jase would speak to the soldiers and get them through. They would then drive all the way to the Stones. There was a real chance that the group could make it to the heritage site without shooting up the checkpoints, but that didn't stop Archie preparing for the eventuality that their ruse wouldn't work.

As he introduced Blondie to Steve, Archie gave the Pleiadian specific instructions to beat the shit out of the soldier if he so much as looked at the men working the checkpoint in the wrong way. Blondie offered his hand to Steve in greeting, and as they shook, Archie knew by the look on Steve's face, that he was getting the message as the big man spoke to him telepathically. Steve's eyes flickered and rolled up into his head for a moment.

"What the…?" Steve said as the handshake broke. "Did he just… I mean…" his speech fell away as he tried to make sense of what had just happened. After a moment of contemplation to make sense of what just happened, he made it clear that they would get no problems from him. Although Archie believed what the soldier had said, he wasn't ready to trust him enough to hand over a weapon just yet.

When Blondie had used telepathy on him, it was in the form of mind to mind speech. However, Archie wondered if the communication could be done in the manner of showing images, as though the recipient was being *shown* stuff, rather than told things. He asked the Pleiadian as they started moving towards the checkpoint.

"I cannot show them anything, I can only communicate in terms of speech," Blondie replied. "I have told them what has happened so far and of the probable invasion by the Draconian's." Archie mulled it over as they approached the roadblock, and came to a conclusion that it seemed plausible that the two men understood the situation better because of the manner of how they were told… telepathically. After all, it wasn't every day that a person could pull off a magic trick like that.

Pulling up at the checkpoint, Jason opened the window and informed the soldier that he had received orders to move up to the staging area. It was a plausible situation. After all, the Special Forces were on a completely different command structure and communications system to the regular army. The guard just nodded, completely disinterested as he signalled them through, and directed them to the off-ramp for the A303.

The cloud cover was thick, and it had started to rain again. As Archie pulled the vehicle on to the road, there was a clap of thunder, causing himself and Blondie to look at each other knowingly. They had just under two miles to get to the Stones, and it wasn't going to take long to get there. Archie wanted to floor it and get there as soon as possible, but instead, he kept the speed within the limit and continued steadily towards their target. He didn't want to attract unwanted attention to their vehicle any more than necessary.

As Archie drove, the group saw a mass of complacent and disinterested soldiers milling around personnel carriers. But as they got closer to the Stones, they started to see men in black, carrying fancy weapons. This lot were anything, but uninterested; they were well switched on, and Archie thought they would be spotted any minute as the Special Forces watched the strange vehicle pass by. A moment later and a thunderous roar emanated from the sky, which took attention away from them as all eyes looked up. There, sitting just in the cloud, was the underside of a massive Arrowhead shaped craft.

"What the fuck is that?" asked Jase with no hint of panic. His voice carried concern, but no panic.

"That is a part of what we're up against, mate. It's a Draconian Battle Cruiser," Archie replied.

"Jesus H Christ!" Steve had seen it too. "I think it's time you gave me a fucking weapon," he demanded. A moment later and all the cogs seemed to fall into place for him. "It all makes sense now. Jase, did you meet anyone when we got back to Hereford? I didn't. The only person I spoke to was the C.O, and I was kept in isolation until he teamed me up with you and the other two. I didn't even have to sign any paperwork for the recall, and I know that's SOP. I fucking knew something was off. I've never trusted that wanker!"

Jason sat for a moment, thinking. "Yeah, same here. I had a feeling that slimy bastard was up to something dodgy when he said there were no forms to fill in for the recall. Now that I think about it, he's the only person who knows we're even here, and that makes me think that we're expendable. No, more than that, I don't think we were walking away from this. He was going to make sure we got slotted." Jason paused for a second. "If we get the chance, we need to put a couple of rounds into his head so that we don't get any problems if we get out of this."

Archie looked at his new team member in the rear-view mirror, and although he felt that the man was on-side, he wasn't ready to fully trust him just yet, "When the time comes, you'll have your rifle, Steve."

"Arch how are we going to deal with that?" Jase asked, pointing to the clouds.

"Hopefully we won't need to," Archie replied. "Apparently, his lot are going to sort it out," he added, nodding in Blondie's direction.

They were about a minute out from the Stones, when the first rounds of incoming started hitting the people carrier. Archie swung the steering wheel to the left and gunned the accelerator. He drove the vehicle straight through the chain-link fence, and into the field. All hell broke loose as bullets were pinging, and thudding into the bodywork. The side windows started smashing, and huge cracks and holes appeared in the front and back screens. They were all trying to get as low as possible, looking for as much cover as they could find. The group had found themselves in a nightmare situation, that they knew it was only going to get worse.

Archie pushed the vehicle hard towards the Stones but was horrified to see a military jeep appear from behind the megalithic rocks and open fire from a roof mounted turret. They were driving headlong into some serious trouble, but they had to push on; they couldn't do anything else. The incoming intensified as Jason kicked out the front windscreen. He brought his rifle up and took aim, firing two rounds at a time - double tapping at the enemy. Steve was screaming for a weapon from the back seat, Archie didn't have a choice anymore, he had to take a chance and hope the man did the right thing.

"Blondie, give Steve his rifle," Archie shouted over the noise.

No more than a few seconds later, the booms of Steve's .50 Calibre Sniper rifle were going off next to Archie's left ear. The sound was so bad that it felt like it was causing Archie's brain to shake inside his skull. Every shot caused him to jump and recoil from the noise; the only consolation was that at least the fire Steve was putting down range was effective.

A second jeep appeared from the other side of the Stones, and Steve instantly switched to firing from his side window. Archie welcomed the slight relief; his ears were ringing, and his lungs were full of cordite. Jase was tapping away like a man possessed, shooting with practised skill at anything that moved. Even Blondie was hanging out of the side, firing his little remote control. From the back of the vehicle, Archie heard a whine, like a defibrillator charging, then a massive blast of energy hit the first jeep, causing it to rise up into the air and explode into flames.

"We need to get into the Henge... we'll have a better chance of holding them off from there," Jason shouted.

The man was absolutely right, but it was easier said than done. The enemy had the same idea, and they looked well embedded behind the giant rocks. Suddenly Archie lost power; the engine must have taken catastrophic damage. As they were coming to a stop, it became evident that it was time to ditch the motor and go for the Stones on foot. They couldn't stay where they were, they had to go for it, or they were dead.

"Grab the weapons and go for the upturned jeep," Archie shouted. The destroyed vehicle was half-way between them and the Stones and was the only cover they had.

The people carrier was still grinding to a halt as the four men jumped out and started running for the cover of the flaming wreck. Archie and Blondie were running like greyhounds, but Steve and Jase were in combat mode as they fired and manoeuvred their way steadily towards the cover. From what Archie could tell, the two men hit with every shot they fired. Now that they were out of the moving people carrier, the pair found their marks with ease as they dropped the driver and the gunner in the second jeep, causing it to veer off.

Blondie reached the burning wreck a fraction ahead of Archie and started opening the weapons bag. As the Earth Born piled into the cover, he pulled out the LMG and opened up on the Stones... hit or miss, he didn't care. He just needed to get the enemy's heads down and provide covering fire for Steve and Jase to reach the jeep. Blondie resumed shooting as soon as his remote recharged. The sheer weight of fire they were putting into the Stones was immense, but it still felt like an age for the two guys to join them at the jeep, though in reality, it was probably no more than a few seconds.

"How many left?" Steve asked, looking over at Jason as he crouched behind the jeep.

"I think there's only a couple left in the stones," he said through heavy breaths. "Come on, lets fucking do this," he added as he started making his way around the left side of the jeep. Steve moved out around the right side. They both stepped forward, fire and manoeuvre – fire and manoeuvre.

"CLEAR! – CLEAR!" they shouted a few seconds later, as they made their way through the Henge.

Archie and Blondie started moving up, but both dropped to the ground as a massive clap of thunder rumbled from above. Looking up, they saw two Draconian fighter Darts heading their way.

"INCOMING!" Archie shouted as loud as he could.

Both, the Pleiadian and the Earth Born got to their feet and started running for the Stones, but as Archie came around the jeep, he noticed a couple of rocket launchers on the ground. He slung the LMG over his shoulder and grabbed them both, hanging one over his other shoulder and holding the other. He got the flash of information but never got the chance to fire one. The ground around him erupted like he was in the middle of an earthquake as the

Darts fired small beams of orange light at him. He tried to run for the cover of the Stones, but he just couldn't move fast enough. A blast hit the ground less than four feet away, and he was thrown through the air, landing on his right side with a big thud. His ears were ringing, and his head was spinning as he tried to figure out where he was. Blasts of energy weapons were raining down around him, but he just couldn't work out what was going on. Everything seemed to be in slow motion.

He could just about make out someone shouting, "MAN DOWN! MAN DOWN," but nothing would compute… he was fucked.

Something grabbed the back of Archie's collar, and he slid along the ground. Steve's rifle was slung across his back, along with one of the launchers, as he pulled Archie backwards toward the Stones.

"Blondie, fucking sort him out," Steve shouted as he dropped Archie behind one of the giant rocks, before pulling his rifle around his body and into his shoulder as he resumed pouring fire into the enemy ranks.

As the Pleiadian got to him, Archie's head began to stop spinning, and his hearing returned. The nausea he'd felt had started to subside, and in the same instant, he remembered what was happening as the blasts from above stopped.

18

Stone Circle

Amesbury

Wiltshire, England

"Why have they stopped firing?" Jase asked.

"They cannot destroy this place. It was built for Spiritual purposes by the Annunaki... a mighty race. If the Draco damage or destroy this Circle of Stones, they will bring the full wrath of its builders upon the Draconian Empire," Blondie said. "That is a war the reptilians could never win."

From his seated position, Archie could see the Darts descending as more streamed out of the Battle Cruiser. They would be on the ground in no time; two had already landed and were starting to spill warriors onto the field.

"REINFORCEMENTS – CONTACT NORTH!" Steve shouted as he opened up with Archie's LMG.

Looking around the corner, Archie could see human squaddies coming from all directions. His little band of fighters were in serious trouble. Flicking his eyes to the landed Darts, he was immediately filled with dread as more and more Draco emptied out onto the grass.

"What the fuck are they?" Jason had seen them too.

"Just fucking kill them" Archie shouted back before turning to Blondie, "Where are your people?"

"There," he said, pointing to the Eastern sky.

Archie looked in the direction that Blondie had indicated to see at least twenty-five Lightships coming in. About three-quarters of them headed straight for the Battle Cruiser and immediately started attacking it with white coloured energy weapons. The others took on the Dart fighters that had now started pouring out of the mothership. The Pleiadian craft was a welcome sight, but it meant little to the fight on the ground.

Archie grabbed the 417 from the holdall and started popping off rounds into the human enemy as Blondie set about hitting the Draco. Jason and Steve were shooting at everything. The game was on.

Incoming rounds were pinging off of the rocks and thudding into the dirt around them. The four defenders each had a sector to cover, Archie was taking West, Blondie North, Steve South, and Jase had East. It made sense for each of them to cover a particular arc, but there were just too many enemy ground forces coming in. It seemed as though they had deployed the entire British Army.

Just when Archie thought it couldn't get any worse, came that dreaded noise; rota blades. Archie turned to see two blacked out helicopters inbound from the South, towards them. *It's squeaky bum time*, he thought.

"Steve – missiles!" he shouted.

"On it."

As he turned back to his sector, Archie was hit in the chest and fell onto his back. He frantically ran his hands over his body to see where the bullet had hit. The hissing snarl made him realise that he hadn't been hit by an incoming round, but rather, a reptilian warrior.

"THEY'RE IN THE LINE! THEY'RE IN THE LINE!" Archie shouted as he got to his feet to take it on.

The giant gecko started running in an effort to get to him before he could raise the 417... it was too late. Archie put five rounds into its face and chest. As the thing face planted into the dirt, Archie pulled out the bowie knife and forced the blade straight into the back of its neck. No sooner had he done it than another Draconian appeared from behind the rock. It started shooting with everything it had. Archie dived into the cover of one of the smaller stones as Blondie gave the fucker a few good blasts from the remote. It was hurt but didn't stop... it charged fast. It apparently didn't like the way Archie had striped up his mate.

As the reptile reached the stone that the Earth Born was hiding behind, Archie rolled out and away from it. He came out of the roll and instantly started putting round after round into it as fast as he could pull the trigger. It took a good ten bullets at close range to put the bastard down. This angry lizard was one hard bastard. As the Draconian hit the ground, Archie put another two rounds into its head for good measure. Afterwards, he changed the mag and got back into position behind the larger rocks to cover his arc.

Things were really heating up as wave after wave of both human and alien enemy poured into their fields of fire. They were well passed squeaky bum time; now, they were at the anal gape stage.

FFWHOOOSH!

Steve had fired off a missile at one of the helicopters. Hitting the mark, the chopper exploding mid-air before it fell to the ground. Jase was covering his mates arc for the few seconds that it took for Steve to get his shot off and sort himself out.

"MISSILE – MISSILE!" Steve was shouting at Archie, but he didn't have a clue what he was talking about; he didn't understand why Steve was saying it to him. "GIVE-ME-THE-FUCKING-MISSILE!"

Archie knew that Steve wanted another missile, but he didn't understand why he was asking him for it. A few seconds later it didn't matter anyway as Blondie dropped the second chopper with a big blast from the remote. At that point, Archie got back into position and noticed that the other launcher was on the ground where Steve had dropped him after he'd been floored from the Dart attack earlier. It must have been over his shoulder or something as Steve dragged him into the cover of the Stones. He couldn't quite remember if the thing had been attached to him or not, but it was irrelevant anyway; the choppers were down.

As Archie resumed firing, it was obvious that Steve had opened up with his .50 again, the noise was deafening. They were all running low on ammunition, and Archie decided that it was time for him to switch to an M4, there were several magazines for those. He saw no point in using the last of the ammo for the 417 on targets close in... and the enemy *was* close now.

The fighting intensified for around fifteen minutes before there was a lull in the battle. It was time to take stock of the situation and count the rounds they had left. The four men gathered in the centre of the stone circle and knelt with their backs to each other, facing outwards so that they could still cover their arcs of fire should the fight begin again, all with the exception of Jason...his arc was being covered by two of the others while he sorted out the weapons. After he had figured out what they had left, he distributed it among the group. Looking at the small stockpile, it quickly became evident that they were in serious trouble. There just wasn't enough in their little armoury to continue the fight much longer. Each man had an M4 and two spare mags. There was one box of rounds for the LMG and Archie had a mag and a half for the 417, while both Jase and Steve had a mag left for their own weapons, and they had one missile. Even with the grenades, of which Archie still had one frag and two stings, they weren't going to last long.

"Can you contact your people?" Archie asked Blondie. "We're going to need them to engage the ground forces, or we're dead."

"They will not attack the humans, you know this," he replied.

"What if the request was to come from me?" Archie wondered just how far he could push what Blondie had told him as to why he had been incarnated as an Earth Born. If what he had been told was true, then there might have been a possibility that he could get the Pleiadian air cover to assist in the ground battle.

"I do not know. Probably not, but I will ask," Blondie said after a moment of thought.

"You do that, because if they don't help, we're fucked!" he said, stating the obvious. "All we need is for them to push and hold the enemy back far enough so that one of your ships can come in and get you off the ground."

"What about you three?" Blondie's voice was dripping with concern as he looked around the group.

"We'll go for that jeep and fight our way out while the enemy is occupied with the air cover," Archie said, not particularly wanting to get on any spaceships. No, he'd rather keep his feet squarely on the ground.

There may have been a lull in the fighting on the ground, but the battle in the sky was still raging. It reminded Archie of a scene from a second world war documentary. There was a significant dog fight going on overhead. Even from his minimal knowledge of aerial combat, his education being none, he could see that the Lightships were an uneven match for the Darts. The Draco were losing ships left, right and centre. It seemed that every time they tried to fire at the Pleiadian ships, their target would blink out and reappear in a different location, with their weapons trained and shooting at their attacker. The Draconian Darts apparently weren't able to do the same and seemed to use a more conventional means of propulsion which left them exposed to incoming fire. Archie was amazed at the capabilities of the Lightships, and he was resolved to find out how they did it; if he survived, that is.

"They will not fight the humans, Archie," Blondie said, clearly frustrated. He'd been in a telepathic argument with the Commander of the Pleiadian fighter wing.

"Why not?" Archie asked, his anger rising.

"Because it is a direct violation of Galactic Law. I informed them that it was your wish. I even expressed that it was your orders, but they still will not attack."

Archie needed to think of a way to change this situation, but the answer was escaping him. It would have to wait, as his attention was pulled away from his trail of thought when another clap of thunder sounded in the middle distance. Looking in the direction of the sound, he saw a second Battle Cruiser dipping below the cloud cover. The enemy was bringing in reinforcements. This wasn't just bad; it was outright shit!

"We need to get the fuck out of here, Arch!" Jase shouted.

Looking around, the only option he could see was the jeep. The only problem was that they would probably be dead before they even got to it. As Archie's mind raced to try to find the answer, Jason started giving orders to Steve. It hit Archie like a bullet to the back, Rank.

"Oi Blondie, if I'm meant to be one of your lot, what was my rank before the incarnation?" Archie shouted.

"High Traton of the Tardran Armies; Counter Insurgency Commander, why?" Blondie answered.

"Did I outrank the Commander of the fighter wing?"

"I see what you're saying... yes. The rank you held was senior to that of ship Traton. They are to yield to Insurgency Traton's will. Although, overall fleet Traton's could override or countermand any Insurgency orders" Blondie knew what Archie was planning, and he liked it.

"Is there a fleet Traton here?"

"No, not to my knowledge," the Pleiadian replied. "They usually command from the homeworld."

"Right, get back on to the Ship Traton, and tell him that *I* am in command and that *I* am ordering him to engage ground targets. If they don't, then the Earth Born mission is doomed to fail. This is not a request, it's a fucking order!" Archie said. He was beginning to accept the role that had been bestowed upon him, and if he were right, the Pleiadian's operating the ships above would have to take the orders he gives and carry them out. "Tell those idiots that we'll all die, and the entire Pleiadian mission on Earth will be at risk." *Let's see them pick the fucking bones out of that*, he thought as he turned his attention back to firing his weapon.

The enemy had started another assault on the Stones, and this time they seemed far more switched on and geared up for it. There was no more blindly running into the defenders' arcs of fire. They were strategically moving with smoke screens and covering fire. There were too many to fend off; it was only a matter of time before Archie and his team were slaughtered.

No sooner had Archie started firing, than the Lightships above opened up on the ground targets. "Fuck me, that was fast," he shouted to Blondie, over the noise.

"You wanted them to hear you. Between the power of the Stones, and your consciousness being opened, it was enough for the Traton to receive your orders," Blondie shouted back between shots. "I did not have time to contact them before we come under fire." If what he was saying was true, it meant that Archie had a link to the Pleiadian's while he was at sites such as this.

As he was firing, Archie heard a voice in his head, apparently from the Traton above, saying that he would answer to the Council for ordering them to break Galactic Law. To say he was surprised was an understatement, he was flabbergasted. *I'm in the middle of a major fire-fight, to save one of* their *people and* their *mission, and I'm having a telepathic row with some muppet about the rights and wrongs of war.* He couldn't help the response he thought back to the Traton. *Fuck off, I'll deal with the Council if I live long enough. But for now, just do what you're fucking told!* He didn't have time for this shit, he had a battle to fight.

Eventually, with enemy numbers dramatically reduced and even though, for the moment they only had the Draco to contend with, Archie and his team still didn't have enough ammunition to take them on. They needed to get Blondie off the ground and get out of there before they were overrun.

"Blondie, it's time to get a ship down and get you out of here!" Archie shouted as the big Pleiadian was shooting the crap out of a Draco warrior that had gotten too close.

"STEVE! STEVE!" Jason was excited about something. "There's the C.O... 3 o'clock... on the jeep. Take his head off!"

The officer was surveying the battlefield through binoculars, as Steve swung the .50 into position and pulled the trigger. The man's head exploded like a watermelon as the large round hit. "Now no-one knows we were here!" Steve shouted back to Jason.

It was a nasty way for someone to die, but Archie didn't feel bad. In fact, he was relieved because it meant that Jason and Steve were in the clear. He had been concerned that when this was all over, the pair would get nabbed, tortured and executed. By the sound of it, the now dead Commanding Officer that had recalled them to duty had been the only person that knew who they were, and now that his brains were spread across the field, he wasn't about to tell anyone else.

19

Stone Circle

Amesbury

Wiltshire, England

The feeling of relief that Jason and Steve were in the clear was beginning to dissipate as a Lightship appeared out of thin air. It came down behind the monument, slightly to the South. It was time to get big bollocks out of here, but no sooner had the ship materialised, than the enemy increased the pressure of their assault. There were at least fifty squaddies and Draco warriors moving forward, all firing, all intent on killing Archie and his little crew.

Archie and his team were covering each other as they worked their way to the Lightship. Fire and move… fire and move… click, click, click… *FUCK,* he was out of ammo.

"I'm out, I'm out!" Archie shouted as he ran.

It was the same situation with everyone, except Blondie and his little remote. The fight was going hand to hand. Shit was about to get real… too real!

"Blondie, get on the ship and fuck off," he shouted before telling the others to run for the jeep.

As the Pleiadian started for the ship, a ramp or door opened from the underside of the rim of the saucer. Archie saw the big man jump in and turn back. There was fear and concern on Blondie's face as he looked to see what was happening on the ground. He was aboard, and even though he knew that he and the other two were likely to die, Archie took comfort in that.

By the time the three men made it to the outer rim of Stones, it was clear they weren't going to make it to the jeep, the lizards were right on top of them. Archie grabbed the Katana from the holdall and moved out towards the vehicle, swinging, chopping, slicing and stabbing everything in front of him. If he was going down, he was going down fighting. Jason and Steve were following his lead with their combat knives.

Archie was about five yards from the jeep, when he heard a scream from behind, the likes of which clearly indicated severe pain. Turning, he saw that Steve was down, a particularly large reptile on top of him, swiping away with its massive claws. In the same instant, there was a hiss to his right. Without looking, he pirouetted in that direction and swiped his blade down hard and fast. He felt good contact through the sword, and he knew that he had hit his target. Without stopping to see who or what he had striped, he headed back towards Steve, who was still on his back trying to fight the lizard off, but he had no chance... the thing was huge. Archie brought the Katana back and with a horizontal blow, took the reptilians head clean off. Looking down, he saw that Steve had suffered some horrific and severe injuries. He knew immediately that the man was going to die. He had seen enough trauma in his life to recognise fatal wounds when he saw them.

"Leave me, leave me, I'm finished," Steve said weakly.

From the right, Archie heard gunfire. Turning, he saw Jason coming towards them with his pistol in his hands and a flash looking rifle over his shoulder. Behind him, he saw where his old friend had gotten the new weaponry; there was a human soldier lying on the ground, covered in blood.

"Leave me, Arch," Steve said again.

"Shut up you prick! I got you into this, and I'm not leaving you or anyone else behind," Archie said as he dragged Steve back towards the megalithic structure.

Bypassing the outer ring of Stones, Archie heaved the fallen man to the inner circle and laid him in as much cover as he could find. On the way in he noticed that the Lightship had gone, and now that he had stopped with Jason covering them, shooting at anything that moved, he saw that the aerial battle was over. There were no Pleiadian ships to be seen, they had all gone.

Looking around, and trying to weigh up their options as Jason tossed him the pistol, Archie realised there *were* no options. There was nowhere to go, and they were on their own. He knew that as soon as Jase was out of ammo, they were dead men. But for now, they were still in the battle, and as long as he drew breath, he was going to fight. *Better to die on my feet, than live on my knees.*

As he brought his eyes down from the heavens, Archie saw a squaddie behind Jason, lining up a shot. Reflexively bringing the pistol up, he put a round through the enemy's forehead. The bullet must have passed Jason's face by less than two inches. He turned to Archie, brought his rifle up and did exactly the same thing, hitting someone or something behind him.

"We're not going to last much longer, mate," Jase said, resigned to the fact that there just wasn't anything more they could do.

They literally sat there shooting until the weapons were dry, then that was it… they waited to die. As he sat there, Archie started thinking about his family; Lucy, the kids, of all the things he was going to miss. Not seeing them grow into adults, getting their first jobs or having their first drink in a pub. He was thinking of how they would take the news of his death or if they'd even be told.

"NO, Fuck this!" Archie said. "We're not dying today!" he was pissed off at the irony of getting killed because he'd done the right thing.

Enemy soldiers started to pour into the Stones, and as they did, Jason and Archie got to their feet and fought hard, with a ferocity that scared even himself; and he was the one doing it. They had managed to take out a good number each, but as soon as the Draco came in, it was over… they were prisoners. That moment of realisation was extraordinarily intense and even emotional. They were caught, and there was nothing they could do but accept the kick-in that they were currently receiving. The blows rained all over Archie's body hard and fast. He tried to protect his head and face, but it was impossible. He felt his jaw crack under the weight of a reptilian punch, his mouth filled with broken teeth and blood. He was struggling to breathe, as his nose caved across his face. He could only hope they wanted them alive, and the beating was just punishment for killing their lizard friends.

Archie tried to keep tabs on Jason, but it was impossible, there was just too much violence, and he lost sight of his old friend almost the instant the brawl started. One particularly hard blow had his head spinning.

After what seemed like an hour's worth of brutal punishment, it all stopped. Archie just lay there spitting teeth, blood and snot, as he tried desperately to get his breath back. The dizziness made him vomit. He knew he was in a bad way when every time he tried to lift his head to look around to see where the other two were, he was sick again. In the end, he gave up trying to find the other's and just laid there, breathing heavily, trying to calm down.

There was some conversation going on between the two enemy factions, but Archie couldn't make out what they were saying. He was just glad of the respite. They left him lying there for what felt like half an hour. Eventually, he got control of his breathing and the spinning in his head began to subside.

He looked up to see that Steve had been left alone during the beating, he was in the same position that Archie had left him after dragging him into cover. Jason though, looked just how Archie felt; like death warmed up. The three men were all still conscious, which was a good sign. He made eye contact with both of them and gave them a wink through his bruised and swollen eye. Their return of the gesture meant that they were still with it. That was *definitely* a good sign, and he felt an instant boost of morale.

Two Draconian warriors grabbed Jason and Archie by the neck and dragged them to their feet. Their hands were forced to their heads and held in place as a squaddie searched them. While this was happening, Archie heard someone say, "Do we know who these people are?"

"No, Sir." The answer boosted Archie's morale even more.

Archie, stand by; when it happens, be fast. At first, he thought he was losing his mind, it took a moment for him to realise that the voice was Blondies. He'd contacted him telepathically.

He was still trying to figure out if what he'd heard was real or if it was just his imagination getting the better of him when it happened. Approximately twenty saucers appeared from nowhere and immediately started firing energy weapons at both the ground and air forces, giving no quarter. In the same instant, Archie kicked out, hitting the soldier in front of him in the groin and instantly dropping him. At the same time, he bent his arms tight and turned in a fast spin; first to the left, then the right, using his elbows to give two punishing blows to the Draconian behind him. This forced it to let go of Archie's right hand, and as he did so, the Earth Born stepped back into the lizard's personal space, brought his elbow down and forced it as hard as he could into its ribs, causing the creature to jolt forward. Archie now had the enemy's right hand in his left and pulled it over his right shoulder, pushed his hip into its body and pulled the reptile over him, sending the bastard crashing to the ground in front of him. The second it hit the dirt; Archie started kicking its face in... only stopping when the thing ceased moving.

Looking around, he saw that Jase was having it too, booting the shit out of another reptile. The enemy had scattered, trying to escape the Pleiadian fire. The Earth Born were back in the fight. Archie grabbed a rifle that had been dropped and opened fire, shooting the bastards in the back as they ran from the Stones. With the enemy beyond the outer ring, Archie looked back to see that Blondie was at the bottom of the ramp of a hovering Lightship.

"Come, quickly," he shouted to the men.

"Jase, we're off, you cover, I'll carry Steve" Archie yelled over the sound of weapons fire.

Switching the fire selector to full auto, Jason let rip as Archie got Steve up onto his shoulder and started towards the saucer. He wasted no time passing the injured man up to Blondie at the bottom of the ramp, before jumping up himself. Once in, he turned and covered Jason's approach. The opening closed the instant the last man was inside.

"Where's the Traton?" Archie asked the big man, murmuring through his broken jaw, "Take me to him." Not only was he well hyped up, but he was also hurt as well. They might be in the relative safety of the ship, but this wasn't over yet.

They left the other two humans in the hands of the Pleiadian crew and made their way through the ship, Blondie leading the way. Again, just as it did on the crashed ship where this all began, the inside of the craft seemed far more massive than it looked from the outside. It was something that had boggled Archie's mind.

"Why do your ships seem bigger on the inside than they look from outside?" the Earth Born asked through a mumble.

"We use an alternate reality drive, which can be used to create a larger interior," Blondie said in his usual low tone. The explanation of the alternate reality drive was fascinating, and Archie found himself wanting to know more, but there was something more pressing at hand that needed to be dealt with. But Blondie's voice told Archie that the big man was concerned about what he intended to do when he met the ships Traton.

Turning through a door off the main hall, they entered the control room. Archie was met by a tall Pleiadian. At over six feet tall, with platinum coloured hair, the man introduced himself as the Group Traton Aldar. As Archie shook hands, he asked where the weapons systems were.

"Why do you want the weapons?" the Traton asked, already knowing the answer.

"Because I'm going to kill everything around the Stones," Archie replied as a matter of fact.

"I would protest, but I know that would not change your mind, would it?" There was resignation in the Traton's voice.

"Absolutely not," Archie said, his tone dripping venom. "Not unless you fucking want some as well?" he snarled, ready to smack the ship's commander in the mouth. "They have to die for the future security of anything we might do on Earth from here on." That wasn't the reason at all, not even close - he wanted revenge, nothing more; just some kind of payback. He felt terrible for his threatening behaviour to a man who had without a doubt, just saved his life, but he couldn't take the chance that anyone on the ground could identify him or his friends and bring the war to his doorstep. No, he had to end it here and now.

Traton Aldar led Archie to a holographic work station with a chair, or more appropriately, a couch in front of it. The thing was a wraparound affair, similar to a seat that you would find in a racing car; however, this was more like a wraparound bed. The operator laid in it, and the thing moulded itself to the form of the person using it. The holographic display had a reticule within it. His instruction was to look at the target, tracking of the eyes would align the targeting system, and *think* fire. Basically, the system worked on thought projection. If he thought short burst, the weapons would fire in short bursts. If he thought continuous burst or *Beam* fire, it would unleash a constant *Beam* of energy at the target... simple. Once an enemy target was locked, the system would calculate whether or not it was moving through the operator's eye movements and thought patterns, then automatically adjust to ensure the blast would hit home.

Once he had settled on the couch, Archie asked the Traton for a continual flypast until he said otherwise. He was amazed at how responsive the targeting system actually was; the reticule followed his eyes exactly. He lined the sights up on a jeep... *FIRE!* Nothing, all that happened was a noise sounded, like an alarm clock.

"What happened?" he asked, looking over at Traton Aldar.

"The Phased Reality Drive is still engaged," he answered. "It means that although we can see the enemy, we are not in the same reality as them, they cannot see us. But we cannot fire on them until we re-phase into the same reality as the target."

"So that's how you can appear and disappear." Archie was starting to understand. "You can literally wink out of this reality to another, target the enemy and reappear firing, then wink out again before they can target you. Clever"

"In essence, yes," Aldar replied. "We are about to re-phase you will hear a tone that will indicate that you can open fire."

As he said it, the tone sounded, and green lighting bordered the workstation. Archie targeted and thought fire repeatedly. The weapons response was as impressive as the targeting. The Lightship zigzagged over the Heritage site as he blasted everything but the Stones themselves. After three passes, nothing on the ground was left moving, and he had destroyed every vehicle he could see, melting them all to slag.

"Traton Aldar, that's it. We're done here" Archie said with relief. "Thank you for your assistance." It was time to go home.

Epilogue

Pleiadian Lightship

Earth

Sol System

As Archie climbed out of the weapons couch, and with the adrenalin dissipating from his body, he felt every ache and pain. The beating he had received had been savage, and now he was really feeling it. He stood like an old man, pained and decrepit. No sooner had he straightened his body, than Jason came through the door to the command room; he looked exactly how Archie felt, limping, swollen and covered in blood. He needed medical attention... they all did. Archie's mind instantly went to Steve. He was almost dead while they were on the ground, his injuries undoubtedly fatal.

"How's Steve?" he asked, fully expecting to be told he was dead.

"He's alive," Jase answered. "He's in their med bay, and they're working on him." Archie felt relieved at the news as he limped towards his old friend.

The two men met in the middle of the deck and hugged, an embrace that said it all. Neither of them had believed they were going to survive what had happened. Yet, here they were, battered, bleeding and bruised, but they *were* alive.

"They're all dead," Archie said, "we're safe."

"Good," Jase replied as he looked around the room. "Are we going somewhere?" he asked, nodding to one of the holographic displays.

"Er, Traton Aldar, where are we going?" Archie asked as he saw stars zipping through the screens.

"Erra" Aldar replied. "We cannot chance taking you home, it is not safe. We have detected many Draconian ships around the planet; several lying in wait to try and detect our electromagnetic signature. They will attempt to destroy us should we appear. We will need to wait until they have resumed normal status. Only then will it be safe enough to return you to your homes." He glanced at the holo-display before continuing. "Besides, your other friend will need to be treated on Erra. His wounds are far too serious to be healed aboard this vessel. The reptilian venom was injected directly into his organs. He *will* die unless we can get him to the medical facilities on the homeworld."

Archie thought for a moment, he wanted to tell Aldar to go fuck himself and take them home, but he knew that Steve would have no chance on Earth. He had experienced the effects of the venom himself, and in his case, it was only injected into his bloodstream through wounds to his face, so he knew intuitively how serious Steve's injuries would be. He had to allow the Traton to do what needed to be done to keep the man alive, or at least give him the best possible chance of survival. After all, Steve did abandon everything he knew to help the Earth Born get the Pleiadian to his people. Archie couldn't leave him now. Besides, visiting an alien world would be an experience that he might never have the opportunity to take again. The more he thought about it, the more it made sense. Going to the Pleiades meant that he might be able to learn more about the alien factions trying to dominate Earth. There was even the possibility that he could garner some method or means to fight against it. All he knew was what Blondie had told him, and if that information was correct, his role wasn't finished. That knowledge brought with it a need for more intelligence and more resources.

Realising he needed to let Lucy know that he wouldn't be coming home, he had Aldar arrange to have the comms adapted to allow him to make a phone call. The conversation with her was a short and emotional affair. Less than thirty minutes ago, he'd thought he'd never see her or hear her voice again. He explained that he would be away for at least a few more weeks, and he would be home when it was safe. The phone call lasted no more than five minutes, but to Archie, it felt like a lifetime. It ended with a tearful "See ya later" and as much as he wanted to keep talking, he couldn't. The ship was already several solar systems away, communication systems were reaching the limit of their range, and there was nothing he could do about it.

Sitting there, alone in a private room, Archie felt as though the weight of the world was on his shoulders. He looked around the compartment and for the first time, actually saw the place for what it was… a Starship. The events of the previous few days had been so intense that he'd had no time to consider the implications of what was happening, but now that the immediate threats were gone, he truly felt fear and panic creep upon him. He had been engaged in warfare, and that was something he'd never considered possible. The more that he thought about it, the more memories of the men and aliens he'd killed came back to him. The sights, the smells, the explosions, the smoke, the contorted bodies, the light, and the darkness, everything came flooding back, causing him to feel sick. He knew that he'd had no choice, that he had to get involved, but the truth was that the things that he'd been forced to do revolted him. He'd get over the thoughts and feelings, but for right now, it all bothered him.

Jason walked through the door as it slid to the side. He had made arrangements for the medical teams to treat the injuries the two men had received during the beating at the Stones.

"The med crew are ready for us, mate," he said quietly.

"Cheers, Jase. Any news on Steve?" Archie was still only able to talk through a mumble.

"No change, Arch. They're still working on him," Jason replied. "They're hopeful that they can stabilise him enough to get him to a place called Erra," he let out a small laugh, "wherever the hell that is?"

"Yeah," Archie snorted back, "it's their homeworld," he paused before speaking again. "Things are never going to be the same, you know that don't you?"

Jason took a deep breath, then answered, "Yep... we're outcasts back home now, mate."

"Yeah, that about sums it up," was all Archie could say.

"Well, it could be worse, Arch. We could be sat on an alien spaceship heading to some alien world, where who knows what is in store for us. *And* we could have been beaten up by giant lizards." He couldn't help but giggle as he said it; it sounded ridiculous, but the irony was, it was actually the reality they had found for themselves.

After spending several minutes laughing at the absurdity of their situation, they both seemed to come to terms with it. They were together, they were alive, and right now that was all that mattered. They could deal with anything else that might come up later. Currently, they just let the relief of piss taking and laughter rule their world.

That was it. Suddenly Archie, Jason, and an unwitting Steve were suddenly Astronauts. They were going farther into the Galaxy than any of NASA's *official* men of space. They were going to the PLEIADES!

ARCHIE

&

COMPANY

WILL RETURN WHEN THE ADVENTURE

CONTINUES

IN

EARTH BORN AGENT

Book 2

in the

NEW PARADIGM SERIES

Thank You for reading my book

If you enjoyed this book, please visit my website and join my mailing list for notification on upcoming release's

https//benedictstonebooks.co.uk

or Email me at

info@benedictstonebooks.co.uk

or follow the

Benedict Stone Books Facebook Page

Printed in Great Britain
by Amazon